"McCarthy always does an excellent job of combining laugh-out-loud humor with sizzling, steamy passion."
—Romance Junkies

Praise for the Tales of Vegas Vampires

Bit the Jackpot

"The sparks fly . . . [a] cute paranormal treat."
—Publishers Weekly

"Imagine *Kindred: The Embraced* done as a comedy, and you'll come close to the feel of this story. Cara's adjustment to the vampire lifestyle and her efforts to overwhelm Seamus with domesticity are a riot . . . This is worth a look if you need a chuckle." *—The Eternal Night*

"[A] fun contemporary tale . . . a delightful read."
—The Best Reviews

"Full of witty dialogue and humorous situations that any reader would find highly entertaining. Lovers of vampire romances, however, should really relish this novel."
—Romance Reviews Today

"More humor and sexy shenanigans explode from McCarthy's second Las Vegas vampire novel. Sure to bring a smile to your face, these characters, with their endearing foibles and their attempts to do the right thing, make this a fun and highly satisfying book." *—Romantic Times*

continued . . .

High Stakes

"[An] amusing, often biting, vampire . . . romantic romp."

—*Midwest Book Review*

"An awesome start to what promises to be a hot, very anticipated new series from popular author Erin McCarthy . . . As far as I am concerned, the more vampire romances from Erin McCarthy, the better. *High Stakes* is hot, sexy, and laugh-out-loud funny. Who knew vampires could be so much fun?"

—*The Best Reviews*

"Erin McCarthy's trademark humor and smoldering, sexy couples keep readers coming back for more. *High Stakes* is erotic fun with a surprisingly darker edge not usually found in previous McCarthy works . . . a fantastic start to a series that is sure to be a winner. Definitely worth the gamble—pick up a copy of *High Stakes* today."

—*Romance Reviews Today*

"[A] fun, witty take on the genre with some intriguing characters. It is always a treat to run into preternatural creatures who aren't obsessed with how dark and tainted they are."

—*Monsters and Critics*

"A funny and steamy new vampire series has hit the market as McCarthy quickly carves out her own niche. The warmth and humor of this book make it an exuberant and charming read."

—*Romantic Times*

Bled Dry

"Ms. McCarthy uses a dry wit to draw the reader into the world of the undead . . . in a market increasingly flooded with vampire stories, Ms. McCarthy's stories shine like gems. Her handling of the idiosyncrasies of both the hero and the heroine is dead on, and the sensuality of the sex scenes is guaranteed to heat up anyone's blood! Five Angels." —*Fallen Angel Reviews*

"*Bled Dry* took only a few pages to have me laughing aloud, though it's hard to say which is foremost, the humor or the suspense. Or the passion. One thing's for sure. The characterization is a delight." —*Romance Reviews Today*

"Humorous." —*The Best Reviews*

"Combines laughs and deep feelings to make it a pure pleasure to read . . . Erin McCarthy manages to make a believer out of me with every story she writes, no matter how out there the plot initially seems. *Bled Dry* is a compelling read!" —*A Romance Review*

"Another biting and exciting tale of the Vegas Vampires . . . Great story, fabulous characters, and a really cool setting. Pick up the entire Vegas Vampire [series] by Ms. McCarthy . . . You'll like it. You'll really like it."

—*Fresh Fiction*

Titles by Erin McCarthy

A DATE WITH THE OTHER SIDE
HEIRESS FOR HIRE
MY IMMORTAL
FALLEN

The Vegas Vampires series

HIGH STAKES
BIT THE JACKPOT
BLED DRY
SUCKER BET

Bit the Jackpot

Erin McCarthy

BERKLEY SENSATION, NEW YORK

THE BERKLEY PUBLISHING GROUP
Published by the Penguin Group
Penguin Group (USA) Inc.
375 Hudson Street, New York, New York 10014, USA
Penguin Group (Canada), 90 Eglinton Avenue East, Suite 700, Toronto, Ontario M4P 2Y3, Canada
(a division of Pearson Penguin Canada Inc.)
Penguin Books Ltd., 80 Strand, London WC2R 0RL, England
Penguin Group Ireland, 25 St. Stephen's Green, Dublin 2, Ireland (a division of Penguin Books Ltd.)
Penguin Group (Australia), 250 Camberwell Road, Camberwell, Victoria 3124, Australia
(a division of Pearson Australia Group Pty. Ltd.)
Penguin Books India Pvt. Ltd., 11 Community Centre, Panchsheel Park, New Delhi—110 017, India
Penguin Group (NZ), 67 Apollo Drive, Rosedale, North Shore 0632, New Zealand
(a division of Pearson New Zealand Ltd.)
Penguin Books (South Africa) (Pty.) Ltd., 24 Sturdee Avenue, Rosebank, Johannesburg 2196,
South Africa

Penguin Books Ltd., Registered Offices: 80 Strand, London WC2R 0RL, England

BIT THE JACKPOT

A Berkley Sensation Book / published by arrangement with the author

PRINTING HISTORY
Berkley Sensation trade edition / December 2006
Berkley Sensation mass-market edition / June 2008

Cover art by Pinglet.
Cover design by Rita Frangie.

For information, address: The Berkley Publishing Group,
a division of Penguin Group (USA) Inc.,
375 Hudson Street, New York, New York 10014.

ISBN: 978-0-425-22299-7

BERKLEY® SENSATION
Berkley Sensation Books are published by The Berkley Publishing Group,
a division of Penguin Group (USA) Inc.,
375 Hudson Street, New York, New York 10014.
BERKLEY SENSATION and the "B" design are trademarks of Penguin Group (USA) Inc.

PRINTED IN THE UNITED STATES OF AMERICA

10 9 8 7 6 5 4 3 2 1

Bit the Jackpot

One

Seamus Fox was a lot of things. Almost four hundred years old. Irish. A vampire. Campaign manager for the residing president of the Vampire Nation.

And baby-sitter. To one paranoid ditzy vampire named Kelsey he'd been stupid enough to give his blood to.

He wasn't exactly sure how his life had come to this—hand-holding the equivalent of a vampiric preschooler and being the spokesperson for some kind of Undead Unsolved Mysteries.

"I've never been to a strip club," Kelsey said. "What are you looking at? You have your serious face on. Like you're thinking."

That made one of them.

Seamus put his glass to his mouth and pretended to take a small sip of the watered-down whiskey. He counted to ten in Gaelic, ripping his eyes off the exotic dancer he'd been watching gyrate with quite a bit of pleasure until Kelsey had reminded him of her presence. Her constant, chattering, needy presence. "I'm just looking for someone."

"Who?" Kelsey shifted her seat closer to his, her long black hair brushing against his arm. "What kind of person do you look for in a strip club?"

Let's see, a stripper, maybe? Seamus fought the urge to roll his eyes. Kelsey was like a cross between a Labrador, a three-year-old child, and a porn star. She rubbed up against him constantly, asked nine hundred questions an hour, and dressed like Frederick's of the Damned Hollywood.

And he was stuck with her because he had been the one to give her blood after another vampire had drained her and left her body in President Carrick's hotel suite. Seamus hadn't even been sure that it was possible to revive a vampire like Kelsey after a total blood draining, but it had been the only humane thing to do, to try and save her, and it had worked. She was restored to her previous vampirism, but now it seemed like she belonged to him. His pet vampire.

Normally she was an inconvenience, but during work hours he at least enlisted her secretarial skills to keep her busy and out of trouble. And off his lap, where she liked to sit whenever she could catch him off guard and slip her skinny rear end onto his legs. Unfortunately, he'd found he was a bit of a bleeding heart, pardon the expression, and couldn't bring himself to be cruel to Kelsey. He usually let her perch on his knee for a minute or two until he felt like Santa Claus with fangs and found an excuse to stand up. Annoying—yes. A potentially growing problem—no doubt. But not the end of the world.

But having her with him, now, when he was watching the most sensual woman he'd seen in two hundred years wrap her naked body around a pole, was downright irritating.

"I'm looking for a stripper, Kelsey."

"Oh."

That went around her brain for a second or two. She pulled up the bodice of her clinging red dress. "Why do you want a stripper?"

Because he was still a man with sexual needs, even though he'd spent over two hundred years trying to pretend he wasn't. But that was no one's business but his.

In reality he was there to find Jodi Madsen, Brittany Baldizzi's aunt, who worked at this strip club behind the scenes choreographing for the girls now that she had retired from dancing herself. It was a long shot that Brittany's Aunt Jodi would have a clue as to who her father was, but it was worth asking. Seamus knew the man was a vampire, but he wanted a name.

His original plan had been to leave Kelsey at a table and go off to find Jodi. Straightforward. Get the job done efficiently in a businesslike manner. That was him. Normally. But then he'd seen this woman moving on stage. The shadow dancer. And he'd experienced something he had thought was gone.

Interest. Desire. The need to taste a woman's flesh, her thick, pumping blood rushing past his teeth, his tongue. The pure thrill of making a woman laugh. Watching her eyes dilate in pleasure.

It all exploded over him again as he turned back and watched the dancer move up and down. A screen hid her, teasing him with only the shadow of her body, the outline of her impressive curves. He was too old, with too many responsibilities, for this kind of adolescent crap. But damn. She could really work that pole.

Her hips thrust forward, caressing and rocking, her back arching, full breasts straining forward. Her hair fell freely down over her naked shoulders, and her ankles swiveled in her high heels.

Seamus wrestled with his conscience. He wasn't here to pick up a woman. He had no time for any sort of relationship, purely sexual or otherwise. Live feeding was never desirable, especially for a man in his position.

"Oooh, you have the hots for her, don't you?" Kelsey said. "I know that look on your face. That's a 'let me do you, baby' look."

Seamus curled his lip at her word choice. He hadn't done anyone in two hundred years. He had devoted his vampire life to penance for his mistakes. That was his burden, his destiny, and it shouldn't change now because he was sexually attracted to a stripper.

"Though I don't see why you want to date a shadow," Kelsey said.

On the other hand . . . Didn't he deserve some kind of release? A little fun in his task-driven life? Having a woman wouldn't compromise his job as Ethan Carrick's presidential campaign manager. The only one preventing Seamus from having a good time was Seamus himself.

And the yoke of responsibility, the burden of guilt, was slowly crushing him. And he was only three hundred and seventy. By the time he reached a millennium, he'd be a shriveled-up recluse with false fangs living off sheep back in Ireland, just to get away from it all.

"Where does the light come from that makes the shadow?" Kelsey asked. "Is she even real or is that like a movie?"

God help him, if there was a God, and he didn't object to assisting a vampire. Seamus couldn't do this. Any. More. Just one night of pleasure. That's all he wanted. Needed.

"I don't know where the light comes from. But she's real." His leg bounced along to the thump of the funky bass music as he considered.

If he focused, his vampire eyes could pick up the rounded tip of the dancer's nipples, the outline of her plump lips behind the screen.

"I'm bored, Seamus. I want to go home." Speaking of lips. Kelsey's red-lipsticked lip jutted out in a pout.

For a finale, the shadow went down deep into some kind of bent-leg, spread-thigh maneuver that had Seamus standing straight up. Holy crap, that was hot. "So go home."

Even uptight campaign managers were entitled to some kind of social life and he hadn't taken blood from a live donor in forty years. Hadn't had sex in two hundred.

He was going to do both tonight. And to hell with the consequences.

"Where are you going?" Kelsey grabbed his hand and rushed to follow him. "Don't leave me! They'll come and get me if I'm not with you."

Kelsey harbored some deep fear that her attacker was going to return and kidnap her. Because Seamus sympathized with her fears, he usually didn't make an issue out of her clinging plastic wrap behavior. But this was different. His first attempt at seduction in a couple hundred years would be better done without Kelsey following him like a bloodsucking dachshund.

"Sit down, Kelsey. I'm going to be two minutes." He tried to gently put her back in her chair and was successful. His vampire strength was greater than hers. "You're fine, I promise. You're a big girl vampire, and I'll be right back."

He made a break for it, running across the room faster than mortals could see, feeling like a bastard and guilty as hell, but desperate for some breathing room. Blowing past the bouncers and to the backstage area, Seamus had an ugly thought.

Maybe the shadow danced behind a screen because she was . . . unattractive.

Moves that could tempt a saint, but a face that only a mother could love.

Then even worse, he wondered . . . did it really matter? She could do some serious hip thrusting.

Which made him a very, very sick vampire.

Clearly, two hundred years without sex was too long if he was hard for a shadow.

Hesitation overcame him, right as he realized the dancer was standing in front of him. He could smell her blood, vanilla lotion, and a light sweat from her dancing exertions. Seamus saw the swish of her dark hair on her shoulders right in front of him as she belted a red Chinese robe around her waist and quickly turned around.

Maybe a strip club wasn't the place to meet a woman. If he really wanted to have an affair, to get the desire out of his system, maybe he could take out an Internet ad. Dull, workaholic, dead Irishman with a fondness for blood seeks hot female for wild nights of mind-melting sex. Must be willing to be bitten.

But that wasn't going to be necessary, Seamus realized when the shadow dancer turned around. She was beautiful, absolutely stunning. She had milky white skin framed by ebony black hair, long cheekbones, a petite bow-shaped mouth with cherry red lips, and a perfectly formed nose. Her eyes were deep brown, almost black, and almond shaped, black eyeliner flaring out from her lids in sexy, sexy cat eyes. She might have reminded him of a porcelain doll if it wasn't for the fact that she had dewy sweat on her forehead and impressive cleavage, her chest heaving from dancing. Seamus could smell her blood pumping quickly through her veins, hear her heart fluttering wildly.

Her eyes went wide in surprise at seeing him, and he knew that she was naked under that flimsy nothing of a robe, which showed her legs and a flash of her navel when she turned.

Oh, yeah. This had definitely been a good idea. What had he been worried about? No one was going to fault him for a little down time, a little physical release. Especially not when faced with a gorgeous dancer with strong thighs.

He fought the urge to let his fangs down.

It was time to exert a little vampire influence on her. With his considerable mind-reading experience, he should have her in bed in ten minutes.

Cara Kim sucked in her breath when she realized a man was standing behind her. God, how long had he been there? Given the sort of lusty, heated look on his face, it was possible he'd seen her putting on her robe. Seen her naked.

Which might not seem like a big deal, since she danced nude for a living, but it had the potential to ruin her night. No man had ever seen her naked *without* the screen in front of her. Not one man ever, because she was arguably the oddest attraction in all of Vegas—the virgin stripper.

Kind of an oxymoron, but Cara nonetheless, and she didn't have any plans to change anytime soon. Sex led women to make mistakes, to lose control of their lives and their emotions, and Cara didn't plan to lose either, ever. She knew enough about herself to understand she had a compulsive personality and a real need to nurture. Bad combo altogether when it came to men and sex, so she chose to abstain from both. She danced because the money was fantastic and she could work nights to pay for her grandmother's nursing home. She did get a certain sensual pleasure from dancing behind the screen, but she didn't want a man to see her naked in the actual flesh. Ever.

This guy looked to have just screwed that conviction up.

Which would only be a minor annoyance if he weren't drop-dead, drop-her-dress gorgeous. Dark hair. Blue eyes. Lots of muscle in all the right places. Capped off with a charming smile. A perfect visual example of why women lost all ability to be rational in the presence of such a fine-looking man.

While Cara's brain assessed him coolly, her body reacted warmly by sending out the nipples as a welcoming crew and turning up the thermostat down south, which annoyed her no end.

"Hi. Could you tell me where I might find Jodi Madsen?" he asked, with just enough of an Irish accent to kick her irritation up a notch.

Every time she thought she was getting ahead in life, she had a roadblock thrown up in front of her. A big, male roadblock. The last time she'd allowed a man to bring her dreams to a halt, she'd wound up betrayed and out ten grand. She did *not* need temptation in the form of a dark-haired Irishman distracting her from her goals.

"No," she said, tightening her robe tie. Maybe if she cut off circulation from the waist down, she wouldn't be so aware of her own nudity.

"Do you know Jodi?" he asked. "Does she work here?"

Cara nodded. "Yes." She was so done with this conversation. He was way too cute and she had the very real feeling he had seen her butt. She wanted her panties on pronto, before she had time to reflect on the fact that she was suddenly aroused after two minutes of meaningless dialogue with a total stranger.

"Alright, then." He tilted his head a little, his smile charming, charming, charming. "So she works here, you know her, you just don't know where I can find her."

Wondering what the hell he wanted with Jodi, she nodded. Maybe he was the club owner. That would explain how he'd gotten past the solid row of bouncers the club employed. Men never managed to get backstage, which was why Cara loved working at this club. Jodi was stage manager and choreographer for all the dancers, so maybe this was her boss. The owner.

Shit. The boss had seen her butt.

"I'm Seamus Fox," he said, holding out his hand.

"Hi," she said, ignoring the hand. She wasn't touching that thing if her life depended on it. The hand was connected to the arm, which was connected to the shoulder, which was broad and muscular, which eventually led across a firm, powerful chest, right down to the bone. Er. Boner. Which she wasn't going anywhere near.

"This is the part where you tell me your name," he said with a wink.

Only if she were stupid. She knew how important it was to protect herself as a dancer from freaks who obsessed over women. Seamus didn't look like a freak, but he did look dangerous. Strong. Well dressed. Sexy, damn it.

"No, this is the part where I walk away. If I see Jodi I'll tell her you're looking for her." She started to turn, but only got half through the pivot.

"Wait." His eyes darted down to her robe. "I saw your show. You dance beautifully. Sensual." Those blue eyes darkened, just went right from pale sky blue to cerulean. Which had to be a trick of the disco light from the stage.

Eyes didn't just completely change color in two seconds. "Your moves are very classy."

Not sure why exactly she was still standing there, Cara licked her lips nervously. She could have sworn she had ordered her feet to walk away and yet she was just frozen in a half-swizzle. A strange sensation stole over her, like a tugging, tingling feeling, in her shoulders, her neck, her skull. She opened her mouth to speak, but realized she couldn't remember what he had just said. Just that it suddenly seemed really important to tell him her name. Urgent.

Her brain battled with the need to open her mouth. Her common sense was screaming no, no, no, he could find her address and phone number on the Internet with her name.

Yet she said, "Cara," before she could stop herself. It just came out with no warning or consent from her.

What the hell? She seethed at herself silently. What was the matter with her? He wasn't *that* good-looking. Okay, yes, he was, but that didn't fully explain why she seemed to have lost her mind. She glared at him, just to let him know the name thing had been a slip, one she wasn't going to repeat.

The glare didn't seem to faze him. He smiled, a beautiful, white teeth grin. "Come have a cup of coffee with me, Cara."

She'd rather die. "No, thank you."

"There's a shop right across the street..." He stopped smiling. "What? What do you mean?"

"I mean no."

Now he looked flat-out shocked. "No? You can't mean no."

"I do." He'd obviously never heard the word *no* before. Maybe he was famous. Probably rich. Used to women dropping at his gorgeous feet. Well, she didn't know if his feet were gorgeous, per se, but given the rest of him she could see, it was highly likely. This would be good for him, to hear no. Take his obviously huge ego down a notch or two.

Seamus stared at her. Hard. His eyebrows rose just a little bit, like he was waiting for something.

Feeling a little weirded out by his intensity, Cara eased to the left, still half-turned. She must be shuffling like a hunchback, but she didn't care. She needed to get away from him, but couldn't seem to force her body to do more than step forward an eighth of an inch at a time. She was either in a dream or she'd suffered some kind of post-dancing paralysis. That had been a really deep cat in the cradle at the end of her routine. She must have sore muscles, or maybe her high heels were too small and she had pinched a nerve.

He smiled, a slow, charming, roguish sort of smile. "Let me walk you to your dressing room. Can I buy you a cup of coffee?"

Umm. Didn't she just say no twice? She attempted another shuffle and moved all of half an inch. Damn it. She was getting really freaked out. Her legs didn't work. So if she couldn't get her own legs to leave, she'd have to force him to take a hint. "Well, that depends. Do you like long walks?"

"Sure." The smile relaxed.

"Do you like sex?" Cara asked in a husky voice, hoping her acting skills were passable.

"Absolutely." His nostrils flared.

"Then take a fucking hike." She'd been dying for months to use that line she'd read in a magazine, and the shocked look on his face was so worth the wait. "I'm not interested, got it?"

For a long second, he stared at her, like he could hypnotize her into having coffee—sex—with him. She half expected a pendulum to start swinging in front of her.

"Hello." She waved her hand in front of his face, starting to get ticked off. "Did you hear me? Not interested. Go away."

He broke eye contact with her, crossed his arms, and shook his head in disgust. "Absolutely unbelievable. I just can't win. I finally decide to live a little and I pick the one woman in Vegas who can shut me out and says no."

Okay, cute guy was psycho.

And she was naked.

"I, um, have to go . . . they'll wonder where I am." She started to turn again, but he touched her arm. Crap. Where the hell was a bouncer when you needed one?

A hideous shriek startled Cara into jumping back three feet. A blur with black hair collided into Seamus.

He swore. "What the hell is the matter with you, Kelsey?"

A tall, thin, gorgeous woman wearing a tiny red dress that boosted up her snow white cleavage was clinging to Seamus. Cara took another step back, damn grateful her legs were finally cooperating, even if she was only able to manage geriatric speed. Time to casually slip away and put some pants on. Leave sexy psycho to his skinny girlfriend.

"They're here, Seamus, I saw them."

"Who?" He sounded impatient, but wrapped his arm around the woman, patting her back. "Kelsey, babe, we've got to get you counseling or something. I can't be with you every possible second of every day."

She sniffled and clung to his chest. "I can't help it . . . I'm sorry. Since they shot me, I just feel scared all the time."

On that note, Cara was out of there. She started increasing her backup shuffle.

"Cara, wait." He glanced at her.

No freaking way. "Look, threesomes aren't my thing. In fact, nothing is my thing, okay? I'm boring and repressed and I have six brothers."

That weird tugging sensation crept over her arms again, across her collarbone and into her face like an invasive, probing, ice-cold finger. Shuddering, Cara whirled around, fast-walked around the corner, and ducked into the dressing room she shared with the other dancers. Slamming the door, she pushed the lock button in, and grabbed her chest.

Geez, she needed to get a new job. Maybe paying for veterinary school and the nursing home with shadow dancing wasn't worth this. That had started to get a little creepy.

"What are you doing?" Dawn asked.

Cara looked at her coworker, sitting in her red thong, touching up her makeup. "This guy followed me." Really strange, sexy guy who had a girlfriend who had been shot and a strange ability to make Cara feel like his fingers were walking up her neck when he wasn't even touching her.

She shivered again just thinking about it, a little scared by the whole encounter. Dawn had no such fear. Adjusting her bra with nipple tassels, she stood up and pushed Cara out of the way. "Where is he? We'll call Bryan. He'll kick his ass."

Bryan was Dawn's bouncer boyfriend. Cara wasn't sure she wanted Bryan confronting Seamus, but she would like an escort to her car. After she got dressed. But before she could reach for her gym bag with her clothes, Dawn was making "uh-uh-uh" sounds.

"Is that him? Standing with that chick?" Dawn had opened the door and was gazing down the hall with a rapt expression on her face.

Cara peered from behind Dawn's shoulder. Seamus was brushing the skinny girl's hair back off her shoulders and looked like he was reassuring her. Freak. "That's him."

"Damn, now that's a man," Dawn enthused. "I'm looking at him, and I swear, my thighs are just spreading automatically."

Bryan, Dawn's bouncer boyfriend, was clearly forgotten. As was the fact that Dawn was wearing only a thong and the bra with nipple tassels as she leaned farther into the hall.

Her friend's reaction annoyed her. "He's not *that* hot." She stole another look down the hall. Okay, so yes he was.

"*Yes*, he is." Dawn turned back to her. "You have to have sex with him and tell me every single detail."

That made her laugh. "No! I'm not interested, Dawn, seriously."

"Okay, then I call dibs on him."

Cara rolled her eyes. "You have a boyfriend and he obviously has a girlfriend."

"So? We could do a partner swap for a night. Bryan likes that kind of kinky shit and with this guy I just might be willing to try it."

Cara did not want to know those things about Bryan and Dawn. "Yuck. Too much information, Dawn." And she wasn't even going to think about why the thought of Dawn with Seamus made her want to strangle Dawn with her nipple tassels.

"You're the prudest stripper I've ever known." Dawn glanced back down the hall. "Shit. Where'd he go? He was there two seconds ago."

Cara stuck her head out farther. Dawn was right. There was no sign of Seamus or the woman. "That's weird. But I'm glad he's gone."

Really. She was.

But when she was sliding her panties on under her robe and felt the sudden desperate sense that Seamus was in danger, she only hesitated for a second. The feeling came hard, a violent splash of red and black emotion, making Cara close her eyes in agony.

"Damn."

"What's the matter?" Dawn asked.

"I have a headache." When the pain subsided, Cara pulled on a pair of jeans and flip-flops without hesitation and headed right for the back alley of the club.

Two

So that hadn't gone according to plan. Seamus patted Kelsey on the back and murmured stupid nothing words to get her to calm down. The dancer, Cara, had bolted after making it quite clear that she wasn't interested in him. His vampire mind-control trick had completely failed.

He had gotten her to offer up her name, but that was it, and even that had been a struggle. She had resisted. Part of him wanted to follow after her and try again. The smarter part of him figured if he did, he'd just wind up with a knee in the groin.

"Alright, let's go home to the casino, Kelsey." He might as well work the rest of the night. Or go to bed early. Alone. No sex for him, no blood unless he wanted a cold plastic bag from his fridge. It was completely depressing.

"Okay, thanks, Seamus, I'm sorry for being such a

pain." Kelsey sniffled and peeled herself off his chest. She wiped under her eyes, dashing away her blood-red tears.

She was one of the few vampires Seamus had actually seen capable of producing tears, but it suited her. Drama and hysterics were Kelsey's personality.

"You're not a pain." He nudged her with his arm and gave her a smile. "You're just paranoid. And too skinny. We need to get more blood on your bones."

She returned a watery smile and followed him out the emergency exit door. Seamus didn't feel like walking back through the club, and this door would probably dump them out into the back parking lot.

The warm Vegas air hit Seamus in the face like a fleece blanket. He had never imagined he would like the heat, the desert, or the glitzy nightlife of Sin City, but he enjoyed the pulse of the city, the ability to hide among mortals completely out in the open.

They weren't in the back parking lot, but a side alley. And immediately Seamus smelled vampire. He scanned the dark, easing Kelsey behind him. He wasn't sure why, but he felt antagonism, danger. Vampire. The air was tinged with a sour scent.

"What's the matter?" she asked, her high-pitched voice bouncing up and down the quiet alley like she'd spoken with a bullhorn.

He was about to tell her to go back in the building, even though he couldn't see anything, when he took a blow to the top of his head that sent him staggering forward, a starburst of colors exploding in front of his eyes. Instinct had him ducking, avoiding a second blow. Seamus arched his arm out and made contact with a thick, full-barreled chest.

His attacker grunted, and as Seamus darted back out of the way, he finally got a good view of him. The guy was heavyset, balding, wearing a silk shirt and dress pants, his gold necklace glinting in the moonlight. With his vampire vision, Seamus could make out doughy jowls, a squat and thick crooked nose, and lids so swollen that his eyes were about as wide as a nickel. Overall, this guy coming at him was one seriously ugly vampire.

Seamus felt a twinge of pity for him that he had to go through eternity looking like the backside of a bulldog. But then the guy landed a fist in Seamus's gut, crunching all his muscles in agony, and his sympathy disappeared.

Especially when he threw a punch, collided with ugly guy's temple with an audible crack, and the guy didn't even lose his footing. Ugly vampire was a strong vampire.

"Go back in the club, Kelsey," he called over his shoulder, as he and the brawny man circled each other. This could take a while.

Seamus was no pretty boy. Back in his youth, he'd been a potato farmer and he had seen his share of fistfights and strength battles. But he'd gone soft lately, spending more time with technology than the treadmill and weight bench. He had the feeling he was going to be very sore in unpleasant places before he and Ugly parted ways.

When he moved to the right, he caught a clear view of Kelsey just standing in the doorway, horror on her pale face. "Dammit, get in the club, Kelsey!"

Faking left, then right, he landed a punch on the guy's kidneys. A howl of rage and pain went up from Ugly, but he didn't even so much as bend over. Not good. Time for Seamus to use his brain, not his brawn, before he got pummeled. Seamus bent over and rammed his head into the guy's gut, throwing off his center of gravity. As Ugly stumbled backward, Seamus kicked his foot out from under him, and the big guy went down with a satisfying thud.

Standing up, feeling a bit pleased with himself, Seamus suddenly realized there was a second guy. And he was holding Kelsey in his meaty, tattooed arms. Shit. This night was officially a complete and total frickin' disaster.

"Let her go," he said with a sigh, wondering why he was wasting his breath.

"No. She's coming with me." And to prove his point, the guy dragged Kelsey backward with him, her legs dangling off the ground, her dress rolling up her thighs and giving Seamus a flash of her red panties.

It was that indignity, that callous treatment of a woman, that made Seamus very angry. Kelsey may be annoying, and she might giggle too much, but she was a human being—okay, an immortal vampire—and she deserved respect. Seamus rushed the guy, and at the last second flew up over his head, and slammed him from behind at the base of the skull with his fist.

The guy stumbled forward, groaning, losing his grip on Kelsey, who hit the dirt.

It was then that Seamus realized Ugly was back on his feet.

And there was a third one. One who was thin and moved with stealth, peeling himself out of the shadows of the building and stepping forward. When he locked eyes with him, Seamus also saw an intelligence in his face that was lacking in the other two.

Well, this was fun.

He couldn't call for assistance because Ethan would hear him. There was no way Seamus would risk the vampire president getting involved in a back-alley fight with rogue vampires. It would be bad press. Seriously bad press.

"Cut his head off," the thin one said, handing a really big nine-inch knife to Ugly.

Let's not and say we did. Seamus gauged how much room he had to maneuver. He was going to guess his flying skills were superior to these two. And despite his leadership role, Seamus sensed the thin one was a young vamp.

Which didn't explain why the guy was able to say, "Come here, Kelsey," walk down the alley toward the street, and actually have Kelsey follow him.

She just stumbled to her feet, fixed her dress, and trotted off after him without one glance in Seamus's direction. So much for loyalty.

This is what he got for his chivalry. His head cut off. That was ironic. It was the guillotine that had almost killed him the first time and changed the course of his vampire life. Now he was about to die the same way.

And he realized that probably no one would mourn him except Ethan.

If these guys didn't kill him, he might just kill *himself* the thought was so damn depressing.

Ringo knew Kelsey was following him, so he walked quickly until he got to the doorway of a closed souvenir shop. Then he turned, took her hand, and pulled her into the darkness with him.

"You're alive." It was a statement, not a question, and he took in her dark eyes, thick black hair, and vibrant red lips, the only splash of color against her alabaster skin. The cleavage-popping dress didn't surprise him. The expression on her face did. Gone was the flirtatious smile, the ditzy wide eyes.

She looked afraid. "Who are you?" she whispered. "Why won't you just leave me alone?"

Letting go of her hand, he rubbed his chin. This was a

twist. She didn't remember him. Just as well. He hadn't realized his target was Kelsey. *Get Fox and his girlfriend,* he'd been told. And he always obeyed orders. If he didn't, his blood supply would be cut off.

It was a job Ringo had understood as a mortal human, and one he did well as a vampire. Hired killer.

But the last time he had seen Kelsey, he had tried to protect her, had watched her get mowed down by a spray of bullets, had seen her die. But that was before he'd been turned to vampire, before he had understood who he was dealing with. Kelsey was clearly a vampire now, too. Maybe she always had been one, though it was a surprise she didn't recognize him.

"You know who I am, Kelsey." He opened his mind to her. She'd been able to read him before, with a clarity that had bugged the hell out of him when he was mortal. He wasn't sure why he let her in now. Why he wanted her to acknowledge that she remembered him.

Maybe because Kelsey was the last shaky link to his mortality. The only person who had known him when he was a man, before the blood lust, and before he'd become Donatelli's fucking minion.

"You're here to kill me," she said, stepping back onto the sidewalk, the streetlight casting a bright glow over her bare shoulders.

"No." He had been. But he couldn't kill Kelsey now that he knew it was her. He'd kill Seamus Fox without a second thought, but he wouldn't kill Kelsey. She represented the last time he'd done something compassionate. He may have been a human until the month before, but he'd lost his humanity years before that. Except for one brief moment when he had actually risked himself to save Kelsey.

She was shaking, her teeth rattling, and her arms wrapped tightly around her middle. He had no sense of recognition from her, just fear.

"Jesus, what the hell did they do to you?" Ringo wasn't any good at mind reading, didn't like picking through people's thoughts, but he tried to probe Kelsey and got nothing but waves of panic. The Kelsey he'd known hadn't ever been afraid. She had been ditzy, annoying, confident. It made his very vivid and cruel imagination wonder what Donatelli had done to her after his men had shot her.

Instead of answering, she crumpled to the sidewalk in a faint, startling the crap out of him so completely that he never even moved to catch her.

"What the fuck!" Did women still faint? The only time he'd seen someone drop like that was when his ex-girlfriend had tripled her diet pill dosage.

Ringo approached Kelsey. She hadn't passed out gracefully. A breast had popped out of her tiny dress and her face was hanging over into the gutter. Her shoe was half off and he had a clear view of some pale inner thighs and red underwear.

He couldn't leave her there like that.

Why did this shit always happen to him? Kicking a garbage can in annoyance, he sent it shooting thirty feet across the street and through a store window. The crash of the shattering glass made him feel better. Lifting her into his arms, Ringo wished he could fly as he started walking.

She stirred long enough to ask, "Where are you taking me?"

He was probably taking them both to hell. But he just said, "Home. I'm taking you home, Kelsey."

Cara couldn't even imagine why she had thought it was a good idea to go out into the alley wearing jeans, flip-flops, and a short satin robe. No bra. No cell phone. No purse.

She had lost her everlovin' mind, and if she hadn't been drinking bottled water only all night, she would swear she'd been drugged. It was the only explanation for why she was crouched in a corner watching Seamus Fox—if that was really his name—brawling with two fat guys in bad outfits.

And they weren't just fighting. They were doing some freaky shit. At first it had looked like normal punches but then Seamus had gone all *Crouching Tiger, Hidden Dragon*, doing moves that looked humanly impossible. He was like a blur in a black T-shirt, and at one point, she could absolutely swear he had actually risen vertically in the air.

She was too scared to move, afraid they might see her if she tried to sneak back in the door. Clearly even though Seamus was outnumbered, she wasn't going to be of any assistance to him. Her major talents in life were dancing naked and animal care. Somehow she didn't think doing a hip rock or clipping his nails would help Seamus at the moment. It would be best to leave them to their beating the crap out of each other thing, but Cara had retreated too far from the door to go back in without being seen.

Cara? Seamus called to her, shattering her illusion that she hadn't been spotted.

Not to mention she was almost certain he hadn't spoken out loud. Just in her head. She licked her lips nervously. *What?* she whispered tentatively, her lips moving automatically even if no sound came out.

Go back in the club, beautiful.

She fell back on her butt, startled that she could hear him so clearly in her head. Yet he wasn't even looking at her. He was slamming one of the big guys into the brick wall.

I'm serious. They want to kill me. Get back inside.

It seemed like a good plan. Get back inside away from big, hairy men throwing punches. But for some reason her legs weren't moving. Leaving Seamus all alone just didn't seem right. She bit her fingernail nervously. If she ran toward the door, she could call 911 and get Seamus help. That would be the smartest thing to do.

She stood up, hugging the wall, staying in the shadows as she inched toward the door.

Right then Seamus leaped six feet in the air in the most unbelievable move Cara had ever seen and kicked one of the guys in the back of the head. It should have dropped the big dude to the ground, but instead, he just growled and bared his teeth. The streetlight was right on his face and Cara had a perfect view of his face and mouth. Of his fangs.

"Arrghh," she said involuntarily, covering her mouth with her hand. Those were not just exceptionally large canines. Those were fangs. And Seamus was leaping through the air like he had superpowers.

Something was very, very wrong here.

Now the big guy had seen her.

"Who are you?" he asked, getting back to his feet after kissing concrete. He took a step toward her, a leer on his face. He wasn't as ugly as the other guy, who was currently in a headlock under Seamus's armpit, but he looked stupid.

"Leave her be. I'll wipe her memory," Seamus said.

Excuse me? That didn't sound pleasant. Cara started fast-walking toward the door.

Stupid cut her off, stepping right in front of her escape path. His nostrils flared. "You smell good."

Cara grimaced. That just didn't sound like a compliment. But to prevent pissing him off, she murmured, "Thank you."

If she ran the other way, toward the street, she could get help. She chanced a glance at Seamus. He still had the ugly guy in his grip, but was getting his head pounded against the wall in retaliation. Cara winced. That must hurt. That was brain damage in the making.

It was up to her to make a break for it. Especially since Stupid was leaning toward her, his mouth wide open.

"I bet you taste really good, too," he said.

Eeew. Time to move it. "What's that?" Cara asked, pointing behind the guy's right shoulder.

"What?" He turned.

She ran like hell to the end of the alley and out into the street.

It was a good plan.

What she hadn't factored in was the possibility of a car driving right in that particular spot.

She popped out with too much momentum to slow down, even as she realized an SUV was only a few feet from her. She felt the impact of the huge car like a massive shove, her brain rattling, her breath sucking right out of her lungs. Then she was hurtling through the air with nothing to hold on to, a scream stuck in her throat.

This could be a problem.

Cara landed, pain ripping through her entire body, crunching and jarring and tearing.

Then with great relief, she passed out.

Three

Seamus smelled Cara's blood flowing before he saw her. The SUV peeled back into reverse and took off, the guy behind the wheel looking panicked, his eyes glassy with shock and alcohol. With the car gone, Seamus had a clear view down the street to where Cara lay in a heap, her leg tucked under her at an awkward angle, blood seeping from her head down onto the street.

He ran, Ugly and Stupid behind him, sniping at each other.

"This is your fault," the one said.

"My fault? What did I do?"

"You had to get distracted. You had to think with your fangs. And now she's dead, Fox isn't, and the other chick is gone."

Seamus half listened, the fact that they knew who he was barely registering. Their attack wasn't random, but he couldn't deal with that at the moment. His concern was for Cara. He kneeled down, digging through her hair to find her neck and search for a pulse. If he strained, he could hear a heartbeat, but it was faint, irregular, and he wasn't sure if it was real or just wishful thinking on his part.

This woman couldn't be dead. If she was, it was his fault. He had approached her backstage, he had reached out to her mentally, connected them. She must have sensed something was happening in the alley and she had walked into the middle of that mess because of him. Guilt was a terrible thing. He had nearly smothered under it back during the Revolution. Had only crawled back out because Ethan had forced him to, and he wasn't at all sure he could do it a second time.

He wasn't finding Cara's pulse. "Damn it." He brushed her long hair out of the way, scooted in closer.

"She's dead, man."

"Fuck you."

"Can I have a little taste now?" the second guy said. "Before her blood gets cold."

Now that made Seamus angry. Very, very angry. He stood up and yanked the knife right out of Ugly's hand. "Get the hell out of here before I drive this through your black heart."

Ugly scoffed. "Try it."

Seamus did. The knife went right into the man's chest, sinking deep with a sick sucking sound.

"Shit, I can't believe you did that." The guy jerked back, swearing and grabbing at his chest. "You bastard!"

His friend laughed and made no move to help him. Seamus reached back and pulled a piece of metal off the ground, car refuse from the accident. Before Stupid even had time to react, Seamus cut off his laughter by stabbing him in the same spot as the other guy. It wouldn't kill either of them, since it wasn't wood, but it would hurt like hell and get them away from Seamus.

"Ow! What'd you do that for?" Stupid looked downright indignant as he glanced down at the injury. "I didn't *mean* for her to wind up dead. Not my fault mortals are so breakable."

"You were going to kill me, weren't you?" Seamus asked, pressing the bottom of his shirt onto Cara's head wound, knowing it was futile, feeling sick and bitter and hating himself.

"Well..." They darted glances at each other, both grimacing and grabbing their chests. "Yes."

"Go away before I cut your damn heads off!"

They took him seriously and shuffled off awkwardly, bitching and moaning to each other.

Seamus stopped pressing at Cara's wound. His shirt fell away, covered in her blood, as he picked up a limp hand, felt for a pulse, any sign of life.

Nothing.

She was so beautiful, even with her face contorted in agony and surprise. Her robe was sliding open, her bare breast pale, her chest still. Seamus rearranged the fabric to cover her back up. Pulled her broken leg out from under her, and brushed her hair off her lips and cheek.

"Damn it." He knew what he was thinking. Knew he shouldn't be. Seamus stood up, paced back and forth. Ignored the hunger that gnawed at his gut from the scent of her blood spilling out over the street. "This is a bad idea."

It wasn't just a bad idea, it was a horrible, dumb-ass idea. They were in the middle of a reelection year, and Ethan was fighting for every single vote. Having his campaign manager turn a mortal just for the hell of it would raise eyebrows. It would undermine Ethan's current presidential policy of vampire population control. The latest polls showed Ethan only had a narrow lead of 52 percent with a 2 percent margin of error.

Turning Cara would be a bad political decision, a complete strategical error.

"Shit, shit, shit." Seamus ran his hand through his hair and glanced down at Cara's body. Blood encircled her head and shoulders in a dark, sticky puddle as Seamus marveled that her eyeliner was perfectly intact on her closed lids, still drawn out into those cat eyes he'd found so sensual.

"Oh, man." He couldn't do it. He just couldn't walk away and leave her like this. It was his fault she was dead, and he had to fix it to the best of his ability.

"Good thing you're used to nightlife, Cara," he said as he dropped back on his haunches, talking out loud to give himself courage. "Look at it this way. Now you'll always be able to find work as a dancer. Your body will never change. That's something." He gathered her limp body in his arms and retreated to the alley. "Right?"

Like she was going to answer. She was dead and was going to stay that way until he stopped dicking around and bit her.

Okay, he could do this. Seamus tilted her head to gain access to her neck. Her head flopped back over his arm, her hair dangling toward the street in a black cloud. He winced. Yep. Definitely dead. Her jugular vein showed clearly through her fair skin and Seamus took a deep breath, bent over, and sank his fangs into her smooth flesh before he could change his mind.

He was acutely aware of the stillness of her body, the lack of a heartbeat, the need to use more effort to pull her blood up into his mouth since her heart wasn't pumping it out to him. There were no thoughts from her either, none of the usual jumble of emotions, confusion, sexual desire, and titillation he had always experienced when he fed from live donors.

Cara was no longer alive and the guilt of that made him draw harder, faster. This wasn't fair, that the one night he decided to forgo his loner status he wound up responsible for another death. And even turned, Cara would be his responsibility, to guide and advise, just like he did with Kelsey since he had revived her.

It was the great truth, illustrated for him all over again. Life for Seamus Fox was not meant to be fun, or filled with pleasure. He had been bound to the land in physical servitude as a mortal. That was his role as a vampire as well, and he needed to accept that, stop fighting against it. Deal with it.

When there was no blood left to draw out, Seamus removed his fangs, sick with the feeling of fullness. Using his teeth, he sliced open his wrist and dribbled blood on Cara's lips. She didn't respond at all, so he forced her mouth open with his fingers and let his blood run down into her mouth. He raised her jaw to encourage swallowing, and after sixty seconds, he sensed her stirring back to life. Felt her arm jerk against his thigh.

Then she started thrashing, jerking her lips away from his blood, her hand slapping weakly at him.

"You're going to be fine, it's okay," he said, in a lame effort to calm her down. He wished he'd had a mother who had comforted him as a child, but his da had been more inclined to cuff Seamus on the head when he was sick, to toughen him up. Whether his mother had agreed with that philosophy was unknown to him since she'd died during his birth. That and the last couple hundred years of avoiding female companionship had left him feeling like an idiot with the whole nurturing thing. He knew nothing about soothing someone's discomfort or fears.

Nor did he understand why Cara was fighting his blood. She kept batting at his wrist, and flinging her head to the side, an expression of distaste on her face. Most mortals clung to the source of vampire blood, and wanted more. Would feed until they burst that first time if they were allowed. This particular mortal, soon to be immortal, was wrinkling her nose like she smelled something rotten.

First she'd resisted his mind-reading attempts. Turned down his offer for coffee. Now she wouldn't take his blood. How many ways could one woman reject him in a night?

He didn't want to find out.

"Come on, Cara, you have to drink it." There was no going back at this point, but if she didn't drink enough blood, she'd be too weak to fully make the change. He wasn't even sure what would happen if she refused to drink. Starvation, he guessed. Which would be horrible to suffer through.

Slashing his other wrist, he let the blood flow freely without making her drink, to let her smell the rich scent, let her hunger recognize it, desire it. He moved her head down into his lap, pinning her lower body to the ground with his leg so she couldn't wiggle away. With his right hand securely in her hair, he took his other wrist and let the blood drop over her mouth again, hoping for better results.

She still frowned and turned her head, but her tongue also popped out and licked a bead off her lips. Relieved, Seamus put his wrist right onto her mouth so she could drink faster. Her hand gripped his knee weakly, like she was going to push him away, but instead she settled down and let him feed her.

"That's it, good. You'll feel better in a minute." He hoped.

After five minutes her eyes suddenly popped open and she wrenched her mouth away from his wrist. "I told you I didn't want any coffee."

He gave a strangled laugh. Even though her face was upside down, he could tell she was mad, her dark eyes spitting fire. It wasn't gratitude or raging lust, but he'd take it. It was a big improvement over dead.

"It's not coffee, babe, that I can promise you."

"It tastes horrible." She rubbed at her lips. "Why am I in your lap? Did you drug me?"

"No." Did he look like a guy who drugged women? He was kind of insulted by that, but would attribute her statement to her recent trauma. "You got hit by a car, Cara." Might as well ease into the whole "you're now a vampire" thing.

Her eyes went wide. "Am I hurt? I feel kind of strange, like I've been drinking cherry bombs. Light-headed . . . hey, is that my blood?"

She grabbed his wrist and yanked it over in front of her face. "It's everywhere, all over you. This is a lot of blood . . . why don't I feel that hurt? Is the ambulance coming?"

Seamus eased his hand away from her as she struggled to get up. Okay, so how did he put this? "Cara, you were hurt. But you've healed because I gave you my blood to drink."

Maybe that didn't sound right.

"Excuse me?" She gaped at him and scrambled onto her elbows, inching away. "I knew you were trouble. The minute I saw you, I said there's trouble, and I was so right. I mean, you did that whole weird staring thing and I told you my name even though I didn't want to, and then I had this bizarre feeling that you were hurt and so I went out into the alley and you were in my head. I mean, I could hear you in my head. And now you're saying you made me drink your blood . . . what kind of sick game are you playing?"

Seamus was trying to find a way to interrupt and explain that he was immortal when she stopped for air.

"I didn't really drink blood, did I?" Her eyes darted down to his wrists, which had healed and closed, but still had blood smeared on them.

"Well . . ." A little help here would be good, since he had no clue how to handle this. But Seamus knew he wasn't going to get any. He'd done this, now he had to make it right.

Cara touched her lips and pulled her fingers back. They were crimson from his blood.

"Holy shit! You made me drink blood. That is sick, sick, sick." She turned on her side and promptly threw up, Seamus's regurgitated blood splashing all over the asphalt.

He darted back to avoid getting hit. "Heaven and hell!" He hadn't expected that. "Cara, calm down, I can explain."

Seamus tried to pull her hair back off her face as she finished retching, but she smacked at him.

"Don't touch me. Oh, my God, look at my puke. It's red." She heaved again.

"Okay, okay, the thing is, Cara, I had to give you my blood. You died. The car hit you, and you died. I gave you my blood because I'm a vampire."

She tilted her head a little to look up at him, on her knees, her hair a curtain shielding half her face. There was a brief pause while he wondered what she was going to say, hope rising in him that maybe she understood. Then she started screaming at the top of her lungs.

"Help! Somebody help me!" She stood up, broken leg clearly healed, and ran back to the nightclub door. "The club's on fire! Everyone out!"

Oh, shit. Seamus sighed. Could he screw this up any more?

With vampire speed, he erased the distance between him and Cara. He slapped closed the door, which she had started to open. "Cara, you can't do that, darlin'." Trying to be gentle, yet firm, he wrapped his arm around her waist.

She kicked and punched him, wiggling wildly. "Let me go, you lunatic."

"I'm not going to hurt you. I want to help you, and everything is going to be okay."

Ignoring his words, she continued to fight to free herself, stomping on his foot and clocking the side of his head with the palm of her hand. That rang his ears a bit, but it wasn't any struggle at all for him to hold her, even with the thrashing.

"Okay, I'm taking you home, and we can discuss this calmly. I'll explain everything to you."

She shrieked, "I'm not going anywhere with you!" That was accompanied by another kick in his shin and an attempt to scratch out his eyes, which he thwarted. Then she reached out and bit his arm, right below his T-shirt sleeve.

He guessed it was an instinctive move, just a survival tactic to escape him, but almost immediately it became more than that. Her bite to hurt became a bite to feed. Seamus felt her new fangs puncture his flesh and eagerly draw on him. The feeling was unexpected and arousing for him, her body flush against his while she drew nourishment from him, her hair brushing against his chest. Seamus shuddered in pleasure, an erection immediately quickly growing firm and thick against her thigh.

Cara sucked and pulled for a long gratifying minute, then she jerked back, his blood on her mouth. Tongue running over her lips, she swallowed hard, distaste clear in the wrinkled moue of her nose and mouth. "What the . . . you're a vampire?"

He nodded.

"I'm a vampire?"

Seamus nodded again, rubbing his free hand along her back, the silkiness of the robe slippery. "Yes."

"No, no, no." She tried to back up again.

It was time to go back to the hotel. "Hold on, Cara." Seamus gripped her firmly, and shot straight up and over the nightclub. They were only a minute from his apartment at the casino, the Ava, if he took to the air.

Cara shrieked in his ear and clamped on his waist with arms and legs. He glanced down into her startled, wild eyes. *I'm taking you home with me,* he said directly into her mind. It was too windy to speak out loud without shouting and he wanted her to understand who he was. What she was now.

Her head shook back and forth and her teeth rattled. "No, I don't want to."

Seamus kissed her forehead, not sure why, but going on instinct. *It will work out, I promise.*

"Are we really flying?"

Yes.

"I'm afraid of heights."

Just don't look down.

Which was absolutely the wrong thing to say to someone who was afraid of heights.

She looked down, spasmed against him, and sank in a dead faint.

When Seamus carried Cara onto Ethan's balcony and knocked on the sliding glass door for someone to let him in, he cursed himself. He couldn't have made a bigger mess out of this if he had planned it.

Alexis, Ethan's wife, pulled back the drapes and unlocked the door, her jaw dropping. "Uhh..." she said as she opened the door and looked him up and down.

"Don't say anything, alright?" He brushed past her with Cara still passed out in his arms. He and Alexis didn't really get along. Truthfully, she'd always annoyed the crap out of him because of her willingness to disregard rules and protocol. Clearly, he had no business judging her now that he had a fledgling vampire in his arms.

"Did I say anything? I wouldn't dream of saying anything." Alexis was wearing sweatpants and a T-shirt and she had her computer on the coffee table, a stack of papers and a half-empty wineglass next to it. "Can I get you anything? A drink? A fresh change of clothes? A membership card to Hypocrites International?"

He supposed he deserved that. He hadn't exactly welcomed Alexis into the Vampire Nation with open arms. "No, thank you. I'm taking her to my room and I'll get us cleaned up there. Sorry to bother you, but my apartment doesn't have a balcony like yours does, and I didn't want to bring her in through the lobby."

She snorted. "I guess not. Want me to call Ethan?"

"No!" he shouted before he could consider it wasn't wise to sound so vehement.

"Chill out." Alexis stared down at Cara. "So, does she have a name? And is there a reason she's covered in blood and passed out? I can hear her breathing so I know she's alive. And I'm assuming it's nothing serious or you'd be calling 911."

"Her name is Cara. She's a stripper I met tonight and she's fine. Now." He wasn't sure he wanted to go into the rest. "And I'd appreciate it if you just kept this quiet for now."

"A stripper? I had no idea you had this kinky side, Seamus." She smirked a little. "But if she would actually like to put on something other than a silk robe when she comes to, I'd be happy to give her a T-shirt."

He hadn't gotten that far in his thought process. He was still somewhere in the *just get her tucked away in his apartment* step. "Thanks. But I'm sure I have a T-shirt if she wants one."

"You really are stubborn, aren't you?" Alexis followed him to the front door.

"I don't know what you're talking about." Seamus cradled Cara against his chest and bent awkwardly to turn the doorknob.

"It kills you to have anyone help you. And I think you would shrivel up and die before you actually *asked* for help."

There wasn't any truth to that. He was not stubborn. He was self-sufficient. He could ask for help if he needed it. "You don't know anything about me. I can ask for help." He stepped out into the hallway. "Look, if it makes you feel better, you can get my key card out of my back pocket. It's in my wallet and I don't think I can reach it."

"Fine, I can do that."

"See? I can ask for help." His body rocked a little as Alexis reached into the back pocket of his jeans.

"Yeah, you just sound like an ungrateful prick doing it, but whatever."

"Is there a reason my wife's hand is on your ass?" Ethan said from several feet behind them.

Shit. Seamus just couldn't catch a break. "She's getting my wallet out."

"I could say a million witty things right now," Alexis said. "But Seamus needs to go, honey. He has a bloody chick in his arms."

"Seamus?" Ethan asked in a quiet, questioning voice.

Alexis was too young of a vampire to figure it out, but Seamus knew Ethan was on to him. Closing his eyes briefly, he turned around and faced his friend, mentor, the vampire who had turned him. "Can we go into my room if we're going to discuss this?"

Ethan studied Cara. "We can discuss it later. Take care of her. And if she needs someone to talk to, I'm sure Alexis would be happy to walk her through the change."

"The change?" Alexis's voice rose as she handed him his key card. "Did you turn her? Seamus!"

"Keep your voice down," Ethan reprimanded. He nudged her toward the open door. Alexis smacked him back but let Ethan push her into their apartment.

"Thanks, Ethan." Seamus adjusted Cara's weight in his arms. "And Kelsey is missing again. We were at the Some Like It Hot nightclub on Spring Mountain and we were attacked. Maybe you can call her."

To his credit, Ethan probably had ten questions, but he didn't ask them. He just nodded. "Absolutely."

"Thanks." Seamus walked down the hall, swiped the key card, stepped into his suite of rooms, and gently laid Cara down on his bed.

Now he had no clue what the hell to do with her.

She was covered in blood. It was on her cheek, chin,

chest, caked in her hair, streaked down her arms, and crusted all over the back of her robe.

The least he could do was wash her face and arms.

And maybe inspiration on what to tell her would hit while he was soaping her up.

Cara was having a really excellent dream where she was an Egyptian queen and a buff slave was washing her, rubbing his big, strong hands up and down her arms, across her neck, and down her chest, causing her nipples to tighten and warmth to pool between her legs.

Lazily, she lounged on her back, and through half-open eyes checked out the slave guy servicing her.

Remarkably, he looked like Seamus Fox, the weirdo from the club. Strange that he would be in her dream, and strange that she didn't remember leaving work after meeting him.

He had that intense look on his face again, just the way he had looked at her in the club. Like he was concentrating, like he could see into her mind, her body, her soul. Cara tensed up as his head bent over her. He was going to lick her nipples, suck them hard, and she was really looking forward to it.

Except instead he froze and said, "Uhh..."

Cara frowned. That didn't sound very Egyptian slave-like. And why did her chin feel wet?

"Egyptian slave?" he said, leaning over her, the washcloth clenched in his hand. "Cara..."

Oh, my God, she wasn't sleeping. She realized it all at once, that she was still in her robe and jeans, that she was in a room she'd never seen before, and that her skin felt damp like Seamus had in reality been washing her. She glanced at the washcloth. Washing off the blood.

She tried to sit up, panic gushing over her. Holy crap, she'd seen some weird alley fight, she'd been hit by a car, she'd thrown up blood.

"Easy now. You're still adjusting to the change." Seamus pushed her onto her back.

"The change?" That's right. He had told her he was a vampire. That she was one now, too. It wasn't a dream. It was a nightmare, and it was her life. "Seamus . . . is that really your name?"

"Yes, it's really my name."

"Am I really a vampire?"

"Yes."

Not what she wanted to hear. Not good, not good at all. Overcome with nine thousand conflicting feelings, all of them ugly and frightened and hysterical, she stared up into his gorgeous face and searched for something—compassion, friendliness, anything. All she saw was discomfort.

"It will be fine," he said.

"I hate you," she replied, and embarrassed herself by bursting into tears.

Seamus dropped the washcloth, put out his hand, and patted her head. "Shit, don't do that. Don't cry, it's okay."

She swatted at his hand. He was petting her like a dog. "Go away and die." Then she started laughing, hysterical snuffling snorts. "But you can't, can you? You can't die."

"No." He shook his head, looking baffled. "And neither can you now."

Pushing hard on his chest, she sat up. She couldn't lie there like that, feeling helpless, him hovering over her. She choked back more sobs and demanded, "Why didn't you leave me dead in the street? I don't want to be a vampire! I don't like the sight of blood. I don't like black. I'm in vet school and I have three dogs and two cats at home."

Just the thought of her animals sent her into a panic. "My babies! What's going to happen to them? I have to call my neighbor so she can let them out in the morning. They're used to me getting home around three."

"Your . . . babies?"

"My dogs. I have two Labs and a Chihuahua, plus a tabby and a tiger." Cara stood up, tugging her robe together at her breasts, and glanced around. Where was the freaking door? She may be dead, but she wasn't Seamus's prisoner. Cara spotted the front door and charged for it.

She got two feet before her legs gave out from under her. The carpet rushed up to meet her and she was two inches from a resounding splat when Seamus grabbed her and scooped her up.

"Whoa . . . take it easy. You need some time before you go tearing off." He smiled down at her as he cradled her in his arms.

It was that charming smile again. The one that pissed her off because she couldn't help but feel her body respond to it. The memory of his hands rubbing over her chest rushed through her mind, making her feel warm and distracted. He really was so damn attractive.

"I'll take care of your pets," he said in a low, gentle voice. "And I didn't leave you on the street dead because it was my fault you were there in the first place. I'm sorry, Cara. I'm very, very sorry."

It was hard to hold on to all of her anger when he looked so full of remorse, so solemn. Cara relaxed in his arms a little, realizing that if he hadn't turned her into a vampire, she would be dead. Something she didn't really like the sound of. Maybe vampire wasn't such a bad deal given the alternative. She would just have to readjust her expectations for her life. But she wanted to go home, be alone, and think.

"You can't go home," he said. "You have to stay with me until I think it's safe for you to leave." He smiled. "And in the meantime, maybe we can explore that Egyptian slave fantasy of yours."

"What?" Cara scrambled to get out of his arms, her cheeks burning. "I don't know what you're talking about!" The bastard was reading her thoughts. Just plucking them right out of her head.

"Yes, I am," he said, with no sign of an apology.

"That's incredibly rude!" Cara managed to get her feet on the ground, but her waist was still trapped in Seamus's grip.

He shrugged. "It's a vampire talent. One I'm good at."

"Well, stop it!" She wiggled in his arms, jerking backward against his grip. All she managed to do was bounce right back into his chest. Her cheek hit his pectoral muscle and her lips tasted the cotton of his T-shirt.

Desperate to get away from him, she bent her knees and dropped down to slip out of his arms, but he just grabbed her shoulders. He had the strength of ten men. The strength of a vampire. He wasn't even struggling to hold her and she suddenly became aware that her face was on his crotch. Her nose was pressing into the denim on his thigh and she could see a bump that wasn't a cell phone.

"Sorry," she said, mortified. This was not a position she'd intended to get into.

"I'm kind of enjoying it," he said, sounding amused. But he still helped her stand until she was facing him.

Cara was breathing hard, feeling dizzy, a sharp burning

sensation in her stomach distracting her. Seamus's lip was right in front of her and it was pink, soft. There was a smell she didn't recognize, sharp and tinny, and saliva pooled in her mouth. She went to lick her lips and bit her tongue by accident.

"You're hungry, aren't you?" Seamus asked, his hands stroking her shoulders. "You smell my blood, Cara. You want more, don't you?"

She wasn't sure what she wanted, just that the world seemed sharper, the colors brighter, the sound amplified and super heightened. Her mouth watered, her eyes narrowed, and she focused on the vein in Seamus's neck, pulsing, pulsing, pulsing.

"Go on," he whispered, pulling her flush against his body. "Take what your body wants."

His hand pushed her closer and closer to him until her lips hovered over his flesh, an inch from his neck. Cara shut her eyes, flicked her tongue out, licked him. His breath caught, and she felt a deep hot hunger rip all the way through her, consume her, inflame her. She wanted with a ferociousness that was as frightening as it was powerful. Cara opened her mouth and bit, sinking her new fangs into his body, instinctively sucking his blood up and over her tongue.

It tasted unpleasant, like alcohol on the rocks, harsh and stinging, but even as her mouth protested, her body rejoiced. She felt it warm her everywhere, winging out in all directions, an erotic, heady elixir of power and satisfaction. Heat pooled in her womb, tugged at her nipples, tickled between her thighs. She spread her legs on either side of his thigh and rocked herself against him, the hardness of his erection catching her own inner thigh with each bump.

She drank and moved, body pressing against his with growing urgency. It felt delicious, frantic, a desperate desire for more, more, more. Seamus cupped her breast, brushing aside her robe while she continued to draw on him, sucking harder and harder, her grip intense, her body flush with pleasure. When he pinched her nipple, she broke the bite and gave a soft cry as she came. The orgasm took her by surprise, stealing her breath, and sending her head flinging back. She ground against him and rode it out, the sharp pleasure intense and all-consuming.

Cara forced her eyes open, sucked in some air, and stared at Seamus as her body shuddered in tiny aftershocks. "Whoa. Does that always happen?" Maybe this vampire thing had fringe benefits. That was the best orgasm she'd ever had.

Seamus shook his head, his eyes dark and filled with lust. "No."

"Too bad." Cara wiped her mouth and grimaced at the blood. "It tastes disgusting in my mouth, but what it does everywhere else . . ." She shivered in pleasure. "Amazing."

He pulled his hand from her breast. "You're amazing, you know that? Gorgeous, just absolutely gorgeous." Seamus brushed her hair off her forehead. "Everything will be fine."

"Okay," she said, because she was feeling too satisfied to care otherwise.

"Now why don't you take a shower while I go check on your animals."

Cara touched Seamus's neck where she had bitten. The holes were quickly healing. She wondered how soon he would let her do that again. "Can you bring my babies here? I'd like to see them."

"Of course I can. I want to help you adjust, Cara. I want

to make sure you're comfortable. Whatever you want, I'll try to give you."

She ran her finger over his flesh where the wound was almost completely gone. He really, really felt good.

"Whatever I want?" She licked her lips again and wondered if there were other places she could bite him.

Four

"Don't let her leave," Seamus told Alexis for the third time.

"I heard you." Alexis rolled her eyes at him.

"And don't let her drink any more blood. She's had enough." More than enough. He'd let her feed off him three times.

"Yes, Dad."

Seamus paced back and forth, not at all sure it was wise to leave Cara with Alexis. "As soon as Ethan gets back from looking for Kelsey, ask him to stay with you and Cara, okay?"

Alexis saluted him in mockery. "Sir, yes, sir."

The water was running in his bathroom, distracting him. He didn't want to leave Cara with Alexis. He didn't want to imagine what she looked like right about now, naked in the shower, water rolling all over those fabulous curves. He still had a lingering pseudo-erection from watching her orgasm, and the thought of her naked, what he could do to her . . .

"Yuck. You're projecting. Close your mind, Seamus." Alexis crossed her arms over her chest and grimaced at him.

Wonderful. Seamus slammed closed the door to his thoughts and rubbed his jaw, incredibly embarrassed. Alexis was the last person in the world he wanted to know he was horny. "I don't know what you're talking about," he said. "I'll be back in half an hour. Call me if you have any questions or anything goes wrong."

"I won't let her leave, I won't let her feed, I won't open the door to strangers, and I won't let her play with stakes," she said, rolling her eyes. "Will you just leave? You could have been there and back six times by now."

Seamus wondered yet again what Ethan saw in Alexis. To each his own, obviously, because Alexis grated on his nerves. In fact, most women annoyed him in some capacity or another. That was why he was celibate and a workaholic instead of a married vampire being nagged between sessions of sex.

Neither was a perfect existence, but listening to Alexis, he decided he'd made the right choice. He may be sexually frustrated, but at least he had peace.

"I'm leaving." He went for the balcony, knowing it was quicker to just jump down to his car than to take the elevator.

"Great. Take your time. No need to worry. Your new girlfriend and I will have fun getting to know each other. We can do each other's makeup and talk about faking orgasms. Complain about men, that sort of thing."

"Great. Thank you," he said, forcing himself to sound nonchalant. She was not going to get him angry. He refused. Instead of arguing with her, he opened the door and shot off the balcony, nervous energy pumping through his body.

What the hell had he done?

And how was he going to corral two Labs and a Chihuahua? He had raised hounds in the eighteenth century, but that had been in England, on Ethan's expansive estate with a multitude of servants and a stable.

What in hell was he supposed to do with animals in a Vegas casino?

Which was why he detoured to an all-night discount superstore and headed for the pet supply aisle.

The minute Seamus left the balcony, Alexis called her husband on his cell phone, watching the bathroom door to make sure Cara didn't come out.

"I'm in the middle of something, beautiful," Ethan said without a hello.

"So am I. Seamus has me baby-sitting his stripper while he goes to get her dogs for her. Her dogs, Ethan. Does this sound like your campaign manager to you? He hasn't even checked the polls once all night." It was starting to freak Alexis out. She could set her clock by Seamus's annoying political hourly updates. "And where is Kelsey?"

Before Alexis had married Ethan, she had been stabbed by a vampire, the same one who had attacked Kelsey. As a result, Alexis felt a certain affinity for Kelsey, since Ethan and Seamus had given them both life back on the same night. Granted, Kelsey had already been a vampire, but she had been drained of all her blood, and would have died, a vampire starvation, had Seamus not given her a significant amount of his blood. When Alexis had stumbled upon Kelsey's body that night, the vampire had still been there, and he stabbed her. Alexis would have died if Ethan hadn't turned her, and she was now worried that maybe there was more to their dual attacks than any of them had realized.

"I found Kelsey. She's at home, in her apartment. She appears to be fine, though quiet, which is odd for her. She doesn't remember getting home either."

"That's weird." Okay, so Kelsey was a little weird. And a ditz. But even she should be able to recall the trip from the strip club alley to her apartment.

The whole thing made Alexis uncomfortable. "Ethan, will you stop by and check on my sister?"

"Brittany? Why? Has she called you? It's almost four in the morning. Isn't she asleep?"

Alexis certainly hoped so. But she worried about her sister, who was the product of their mother's affair with a vampire. Seamus was determined to uncover his identity, and had considered Aunt Jodi a possible lead. Brittany had vampire blood, but no powers, and was trusting to an extreme. Alexis had made worrying for her practically a full-time job. "She hasn't called, but I don't know . . . this whole thing is making me nervous. And Brittany's been depressed since she had sex with Corbin and he disappeared like five minutes later."

"I still can't believe she slept with the Frenchman, arguably the most controversial vampire in the entire Vampire Nation."

That irritated Alexis. "Well, it's not like she knew! He didn't tell her he was a banished research scientist vampire, setting off undead debates about the ethics of immortality with his search for a 'cure' to vampirism. I guess that didn't pop up first thing, though I can't imagine why not. Please. You people walk around and act like you're normal, and the next thing we know, we're in bed with a vampire."

"Are you in bed with a vampire? Right now?" Ethan's voice got hard, jealous, violent like the warrior he'd been in his youth.

Please. Alexis often marveled that even though he was nine hundred years old, Ethan could still act like he was a twenty-year-old frat boy in a bar brawl.

"Yes. So go check on my sister and hurry home so you can watch."

"Alexis..." he growled.

She made a kissy sound into the phone and said, "Love you," before hanging up on him.

That would light a fire under his ass.

"I need a cage and a leash for my girlfriend," Seamus told the store clerk, startled as hell when the word *girlfriend* just popped out of his mouth. He was attracted to Cara, he felt extremely guilty for the way the night had played out, but *girlfriend* was taking it too far, even if it was just easier to call her that than explain his whole life story to a stranger.

"Yeah, don't we all," the twenty-year-old clerk said, a grin splitting his wan face.

Huh? Seamus looked at the guy blankly for a second before realizing what exactly he'd said. "I mean for her dogs."

"Right." The guy's finger came out and he made a sound with his teeth. "Probably better to use handcuffs on the girlfriend anyway."

Seamus ignored that and pointed to a cage in front of him. "Is this big enough for a Lab, you think?"

The clerk scratched his chin, stroking his little fuzzy beard. "How long of a trip?"

"Just ten minutes. My girlfriend, she got hit by a car." Always go with the truth when you can. "And she's going to be moving in with me for a while until she's better. But she's insisting the pets come, too, and man, I'm just not sure this is such a good idea. Two Labs, a Chihuahua, and two cats."

He whistled. "Whoa. Major animal lover. But that's not really the problem, is it? I can tell. You're a little worried about the whole cohabitation thing, aren't you?"

Yes, he was. Terrified. "Well, you know, this is a big deal. It's a lot of responsibility, and we're going to be together all the time, and I'm used to my privacy . . ."

Seamus was whining to the store clerk. The night was officially complete.

"I hear ya. Nothing changes a relationship like living together. It's just one step away from walking down the aisle and that can be a little scary."

"Exactly." He was already responsible for Kelsey. For Ethan's presidential campaign. For finding Brittany's father. Now he was responsible for keeping Cara by his side until she was ready to live on her own. And Cara came with pets and an incredibly hot body. Together it was an overwhelming package.

"Are you in love with her?"

"No." He had been in love only once, with Marie, and look at how that had turned out. Subconsciously, he touched the scar on his neck. He could admit to some lust for Cara, but he wasn't taking the love train again.

"Then you're crazy letting all those damn dogs into your place."

He was starting to think he *had* lost his mind. Along with his common sense, his edge, and his rationale.

Not to mention the two hundred and thirty-two dollars he was spending on pet supplies.

Cara toweled herself dry, amazed at how every move felt sharper, crisper, like she had spent the first twenty-eight years of her life moving through mud and now she was free. Everything shifted faster, caught in her fingers quicker, and she felt vibrant, healthy, strong. That was interesting, appealing even.

But then there was the anger and embarrassment. Seamus Fox had wrecked her life. Flirted with her, tried to vampire mind control her, gotten her killed, and told her she had to stay with him, a virtual prisoner, until he said otherwise. And how had she reacted? By having an orgasm while humping his thigh.

She wanted to die.

Except she was dead already.

This was why she was still a virgin. Because sex was a way for men to control women. Keep them barefoot and pregnant and under their thumb. She wasn't going to buy into that. No matter how good it had felt.

And it had felt good.

Cara shivered as her body warmed in memory. She took the towel and wiped the steam off the mirror. Then screamed at the top of her lungs. She dropped the towel—which had been dangling in the air in the mirror with no hand attached to it—and backed up.

She had no reflection in the mirror. She really was dead. She really was a bloodsucking vampire. And she liked it. She'd had an orgasm while sucking blood. Her life as she knew it was totally over. How could she ever explain this to her grandmother?

There was a knock at the door. "Are you okay?"

It was a woman. "Yes." No. Cara grabbed her panties

and slipped them on. "Umm . . . who are you? Where's Seamus?" So she could beat the crap out of him for ruining her life.

"I'm Alexis, Ethan's wife. Seamus went to get your dogs, but he thought it would be better if you weren't alone."

So he could keep her prisoner. "Are you a vampire, too?" Cara grabbed her pants and dragged them on, trying to ignore the blood crusted above the knee.

"Yes. I'm two months young." Alexis had a firm, no-nonsense voice that Cara appreciated even as she was feeling a bit hysterical.

"Cara, do you need some new clothes? Yours looked like they should be tossed in the trash."

Needing to see another vampire besides Seamus and the two loser thugs in the alley, Cara wrapped the bath towel around her chest and opened the door. "Thanks for the offer," she said to the petite woman with blond hair standing in front of her wearing sweatpants. Alexis looked so completely normal that Cara relaxed a little. "I could use a T-shirt."

"I thought so." Alexis held out a dark green shirt. "I tried to tell Seamus, but he swore he had it under control, then of course, he completely forgot, didn't he?" She shook her head. "He has tunnel vision—focuses on one thing and ignores everything else. And usually the tunnel vision is something he wants, you know what I mean?"

"No." Cara took the shirt and bunched it against her chest. "I don't know Seamus at all. I just met him tonight." And her entire future rested in his controlling, tunnel vision, firm, vampire hands.

She hated him at the same time she wanted him.

"Why don't you finish getting dressed and then come out into the living room? You can ask me anything you want about becoming a vampire. It's not so bad, really. It has some definite perks."

Cara had experienced one already. One she was going to have to resist in the future if she wanted to retain any sort of dignity whatsoever.

"I just want to know where I am and how I can get home."

Alexis rocked back on her heels. "Well... you're at the Ava, the casino and hotel owned by my husband. You're in Seamus's apartment. Ethan and I live down the hall, and there are approximately six vampire bodyguards living in between us and the elevator. Ethan is president of the Vampire Nation and Seamus is his campaign manager. We're six weeks out from the election and... sweetie?" Alexis shot her a look of sympathy.

"Yes?" Cara asked, heart pounding. Vampire elections? What the hell was that?

"Seamus doesn't want you to leave. Which means you'll have to get past him and the six bodyguards. A couple of them aren't the swiftest undead guys I've ever met, but pulling the wool over all six at once might be tough."

"So I'm a prisoner? Indefinitely?" She'd go insane. She didn't like being idle, she didn't like being told what to do, she didn't like her whole world turning upside down and being tossed out like yesterday's garbage.

"Give yourself a day or two to adjust to the change," Alexis said. "Then if the look on Seamus's face when he brought you in here is any indication, you could have him eating out of your hand in a week if you want to."

What she wanted him eating out of and what she wanted intellectually were two different things. Cara tightened the grip on her towel. "I'd rather beat the crap out of him."

"That could be fun, too."

"Okay, listen." Seamus got down on his hands and knees for the ninth time and peered under Cara's leather couch. Two pairs of cat eyes stared back at him. "I'm taking you to Cara. I swear. Vampire honor. But I can't do that if you don't come out."

All his encouraging pep talk earned him was a defiant hiss from the one on the left and a disdainful sneer from the one on the right. "This is ridiculous." Seamus stood and picked up one end of the couch and flipped it right up on its side. "What do you think of that, boys? No hiding place left."

He reached down for the orange tabby as the black one shot between his legs and tripped him. He slammed his shoulder into the couch he had just stood up and his hip knocked the undersprings, rocking the whole thing precariously. He grabbed at the orange cat again, out of balance, out of breath, and pissed off. He'd been playing this game for twenty minutes. He was a four-hundred-year-old vampire, with exceptional hearing, speed, and strength. Yet these cats were besting him because he was afraid to hurt them, and the whole thing was definitely getting old.

A fistful of fur and fat in his hand, he tried to drag the cat back toward him, but it bit his hand and wiggled away, leaping onto an end table and knocking Cara's glass-base lamp off.

"Shit." The lamp broke, spraying shards of glass all over the hardwood floor, and the two Labradors started barking loudly in the kitchen, where they were cowering away from him. The Chihuahua snarled and ran in hysterical laps back and forth on the dining room table, where Seamus had set it until he could figure out what to do with it. It couldn't get down off the high table with its short legs, but it was howling like an Irish banshee.

Seamus pulled himself back to full height, only to turn and find the black cat standing on the arm of the couch, four feet in the air. He reached out for it, and it bit him on the nose.

"Bastard!" That stung. Seamus blinked hard and abandoned the cat project.

He opened the door of the largest crate in preparation and went for the black Labs. They had the good sense to be afraid of him. They must have sensed his vampire blood, because they cowered and snarled and backed away a step for each he took in their direction. Seamus leaned over, stared into the one's eyes with all his concentration, and told him, "Get in the crate."

Without moving, the dog barked twice, which Seamus decided was the canine equivalent of "Fuck you."

He really didn't want to use force with Cara's animals. With his strength and speed, he could wrestle them into submission, but he didn't like getting rough. He had enjoyed raising dogs in the eighteenth century. He liked them, and usually they liked him. Cara's dogs were like her—they wanted him to go to hell.

When he took another step forward, the one dog growled at him and bared his teeth.

"Mine are bigger than yours, buddy," Seamus told him and flashed his own fangs.

If a dog could frown, this one was doing it. Its brow furrowed and then it skirted around the doorway and shot down the hall toward the bedroom.

"Damn. I scared it."

At a loss, Seamus glanced over at the door. He smelled vampire. There was a knock, then he heard Ethan.

"It's me, open the door."

He did and Ethan stared at him for a second, assessing his appearance. One brow rose. "Need some help?"

"Yes. These animals are psychotic." He stepped back to let Ethan in, glad for reinforcements.

"What do we have?"

"Two Labs that think I'm the devil, an obnoxious Chihuahua that thinks he's the devil, and two cats that really are the devil."

Ethan fought a grin.

"What?" Seamus turned, unlatched the smallest crate, and lifted the Chihuahua off the table one-handed. Trying to be gentle but firm, he rammed it into the cage and slammed the door shut. "Just cool it, Satan."

"Nothing." Ethan went into the kitchen, sending the other dog streaking out into the living room. It spotted Seamus, panicked, and vaulted down the hallway toward his companion. "It's just nice to see you taking an interest in a woman again," Ethan called as he opened cabinets in Cara's kitchen and closed them again.

This was not interest in a woman. This was insanity. "Cara is not a woman. She is a mistake I made that I'm going to pay for indefinitely. I'm already paying." He curled his lip at the brown Chihuahua, whose little sausage body quivered in indignation. "To the tune of two hundred and thirty bucks and five furry pains in the arse."

His native brogue tended to increase when he was annoyed. At the moment, he sounded like he'd just stepped out of the potato field. "And what the hell are you doing?" The can opener was whirring in the kitchen. He headed for the doorway. "Last time I checked, you don't eat solids."

"Tuna," Ethan said, holding up a can.

"That smells disgusting." Like rotting corpse. Bad blood. Sweaty men. All mixed together.

"Cats love it."

And to prove his point, both cats appeared out of nowhere and rubbed against Ethan's legs.

Annoyed, Seamus said, "Aw, isn't that cute? You and your two kitties. Bet your wife would like a cat for Christmas."

"Over my dead body," Ethan said.

They looked at each other and laughed.

Ethan shoved the can of food into the open crate and both cats leapt onto the coffee table and straight in. He latched the door closed. "Three down, two to go."

Seamus rubbed his temples and gave a rueful shake of his head. "How in hell did I get myself into this?"

"I think it's called lust."

Heading down the hall, Seamus called back, "I think it's called stupidity."

Then he stepped into Cara's bedroom and almost had a heart attack. The dogs were crouched down on the purple throw rug, but he barely spared them a glance. What had caught his attention was the bed. It was big, white wrought iron, with a bunch of material draped over it from a hook in the ceiling, making it look sexy and exotic, like Cara. It was unmade, the lavender sheets rumpled and shoved aside, and the whole room smelled like... woman. Soft and floral and alluring. There was a red bra tossed on the floor, a pair of jeans bunched on an easy chair, and various lotions and makeup scattered across her dresser.

But what stopped him dead in his tracks, robbed him of all breath and all coherent thought, was the thing lying in the middle of her bed, like she'd tossed it aside negligently after getting up.

"What . . . what am I looking at?" he asked Ethan, wanting confirmation.

"Where?" Ethan came up behind him and looked in the room. Seamus knew the minute he saw it because his posture stiffened. "Holy crap. Uh, well, shit. It's a vibrator."

That's what Seamus had thought. He ran his fingers through his hair and tried not to stare at it. "You were definitely right," he said, feeling a little weak, like he'd lost all of his brain blood to his massive erection. "It's lust."

"Why don't I get the dogs while you stand there and drool."

Seamus absently glanced down at the Labs, reaching for the nearest one and scratching the backs of his ears, digging his fingers into the warm fur and flesh. "Why, Ethan? Why did I have to pick a stripper? Someone this . . ." He nodded to the purple vibrator. Damn, that was unbelievable. It even matched the rest of her bedroom. "This sensual. Confident in her own sexuality."

She was going to eat him alive.

"I think you answered your own question. And the dog seems to have warmed up to you."

Seamus glanced down at the dog in surprise. Its eyes were half-closed, tongue lolling out of its mouth in ecstasy as Seamus rubbed and scratched his head. "Well, at least somebody likes me."

The red bra leaped out at him again when he gave another wary glance around the room. "I guess I should pack some of her things. I can't let her leave my place until I can trust she understands how to live in her new life, according to our rules."

"Get the dog in the crate while he's being so mellow and I'll pack a bag."

Seamus frowned. "I don't think you should be touching

Cara's clothes." The image of Ethan pawing through her drawers didn't sit well with him.

"And you should?" Ethan opened the closet and pulled out a red suitcase with wheels. "At least I won't get aroused by it. If you do it, we'll be here all day while you investigate every article of clothing she owns."

Ethan yanked three pairs of jeans off their hangers and tossed them into the suitcase with brutal efficiency.

Seamus felt a little better, and he looked down at the dog. "You're coming with me, kiddo. We need to get out of here before I do something even stupider than I already have."

Since the urge to poke in all of Cara's drawers in pursuit of sex toys to feed his very active imagination was intense, he backed up, coaxing the dog with him.

Let Ethan deal with it. He needed to get the hell out of her bedroom.

Ethan watched Seamus retreat like the whole Royal Navy was bearing down on him and shook his head. They had been friends for a long time. Fought on three continents and in six wars together and he'd seen Seamus like this only once before. With Marie.

That little witch had nearly destroyed Seamus, and he had spent the last two hundred years in enforced solitude because of her. It was unnatural to live the way Seamus did, with no relationships, no sex, no hobbies. Just work, all the time.

A woman like Cara could be good for Seamus. Help loosen him up. Make him understand that there was more to life than politics and that not everything could be resolved by launching an opinion poll and stating the data.

Making sure Seamus wasn't near the doorway, Ethan

took one of Cara's little cotton T-shirts and leaned over the bed. Using it like an oven mitt, he picked up the vibrator and tossed it into her suitcase. That ought to get a conversation going between Seamus and Cara when she found that in her bag.

On top of it, he piled more shirts, a whole handful of undergarments, a makeup bag off her dresser, and a pair of gym shoes.

Whistling, he zipped it closed. Alexis would be impressed with his quick thinking. His wife always commented that Seamus would be more pleasant if he were having sex.

Damn, Ethan was just brilliant.

Five

Cara was having a hard time staying awake. Her eyelids kept slipping closed and her body felt sluggish, exhausted.

"I'm sorry," she told Alexis as she yawned for the ninth time. "I don't mean to be rude."

It wasn't Alexis's company that was dragging her down. Alexis was funny and matter-of-fact, and had told Cara all kinds of interesting things about the Vampire Nation and Seamus's role in Ethan's campaign. It seemed she had the blood from one very uptight vampire.

But now she was sleepy and it was taking everything she had to stay awake and vertical.

"Don't worry about it. Go to sleep if you're tired. You're still adjusting to the change."

Cara slid down in the couch, tucking her feet under one of the cushions. "I wanted to stay awake to see my animals, but I don't think I'm going to make it."

"I'm sure Seamus has it under control. He may be boring and rude, but he's very thorough."

Odd, but Cara wouldn't have thought of Seamus as either of those adjectives. She might have said persistent, intense, sexy, and domineering, but definitely not boring. And while he was confident, and had ruined her life and given her a really embarrassing orgasm that she wished she could forget, she wouldn't call him rude either.

Not to mention he was very cute.

"Cute?" Alexis said, her legs crossed as she sat in the big overstuffed chair. "You think Seamus is cute?"

"Did I say that out loud?" Cara was so tired, she wasn't sure what she was saying anymore. "Or are you doing that mind-reading thing?"

"Yep. Very annoying vampire trick, isn't it? Lock your thoughts around Seamus unless you want him hearing that he's cute. Personally, I wouldn't advise it. Not if you want to get out of here."

Yes, she wanted out of there. Her life as she knew it was gone. But she wanted out of Seamus's apartment. It was the only thing she was sure of before she collapsed into total oblivion.

When she woke up again, she was in a bed that wasn't hers and someone was warm and breathing deeply beside her. She hoped beyond anything it was Alexis, but somehow she really doubted Ethan's wife would be sleeping with her. Which meant it had to be Seamus, and the thought of being in bed with Seamus made her heart race from anger and something that might be desire, if she were honest with herself, which she didn't intend to be.

Nervous and disoriented, Cara became aware she was

still wearing her jeans and the borrowed T-shirt—thank God she wasn't naked—and the room was dark, the drapes drawn. She tentatively rolled on her side, prepared to meet her maker, literally. Instead of coming face-to-face with Seamus, she saw it was one of her Labs, Button, lying next to her.

Her old friend, familiar and cuddly, was immeasurably better than a sexy vampire in bed with her.

"Hey, sweet baby," she said in complete relief, petting her dog's head. He opened his eyes for a brief second, then snuffled back into sleep.

It was so normal, his reaction so uninterested and typical, that she wanted to cry in gratitude. She could give up a lot of things, but never her babies.

"Button's such a good baby," she murmured, snuggling in closer to him, wanting comfort and loving. "Where are Fritz and Mr. Spock, hmm?"

"Mr. Spock? Who the hell did you name Mr. Spock?"

Startled, Cara glanced over and saw Seamus standing in the doorway with Fritz at his side. Despite the darkness, she could see him clearly. He was wearing lounge pants and a Notre Dame T-shirt. His fingers played idly in her dog's back fur and Fritz looked perfectly content to be fondled by his new friend.

"Mr. Spock is my Chihuahua. Where is he?" Cara made sure the navy bed sheet was still over most of her body. Being around Seamus made her feel naked.

"He's scarfing down some really expensive dog food in my kitchen. I can't believe you named him Mr. Spock. No wonder he's such an asshole. I would be, too, if that was my name." Seamus came into the room, Fritz following along beside him like he was tethered to his leg.

"He's not an asshole!" Cara sat up, indignant. No one

messed with her fur babies. "I named him Mr. Spock because of his ears, and he's very sweet." And how dare he walk around with Fritz like he was *his* dog?

"If that's sweet, I'd hate to see pissed off." Seamus sat down on the bed by Cara's feet, his legs spread and his forearms on his thighs, hands cupped together. Fritz trotted in between his knees and shamelessly rubbed his head under Seamus's hands.

"How are you feeling?"

"Are you talking to me or the dog?" she asked in annoyance. "Because he looks pretty content."

"He likes me," Seamus said, making cutesy faces at her dog. "Don't ya, buddy? Yep, we're good friends now, aren't we?"

Fritz gave a happy bark.

Cara bit her lip and tried not to feel jealous. It didn't work.

Seamus turned to her. "But I meant you, actually. How are you feeling?"

That was a good question. Cara thought about it. She still felt a little tired, but otherwise fine. Great, in fact. Strong and highly aware of the room around her, of texture on her skin, the sound of the air-conditioning humming, and the amazing ability to see even though the room was dark. Physically, she was the new and improved Cara.

Mentally? She was feeling a little stressed, to put it politely.

"I'm fine." Total lie. Her whole life had been altered forever. She was borderline hysterical and altogether terrified, yet she had no intention of letting him know how vulnerable she felt.

"I brought a suitcase full of clothes and stuff from your apartment. It's in the corner by the closet." He gestured in that direction. "Why don't you get changed and we can give you a tour of the casino and discuss some relevant... issues."

"What time is it?" She felt like she'd slept for hours, yet she sensed it was still dark outside.

"Just past midnight."

She stared at Seamus blankly. "But I didn't leave the club until almost two. How can it be midnight?"

"It's midnight on Thursday. You slept through the day."

"Thursday?" Cara shoved back the blankets. "Shit! I'm late for work." She swung her legs around until she was sitting next to Seamus, looking around frantically for her suitcase. She did not want to lose this job. It paid well, and the management understood her appeal to clientele was the mystery of the screen. Never had they asked her to dance without it, which kept her happy.

"I called you in sick for the next two weeks. Your manager was very understanding when I explained you got hit by a car."

Cara stopped en route to her suitcase and swung around. "You did *what*? Maybe we need to discuss our issues right now, because you cannot just walk into my life and take charge. Rule number one: Back off."

Furious, she glared at him. He just petted Fritz and stared back at her, very calm and confident.

"Rule number two," he said. "Until I am convinced you understand all facets of your new life, and I'm assured of your safety from the two vampires who attacked us in the alley, you will not be working at the club. You will not be leaving this casino, or even this apartment, without an appropriate escort."

"That's ridiculous!"

"It's for your own good."

"What are you, my dad?" Cara stomped over to her suitcase, so angry she was on the verge of tears. She could not, would not, stay with him, doing whatever he wanted. She had always lived her life on her terms, free from the suffocating domination of men. The one time she had given up control, let herself fall in love, she'd only lived to regret it. She wanted to maul Seamus for doing this to her.

When she bent over to unzip her suitcase, her head spun a little, and her stomach burned. She tried to ignore it.

"No, fatherly is not how I feel about you."

Determined to ignore the sensual ripple moving over her body at the sexy huskiness in his voice, she zipped the suitcase open, still upright, and let the contents slide out toward the floor in a pile of bunched clothing. "I don't want to stay here," she said firmly.

"I know. But you don't have a choice." Seamus drummed his thumbs on his knees. "It's to protect you, Cara. To protect every vampire in the nation. If you stumble around not knowing what you're doing, you risk your exposure—and therefore our exposure—to mortals. Or you could inadvertently break our rules and bring censure down on yourself. I can't allow that."

"Alexis said you're anal to a fault." She pawed through the pile looking for some clean panties. And a bra would be really helpful. It was dangerous to walk around Seamus in a tight T-shirt without one.

"I'm very organized. Thorough. If that's a flaw to Alexis, clearly we don't agree."

Yes, he was thorough. There was everything she could need in her suitcase: toiletries, makeup bag, hairbrush, blow-dryer, pj's, matching bra and panty sets, an assortment of jeans and shirts, and gym shoes.

He had even packed her vibrator.

Cara felt her cheeks go hot. He must have gone through her dresser drawers. He must have found *that* drawer. The one that had various forms of stress relief, as she liked to think of it. He must have packed it to embarrass her, but somehow that didn't seem like something Seamus would do. Her first assessment made more sense—that he was just thorough, gathering everything he thought she might want.

Because she remembered that it hadn't been in her drawer at all. She'd left it out on the bed. In full view. After using it. Oh, help.

He must have assumed it was a necessity to her if it was out and ready to go.

Could she be any more mortified?

"What's the matter? Did I forget something? I can go back for you or we can buy anything you need in the casino. There are a dozen shops downstairs."

That he could sound so innocent, so helpful, ticked her off. "Ones that sell these?" She picked up the vibrator and waved it in the air, wanting to make it clear to him she wasn't addicted to it or anything. She wasn't embarrassed she had it, but she sure in hell didn't want him to think she *needed* it. "Thanks for packing it, but I could have gone a few days without it."

Seamus's jaw dropped. "I didn't pack that! Ethan packed your bag."

That made her roll her eyes. "Oh, right. Like Ethan, a married man, would just scoop up my vibrator."

"Maybe he didn't know what it was," Seamus said, but he was lying. Cara could tell by the way his eyes darted off her and onto Fritz.

"How old is Ethan?"

"Nine hundred and something."

Jesus. That almost sidetracked Cara. But she managed to give Seamus another glare. "Then he knows what it is, give me a break. And just admit it. You put it in here to piss me off."

"I did not put it in there," he said, his voice rising in anger. "But if it had been me, I wouldn't have packed it to piss you off. I would have packed it because it's damn hot to picture you using it on yourself."

Cara was sorry she'd brought it up. Because now they were staring at each other, both angry, both breathing hard, Seamus looking hot and bothered, Cara feeling hot and bothered. She would not picture lying on Seamus's bed, moaning in pleasure, legs spread, Seamus standing at the bottom of the bed watching her, his eyes dark, erection thick.

"Cara . . . I can see your thoughts," Seamus said, his words trailing off into a groan.

"Shit! Stop doing that." She buried her face in her hands and rubbed hard, like that would erase the mental image of her going to town with Seamus as an audience. The burn in her stomach grew stronger. "Well, just so you know, I had it out because I was cleaning my dresser drawers, reorganizing. I don't *need* it."

"Okay," he said, but he didn't look like he believed her. "It's none of my business, you don't have to explain yourself to me."

"Exactly." She shoved the vibrator in an outside pocket on the suitcase so she wouldn't have to look at it. When she saw it alongside Seamus, it made her want to rethink her whole no-men philosophy. Being with him seemed so much more appealing than a date with a jelly vibe. And that was very dangerous thinking.

"And even if I was attracted to you and did want to watch you satisfying yourself—not that I'm saying I am—it wouldn't be a good idea to act on that feeling."

"Right." She thought. Cara rubbed her stomach. That burning was getting worse. It felt like an ulcer was forming and spreading right as she was sitting there.

"Hungry?" he asked, standing up. Seamus clapped his hands and both Fritz and Button bounded toward the bedroom door and out into the living room. He closed the door shut behind them.

"I... don't know." Was that hunger? It felt more like pain. Growing more vivid and agonizing with each passing second.

Seamus lifted his wrist to his mouth and slashed his skin open with his teeth. Immediately Cara smelled the blood, warm and vital, and her stomach cramped convulsively. "Yes, I think I'm hungry." Ravenous.

"We'll let you feed, then we'll discuss what you need to know about being a vampire."

"So that I can go home." Her eyes locked onto the beads of blood flowing from Seamus's wrist, trickling across his skin like a robust red wine. It looked delicious. It smelled even better. Cara licked her lips and swallowed hard, fighting the urge to leap up and cover it with her mouth.

"Yes, so you can go home. I don't want to keep you here either, Cara. You are a distraction for me." Seamus sat back down on the bed and flexed his fist several times. "Come sit with me."

He didn't have to ask her twice, especially now that the blood was flowing freely, all down to his elbow, and pooling in a delicious little puddle above his palm.

She walked toward him. "Why am I a distraction to you?"

Seamus took her hand and turned her around so she was facing away from him. "Sit right here, in front of me, inside my legs."

Nostrils flaring, Cara did what he asked, settling herself between his thighs on the edge of the bed, staring at the closet. She closed her eyes and breathed deeply, her body excited and alive and desperate all at once.

"You're a distraction because I am attracted to you. I have a personal policy of staying the hell away from women, and each minute I'm with you, you test that resolve." And as if to prove that point, he ran his lips along her temple, slipping his left hand around her waist, gently stroking.

"I have a personal policy to stay away from men." Cara turned toward his wrist. "And you're testing my resolve, too." Seamus put his bloody flesh on her lips and Cara licked through the fluid.

"Then we should definitely concentrate on getting you ready to go home," he said, even as his fingers trailed down between her thighs and stroked across the front of her jeans.

"Absolutely." The blood still tasted disgusting to her, but her body needed it, in a way that made the taste irrelevant. She sucked and swallowed, closing her eyes in pleasure. "Oh," she moaned. "That feels better."

"Good," Seamus whispered into her ear. He popped the button on her jeans while she drank from him, and his hand slipped between her panties and jeans to cup her, his touch hot and firm.

Damn, that was good. She never thought to stop his touch, to push him away. She wanted the sensation of his stroking her, welcomed his touch, the way it added to the pleasure of the blood, the hot need pulsing and spiraling higher and higher.

Cara drank harder, testing her new fangs by puncturing Seamus's flesh herself. He gave a groan of surprised pleasure. Cara leaned back, her backside bumping against his erection. She started a rocking rhythm, bumping back to hit his body, thrusting forward to put pressure from his hand on her. She gripped his arm with her fingers and sucked harder still, drinking faster, her excitement rising like helium, inflating her from the inside.

Seamus yanked her panties aside and slid his finger across her wet heat. They both moaned. He started thrusting forward when she would bump back, so they were colliding together violently, mimicking sex, sending shivers of arousal throughout her body.

"You like to feed from me, don't you?" he asked, dipping his finger down into her, then pulling it back, slippery and elusive as it teased around her clitoris.

She nodded, not wanting to take her mouth off his flesh. Wiggling to try and force his finger where she wanted it, she felt herself careening closer and closer to explosion. He was barely doing anything, but every inch of her was zinging with pleasure, tense with desire, and the quest for violent satisfaction.

Stroking in her faster and faster, thrusting against her, Seamus buried his lips along the back of her neck, pushing her hair out of the way with his mouth. When he bit her, teeth sinking into her flesh unexpectedly, sharp and powerful, Cara broke her own hold on his wrist long enough to suck in a shocked breath.

Then she came in a rip-roaring orgasm that would have sent her shooting to the floor if his hand wasn't holding her in place, his teeth firmly buried inside her neck.

The shocking spasms rocked out from the center of her body, drenching her in ecstasy as Seamus pushed inside her with a finger, and pulled out of her with his fangs. She swallowed the blood in her mouth, accidentally biting her lip in her excitement.

"Oh, my." Wiping at her lips, Cara rocked one last time against Seamus. "I thought you said that doesn't happen every time."

"It doesn't."

"Oh." She thought about that for a second, her body reacting to the blood, her energy kicking up, her limbs tingling. Shoving her hair back, she closed her eyes against the light-headedness the orgasm had given her. Her brain was scattered, but when she pulled it together, she realized something. "So . . ."

"That means we have a problem."

His erection snugly between her cheeks, hand still down her pants, Cara knew he was right. If she did this every time she drank blood around Seamus, she could forget about her independence. She'd morph into his love slave, begging him for more while offering to do his laundry. She would pout when he was late, feel jealousy when he glanced at other women, and would constantly worry about her weight. In short, she would become her mother, the way she'd been with Cara's jerk of a father.

No thanks.

"You have to let me leave," she said, trying to stand up. His hand in her pants kept her firmly in his lap.

"You have to learn how to be a vampire first."

"Then start teaching." She grabbed his wrist and pulled him out of her panties. What was he waiting for, a private escort out of there? "I mean, about other things than this."

Seamus thought if anyone was going to be the teacher in this relationship, it should be Cara. She was the most sensual woman he'd ever met. She danced naked—damn well, he might add—she had a vibrator that matched her décor, and she twice now had embraced the eroticism that feeding could inspire and had had an orgasm.

Neither time had she apologized or looked all that embarrassed. In fact, at the moment, as she stood up, she had a sly little smile of satisfaction on her face, despite her no-nonsense words.

She wanted to leave. He got it. But was there any reason they couldn't fully explore the attraction between them while he taught her all things vampire? And she taught him all things hot and sexy? That was what he had wanted when he'd gone to speak to her in the first place. An explosive affair. A rediscovery of sexual pleasure with a woman who appreciated an orgasm for the sake of an orgasm.

No commitment, no ties, just some amazingly hot sex to get him through another two hundred years.

It was sounding better and better and he wanted another nip at her flesh.

Cara yanked open the bedroom door. All three dogs tumbled into the room. The cats followed a second later at a more leisurely, blasé pace.

Satan dashed over to Seamus, his tiny legs a blur as he ran right up to him, gave a little leap in the air, and started barking violently. Seamus looked down at him. "What?" He and the Chihuahua weren't coming to terms with each other yet.

"Does he need to go out?" Cara asked, down on her knees petting a dog and a cat at the same time.

"I have no idea." It's not like the dog was crossing his

legs or anything. How the hell was Seamus supposed to know? "We're going to have to hire a dog walker for during the day when you're sleeping. Day life isn't an easy feat for a young vampire. Especially since you're used to the night shift anyway." And he really didn't want any doggie accidents in his apartment. The carpet had just been cleaned.

Cara didn't say anything, but her lips pursed. A second later, she said, "Why can't I just walk them at night? They can sleep during the day with me."

Seamus sighed. "You could do that, but is it fair to the dogs to never go outside during the day?"

Her face went pale. She looked like she'd been slapped.

"Cara . . ." He didn't know what the hell to say. Reality was a bitch.

"Get out."

"What?" Her face was buried in Fritz's fur, but he was almost certain she'd told him to leave.

"Get out! I want to change."

She looked dangerously close to tears, so Seamus didn't even hesitate. She wanted him gone, he was out of there. A woman in tears was the last thing he knew how to deal with.

Not sure whether to shut the door or not, he left it open, but Cara slammed it the second he cleared the door frame.

"Don't worry, I don't need my heels," he murmured.

"I heard that!" Cara called, her voice shaky.

Okay. Seamus would just take himself off down the hall, thanks. His dining room had a table, but he used it and the sideboard as a home office since he didn't need it for meals. He popped open his laptop, checked the schedule for the week, and cleared out his e-mail. They had only five weeks until the election.

The numbers from the latest poll danced in front of his eyes. Ethan and his opponent, Donatelli, were almost neck and neck.

Donatelli was winning with young vampires, and those who were called Impures, born to rogue vampires and mortal women, like Brittany Baldizzi had been. Donatelli supported finding these mortals with vampire blood and turning them. Ethan opposed the practice, feeling it was a dangerous policy of population explosion. The more vampires, the greater the risk of exposure. There was also some question of whether or not Impures had full consent in their turning.

Seamus rubbed his temples. Ethan had one last major trip scheduled to New York. They had just spent the summer on the campaign trail, traveling from Saint Petersburg to Berlin and on to Paris. They'd done a flyby down in South America before heading back to the States. They were doing everything they could to win another term.

But Seamus was worried. Very worried. And instead of planning strategy or ferreting out Brittany's father, he had turned a stripper. It was like spitting on vampire policy. He clicked on his Excel spreadsheet for Ethan's appearances for the remainder of the month. He was doing another debate, a fund-raiser dinner, and a speech at the United Bloodworkers Union. It didn't feel like enough.

Cara could jeopardize the campaign. If she did something inappropriate, they'd be in trouble. Hell, her mere existence was going to cause a lot of eyebrows to shoot up. Seamus was known to toe the line, always. They would take Cara and turn her into an issue, make her a statement of the Carrick policy's weaknesses.

If Ethan lost the election over this, Seamus would never forgive himself.

Which meant Cara was not going to be able to leave Seamus's side until the election was over. She wasn't going to be able to even leave the casino.

This was not going to go over big with her.

Seamus wondered if there was a way to convince her he was right that didn't involve tears or screaming.

He'd much prefer it involve orgasms, and one for him, too, this time.

But the look on her face when she stomped her way into the dining room convinced him he was going to have to try an alternate form of persuasion initially. One that didn't involve him letting her feed off him. He still couldn't believe he had done that. More than once. It was totally against the rules and completely unnecessary. He had an entire fridge of bagged blood he could be giving her. Instead, he was slitting his wrist and letting her take from him because it gave him immense pleasure to feel her drawing on him, to see the ecstasy on her face, to feel like if he gave her his older, more powerful blood, it would somehow make up for the guilt he had.

And it really bothered him that she kept insisting his blood tasted bad. A small, illogical part of him didn't want her to taste mortal blood from a bag, decide it was delicious, and disdain his offerings. Right now she needed him, wanted him.

And he needed counseling. He'd lost his ever-lovin' undead mind.

"What are you doing?" she asked, peering over his shoulder.

"Just checking e-mail, verifying Ethan's schedule for the week, checking the election polls." Thinking about her.

"So you really are Ethan's campaign manager?"

"Yes."

"How old are you?" she asked, crossing her arms over her chest. She'd changed into clean jeans and a red T-shirt that hugged her very impressive breasts.

"Three hundred and seventy-one last April."

"Are you Irish?"

"Yes. Are you Korean?" He wanted to know who Cara was, her likes, dislikes, what made her tick. They were going to be living together for a while, and it was important they talk, find some common ground.

"A quarter Korean. The other three-fourths, who knows, something European." She gestured to the very chest he'd been ogling with a rueful look. "No Asian woman has a chest like this naturally."

"And yours is? Natural?" That pleased him more than it should.

She leaned against the table, dogs hovering around her ankles. "Yes. Not that it's any of your business.

"I need to call my grandmother's nursing home and give them this number. My grandma is pretty far gone with dementia, and I want them to know how to reach me."

"Sure, I understand. I can call the nursing home tomorrow if you have trouble staying awake past sunrise." Seamus pushed his chair back from the table and crossed his leg over his knee. "Anything else you want to know?"

"How did you become a vampire?"

That was easy enough. "I was an Irish farmer until Cromwell. Then I defied my father and joined the rebellion against the English. I was a good soldier, until I met Ethan. He ran his sword through me. Then for whatever reason, he pulled me off that field and gave me this life back."

"So it's his fault you died? And he felt guilty and made you a vampire?"

"Yes." He had always been grateful to Ethan for that. War was war and by all rights he should have died.

"Hmmm . . . I see a pattern here. Sounds exactly like what you did with me."

Where was Freud when you needed him? "Maybe."

"So give me the book of rules. I want to study all this and go home. I don't know how I'm going to go to school, since there aren't any night classes, but I want to be in my own apartment at least. And I can't be gone for more than two weeks at work or they'll replace me."

Her hand was out. Seamus stared at her in disbelief. "Cara, I don't have a written manual for vampirism. The rules are verbal for the vast majority of us. There are hard copies, but only the ancients and the president have access to them."

Cara crossed her arms. "How am I supposed to know if I'm doing it wrong or right?"

"I'll tell you."

"I don't want to be with you," she said, her teeth grinding together.

"Sorry." He meant that. Sort of. "But that's the way it is."

She made a hideous noise and threw her arms up in the air. "You're like a block of wood. You're *impenetrable.* Your expression never changes. You always look vaguely annoyed. Even when I'm . . . you know"—her voice dropped down to normal tones—"you don't even react. You don't try to have sex with me. Not that I want you to. But you don't even try. Are you gay?"

"No!" This was why he avoided women. They were freaking crazy. How could she not notice his erection? How could she not see his drool when he looked at her?

And why did she want to *penetrate* him in the first place? She didn't even seem to like him.

"I am not gay. And I don't try to have sex with you because I don't want to take advantage of you when you're confused and adjusting."

"I'm confused?"

"You're not?" Was she saying she wanted to have sex with him? Seamus felt an erection spring up of nowhere.

"I don't think so." She chewed her bottom lip.

Very convincing. "Uhh . . . what are you in school for?" When in doubt—confusion, cluelessness, utter know-nothingness—change the subject.

Cara frowned. "I'm in veterinarian school. I intended to be an animal doctor, though this has the potential to seriously screw that up."

Well, that explained the fur menagerie. "Maybe you can take some of your classes online." Seamus loved the Internet. It was the best invention since electricity.

"I hope so."

Then to his utter horror, she gave a sniffle.

"I've worked so hard . . . dancing at night, classes and studying all day . . ." Her words wobbled and her lip trembled.

Oh, crap. "Cara, I'm sorry. I really am. I'll help you figure it out. We'll get it all worked out and everything will be fine." Or he'd impale himself. He couldn't stand to see the look of unhappiness on her face, knowing this was all his fault.

She pressed her mouth with her palm and took several breaths like she was getting herself under control. "Why did you approach me last night? Was it to feed off me?"

"Well." He should have known he'd be called to the mat for this sooner or later. Honesty seemed like the wisest course. That's what he always told Ethan when campaigning. Just come clean and apologize or it will bite you in the ass later.

"Normally we discourage live feeding from mortals. I haven't live-fed in a couple hundred years. But last night I saw you dancing. I was attracted to you, to the way you move, the way you understand your own body." He felt hard just remembering. It didn't help that her eyes were dilating, that he could feel sexual tension vibrating between them harder, faster, and louder than that little toy of hers could ever manage. "I wanted to seduce you. That was my primary goal."

Her cheeks went pink. "You wanted to have sex with me?"

He nodded. "I thought I might encourage you with a little vampire persuasion." Which sounded cheap and disgusting now that he was repeating it out loud. He was such an Irish pig. "But I assure you I wouldn't have done anything you didn't want me to do." Like that made it sound any better.

"So I looked like the kind of woman who would be up for a good time?"

He wasn't going to answer that on the grounds that she might castrate him.

Instead, he said, "I thought you were beautiful. The first woman to tempt me into impulsiveness in two hundred years. Clearly I should have put more thought into it, given the way it's turned out."

"Clearly."

But to his relief, the trembling lip was gone, and she didn't appear all that upset.

Seamus turned to print off a fresh copy of the week's agenda, grateful to have dodged that silver bullet.

He wasn't prepared for Cara to insert her curvy, sexy body between him and the computer screen. Startled, he found himself eye to eye with her breasts. Whoa, boy. Much better than his geometric shapes screen saver.

When he managed to drag his eyes off her chest and look higher, he watched in fascination as her lips opened sensually and her hips swiveled toward him.

"How about a lap dance, soldier?"

Six

Ringo paced back and forth in the back of Donatelli's luxurious suite in the Venetian hotel and tried to ignore Smith's complaints and whining.

"It wasn't my fault, Mr. Donatelli, I'm telling you. The woman distracted me."

"The woman." Donatelli unfolded his linen napkin and placed it in his lap as he sat at the ornate round table in the sitting area. "The woman distracted you?"

His voice was calm, and he wasn't even looking at Smith, but Ringo knew he was angry. His temple pulsed and his shoulders were rigid. "That is the second mortal woman to distract you in recent months. The second mortal woman you've killed."

"I didn't kill her!" The color blanched from Smith's beefy face. He went from vampire pale to nearly translucent.

"But you did kill Alexis Baldizzi, didn't you?"

Ringo stopped pacing and studied Smith's reaction. He hadn't known Donatelli was responsible for Alexis's mortal death, however inadvertent. Donatelli's strategies were never clear to him. Ringo just did what he was told to do, like a dead doormat. Donatelli yelled, he jumped, and in return he got blood delivered to him laced with nicotine, alcohol, and an irresistible hint of heroin.

He hated Donatelli, hated his dependence, but knew he wasn't strong enough as either a vampire or a man to attempt to escape both his master and his addiction to drug blood.

Smith didn't answer Donatelli directly, clearly recognizing his guilt in killing Alexis Baldizzi. "The woman last night, I don't even know who she was. She was just there all of a sudden, screaming and running, and . . . and . . . a car hit her."

"Does she belong to Fox?"

"I don't know."

Ringo did. He had watched from the shadows, sensed that she was moving on Fox's orders, that they were mind linked. Perhaps lovers, perhaps his blood donor. Which from what Ringo had learned in the past two months was against Carrick's political views. Carrick supposedly didn't believe in mortal slaves.

"Thank you, Smith. You may return to your room."

"Yes, Mr. Donatelli." Smith looked relieved, his thick shoulders sagging in his ill-fitting gray suit. He turned toward the door.

"Oh, and one more thing before you go." Donatelli sipped from his wineglass, the thick scent of blood filling Ringo's nostrils and making his stomach clench. Donatelli tilted the glass, staring at it, running his tongue along his thin bottom lip to catch a stray drop. He had the look of a weasel—thin, wiry, sly, dark eyes filled with malice. "Mr. Smith, no feedings for you until Tuesday."

Smith stopped near the door and turned, jaw dropping. "Five days without feeding? Mr. Donatelli, no, you can't do that!"

"Make that six."

Smith shut up. Ringo went cold as he watched the panic in Smith's eyes. Like a cruel parent, Donatelli waved his hand. "Go on. To your room. Think about what you've done and why it was wrong."

Something like a whimper came from Smith's big frame, but he left, the door closing quietly behind him.

Ringo hesitated, but only for a second. Then while Donatelli took another deep swallow of blood, he told him, "Mr. Donatelli, I think the woman is Fox's. I sensed a mind link between them. I sensed his fear for her."

"She was mortal, correct? Smith wasn't wrong about that, too, was he?" Donatelli turned and looked at him, his dark eyes amused.

"No. I didn't see her die, though. I was chasing Kelsey."

"And she outran you?"

Ringo kept his mind tightly closed and gave a casual shrug, hands in the pockets of his linen pants. "She's older than me, and had a head start. Would you like me to pay her a surprise visit?" And kill her, was implied, though Ringo wasn't sure he could do it. He was hoping he could play a game of his own, to protect mostly himself, but Kelsey as well.

A week without feeding would be death for a vampire. At least one his young age, and addicted to drug blood. And for whatever reason, Ringo did not want to die.

"Perhaps. Let me think about it."

"Her memory's gone. She doesn't remember anything. Not me. Not anything about that night." The night Smith had shot Kelsey with a full round of bullets, then drained her entirely of blood. The night Donatelli had turned Ringo into a vampire.

"But she is under Fox's protection?"

"It looks that way. But I think the mortal woman is his true weakness. Maybe his feeding source."

"Smith says she was killed."

"Does that matter? If he had one feeding source, maybe he has another, and another. Which makes him a hypocrite. Which makes Carrick look bad. Or maybe he took this dead mortal and turned her. That wouldn't make Seamus Fox and President Carrick look very good to voters, would it?" Ringo's palms were wet with vampire sweat in his pockets, but he stood as casually as he could. Met Donatelli's eye straight on.

"You've given me something to think about, Mr. Columbia. Sit down and join me for dinner."

A snap of his finger and suddenly there was a short, curvy woman with pink cheeks and bouncy blond hair that swished over her back as she walked into the sitting area from what Ringo had thought was the bathroom. She wore a tiny miniskirt, and a lacy sleeveless top, and she carried a goblet of blood in her hands. She set it on the table and glanced at Donatelli for approval, her body leaning slightly toward him, breasts out, neck arched, pulse pumping, pumping, pumping in excitement and anticipation. Ringo could see bruising on her arms and her neck, but she still glowed with health, her eyes dilated with desire.

She was very much mortal, very clearly addicted to the

pleasure of giving her blood without a glamour, to the draw of power that came from Donatelli, and the vampire sensations he could give her as he fed from her. The smell of her filled Ringo's nostrils, her warm mortal flesh dewy and loamy to his heightened vampire olfactory senses. She was plumper than he had liked women when he was alive. He'd always felt suffocated by all those curves and rolls. But as a vampire, her soft, juicy flesh appealed to him, made his mouth water and his nostrils flare.

The girl was aroused, and now so was Ringo, to his embarrassment.

"Why don't you drink this glass here first." Donatelli gestured to the goblet. "A special blend for you."

Ringo didn't need to be asked twice. He brushed past the girl, who gasped at his speed, and dropped into the chair opposite Donatelli.

"Then when you're finished with that..."

It was half gone already. He'd learned to toss it back like a shot. One, because his body craved the blood desperately, and all its soothing, lethargic properties, and two, because he was never certain it wouldn't be taken right back away from him before he could drink it.

"...why don't you and Katie spend some time together?" He nodded in the blonde's direction.

Ringo slapped the empty glass down and stared across the table at Donatelli. The blood was slipping and winding through him, easing his aches and stroking his extremities into a hot, pleasant boil. He hadn't seen this coming. It was either a trick, or he had been elevated to Donatelli's inner circle. Or perhaps it was one more way to enslave him. He'd never been allowed to feed directly from a living source before, and just the thought sent his heart racing, his fingers twitching, his dick swelling hard and eager.

He chanced a glance at Katie, curious what her reaction would be. She was pouting.

"I thought I was going to be with you tonight, Donnie."

Ringo just about swallowed his tongue. Donnie? That almost drew a laugh from him for the first time in months.

Donatelli reached for her and she sidled around the table to him. He wrapped an arm around her waist and pulled her against his side. "Don't stick your lip out like that at me or I'll bite it."

Her breath caught in obvious excitement, anticipation. "Okay."

Laughing, he patted her backside. "Later, pet. First I want you to go with Mr. Columbia and let him taste how sweet you are. Then when you're finished I have a present for you."

"A present?" Apparently that was enough inducement. She moved back around the table and smiled at him. "Hi."

Ringo wanted to say no to what Donatelli was offering, but knew he wouldn't. Knew he couldn't.

"Take him to the bed, precious, and take off your clothes so he can see your pretty body."

"Okay." She pivoted again and started across the room toward the big king-size bed, already peeling off her ivory lace top.

"Better hurry," Donatelli told him with a conspiratorial smile. "She'll start without you."

Ringo knocked his chair over when he stood up, forgetting his vampire strength in his eagerness.

"Don't limit yourself to the neck, which is very cliché. Bite her wherever you like, though you might wish to know she's fond of the deviant." Donatelli took another sip from his glass.

Katie had dropped her miniskirt to the floor after the shirt, and was walking nude up the two steps to the bedroom. She glanced over her shoulder with a small, flirty smile.

"Don't take too much blood. I'm rather attached to her. I'd be mildly distraught if you killed her."

At those words, Ringo paused. He didn't want to do this. This was a mistake. This was another way for Donatelli to enslave him, hold him under his command, force him to do his dirty work.

His body screamed at him to do it, to take it, to fuck her, and suck her blood. But somewhere in his mind he protested just as loudly. He shouldn't. He already despised himself, what he had become, what he was.

Katie gave a huff of exasperation when she realized he wasn't following her. She came back down the steps, more flouncing than seductive. "Come on."

Her breasts collided with his chest, her pelvis pressed against his erection.

Then she nipped his bottom lip, and Ringo gave in to what he was, what he had become, what he'd always been.

Cara knew offering a lap dance was a calculated risk. Because she didn't really want Seamus to take her up on it. She'd never danced down on a guy in her life. Swiveling on a pole behind a screen was a whole different mind-set than swiveling on a man, and prior to Seamus, she'd never really wanted to perform the latter move. At the moment, though, she had to admit, a small part of her was tempted to do it and shock that bland look off his face. The other, more restrained part of her personality was cringing inside at the thought of having to actually go through with it.

But she had suggested it because she was angry that he had seen her as nothing more than a sex object, as a stripper. She had convinced herself that she was an artist, a dancer, a solo act hidden behind the screen, and when he'd confessed he'd wanted to have sex with her, it had made her feel cheap, degraded.

Which was stupid. She danced naked. Did she expect he would look at her and leap to the conclusion she was a genius?

She needed a vampire reality check.

Seamus needed three. Right, left, and center.

If they were stuck together, even temporarily, she didn't want to be the only one off-kilter. She had to shove him sideways as well.

"Cara?" Seamus asked her breasts.

"Yes?" She put her hands in his black hair. Even though it was short, it was thick and soft, and she couldn't help but enjoy the feel of it as she gripped.

"What are you doing?"

At the moment, she was only standing in front of him, but given the husky sound of his voice, that was enough.

"I'm waiting for your answer." Picking through his hair, she found a smooth, satin scar.

He cleared his throat. "Well, um, is there a reason you're offering . . . what you offered?"

"Maybe I'm fishing for a compliment. Maybe I thought you'd enjoy it." She ran her finger back and forth over the three-inch-long line again. "How did you get this scar?"

"My father dropped a scythe on my head in the barn. Nearly bled to death."

That it had happened over three hundred years earlier made her shiver. Seamus wasn't going to age. Ever. And neither was she. It was a sobering, scary thought.

"I'd enjoy it."

She shifted her gaze down to his face when his hands landed on her waist. "What?"

"I'm saying yes to your offer of a dance."

Shit. She had been positive he'd say no.

He must have seen her surprise because he gave her a slow, sensual smile that made her breath catch.

"You're a beautiful dancer, Cara. And despite what you said earlier about me not reacting to you, I pretty much only need to glance at you and I'm turned on. I'd be insane to turn down your very gracious offer."

His accent had gotten deeper with each word.

She liked the way he sounded—aroused and arrogant.

"Why am I so attracted to you?" she asked, genuinely puzzled at the same time she gave a tentative swivel of her hips, testing her balance as she spread her legs on either side of his thighs.

Seamus's fingers trailed over her waist, his eyes clouding with lust. "I don't know, but I'm just as attracted to you. And I don't believe in destiny anymore. Random, capricious things happen, and we react. Nothing happens for a reason. But that doesn't mean we can't enjoy them all the same."

The words weren't bitter or cold. Just matter-of-fact. But they made her feel unaccountably sad.

She'd never thought about destiny as irrefutable either. Her whole adult life had been spent trying to shape and mold her own future, to maintain control. It wasn't destiny that determined her actions—she did. But on the other hand, she wasn't sure she believed in total randomness either. Look at how she had tried to control her relationship with Marcus, and the awful, humiliating way it had ended. That had been two years ago, and in all that time, she had never managed to convince herself that it had been for the best that it had ended the way it had. She didn't know now why she was so attracted to this man—vampire—in front of her.

All she knew was that Seamus Fox was dangerous to her control, to everything she had worked for. All that dignity she had wrapped around herself like a blanket after she'd found out Marcus had cheated on her about nine times over.

Yet despite her fear, she wanted Seamus, desired him in a way she had never, ever wanted her ex. Her need for Seamus was exciting, sexy.

Even as she thought it, her body was warming under his stare, limbering up and relaxing. It should have felt odd to be arching her back, thrusting her breasts toward him, rocking her hips slowly, but it didn't. She wanted to feel desirable, wanted Seamus to appreciate how he had disrupted both their lives. Realize that there was something that flowed between them that had her on edge, confused, desperate.

"So this is random?" Cara brushed her chest against his as she undid the button on her pants. That was the only explanation for why she was even doing this.

"Very." Seamus moved his lips over her jaw. His fingers shoved her jeans down the second she undid the zipper.

She shimmied out of them, aware she was wearing rather ordinary stretchy seamless hot pink panties. But they covered her backside, and she needed that for the moment. "Does this feel randomly good or randomly bad?"

Heart thumping, Cara held on to Seamus's shoulders and climbed fully into his lap. Given the grunt/groan he gave, he hadn't been expecting that.

"Randomly good." And as if to prove it, he grabbed her hot pink panty–covered ass. "Cara."

"Yes?" She got some leverage and moved up and down, hips turning, back rolling, breasts giving a little bounce. He had nice, hard thighs, and she was starting to get turned on all over again. He seemed to have that kind of effect on her.

He ground his hands into her taut flesh, lifted his own hips to crash against her. "I don't know. Was I saying something?"

"I think so." Cara leaned against his shoulder, breathed hard as overwhelming need rolled over her. "Don't you remember?"

"No." He nuzzled her neck, licked her flesh.

She shivered in anticipation. He was going to bite her. She wanted him to. Bite her hard, mark her, make her have yet another orgasm. She felt greedy and excited and aware that she was different, sharper, stronger. Hornier.

"Take your panties off. Let me inside you."

The teasing tip of his fangs put pressure on her skin, distracting her. It felt so good, the rocking, the heat, the hard push of his hands on her waist, his teeth torturing a tingle of anticipation from her body.

But when he lifted her backside, began shoving down her panties, she snapped back to reality. There was something he didn't know about her, didn't understand.

"We can't."

"Why not?" He continued fighting with her underwear even as she tried to wiggle back out of his reach.

"Because I'm a virgin." She was starting to panic now. She didn't want to sleep with Seamus Fox. Not when she seemed to have no control over herself. Not when she was at the mercy of her new urges, not when she was confusing feeding with sensuality, and was clearly exhibiting some kind of bizarre infatuation for the man who had saved her from death.

Seamus stopped moving. Then he burst out laughing. "A virgin? Please."

Please what? Feeling like she'd been slapped, Cara jerked back off his lap and planted her feet firmly on the ground. "Yes, a virgin."

"If you don't want to have sex with me just yet, all you have to do is say that." Seamus shook his head, a grin still plastered on his face. "You don't have to lie."

"I am a virgin."

"Whatever." He patted her butt.

Cara moved out of his reach and pulled her pants up. That was it. She did not want to see Seamus for the rest of the night. He could take his vampire persuasion, sarcasm, and dickheadedness, and leave her alone.

"Get out." She would not suffer any more humiliation.

The smile fell off his face. "Oh, shit, are we starting this again? I thought you were over that."

Zipping her jeans, she headed in the direction of the bedroom, so frustrated she wanted to scream "Die vampire scum!" at the top of her lungs.

"And this is my apartment, by the way."

"Then I'll leave." Cara yanked her suitcase up, forgetting her new strength. The little wheeled bag hit the ceiling, scraped the plaster, and ricocheted back down to the carpet.

"You can't leave."

As if he hadn't told her ninety times. "This topic is getting boring. I'm leaving. And you can't stop me."

Fueled by indignation and irritation, Cara called her animals, ran to the front door, threw it open, and tore out into the hallway with her suitcase, not sure where in the hell she was going, but wanting away from Seamus.

It wasn't a big surprise that he followed her. What was startling was how fast he got there. In about one point six seconds he was at her back, another blink and he was in front of her. She slammed into his chest, unable to stop herself, and he stumbled back a few feet, causing her to trip over her suitcase. They hovered together, tangled arms and ankles, for a movielike hang time, then they both crashed to the floor, Cara knocking hard on Seamus's rib.

"Ooff." She pushed on him, trying to roll over, sit up, scramble away in some way, shape, or form to get the hell out of contact with him.

Seamus just put one palm on her butt and was able to hold her flat against him. She wiggled harder, ticked that he was stronger than her. "Let me up."

"No. We need to talk."

A door opened to the right. Cara glanced over. Saw two pairs of feet. One male, given the black socks and big size, the other female, polish on the naked toes.

"You know, you might want to take that sort of thing to your room," a voice said.

Cara closed her eyes. She had a horrible feeling it was Ethan.

"Seamus Fox, you old dog. I had no idea you had it in you." That was definitely Alexis, amusement heavy in her voice.

"Do you mind?" Seamus said with great dignity. "We were having a private conversation."

"Is that what we're calling it these days? We really have gotten too politically correct."

Cara shoved backward, trying to break Seamus's grip. "Let me go!"

"No." He locked eyes with her, and Cara saw that he would hold her there for the rest of their immortal lives if she didn't try another tactic. Seamus was as stubborn as she was. As if to prove it, he rolled, forcing her on her back, his legs and chest weighing down on her.

Fortunately, Alexis intervened before Cara screamed expletives at him, or worse, kissed him. She'd never kissed him, and she suddenly had the urge to do that. Just place her lips on his and taste his warm flesh.

"Well, this is cute and all, but seriously, you guys need to go into your room. Or better yet, Ethan and Seamus can work and Cara and I can go hang out."

Seamus stared down at her, his breath landing on her cheek, hot and rapid. He smelled delicious to her, like salsa—tangy and sweet. Her head pressed against the hard floor, but she was only vaguely aware of it. There was only him, his Irish blue eyes stroking her, stripping her, worshiping her. She relaxed her thighs apart, wanting his erection to rest more fully against her.

It seemed like a wonderful idea to just reach up, to touch his lip with her finger, run her touch along the warm fullness.

His mind reached out to hers, a persistent brushing of his thoughts over hers.

Let me make love to you.

She wanted to . . . hell, that was an understatement. She

needed it with a primal fierceness that scared her. And she would have said yes, except that she never got the chance. Her mouth was opening when Seamus jerked back with a curse.

"Hell!"

"What?" Cara suddenly remembered they were lying in the hotel hallway. She sat up and tugged her T-shirt down over her waistband.

"Satan bit me, the annoying little shit." He was glaring at her Chihuahua.

Mr. Spock sat on his haunches, his little tail wagging. He looked adorable. Cara wondered if Seamus had thought to pack Mr. Spock's clothes. He had half a dozen adorable sweaters and T-shirts.

"That little dog couldn't have possibly hurt you," Alexis said, leaning against the door frame, arms folded.

"It didn't hurt. It pissed me off."

"Everything pisses you off," Cara said with a sniff, the mood broken, thank goodness.

"You trying to leave pisses me off." He stood up, held out his hand for her.

She ignored it and scrambled to her feet.

"Seamus, do you have anything for me tonight or can Alexis and I go back inside and leave you to your little domestic drama?" Ethan was smirking next to his wife.

Seamus glared. "I need to talk to you, actually." He turned back to Cara. "Get back in the apartment."

That infuriated her. "No."

"I'll pick you up and haul you back if I have to."

How could he do that? Go from seductive and caring to bossy bastard? Cara felt angry tears blurring her vision.

"Whoa, whoa." Alexis stuck her hand up in a T shape.

"Time out. Seamus, go do your thing with Ethan. Cara and I are going downstairs to have some girl time."

When Seamus opened his mouth, she added, "Don't worry, we'll take bodyguards. We'll be fine. How much trouble could we get into in our own casino?"

Seven

"Seamus, could I offer a bit of advice?" Ethan asked, as he glanced through the schedule Seamus had handed him.

"Sure." Seamus lifted the orange cat off his notebook computer and dropped him on the floor. A tuft of fur wafted up and stuck on Seamus's lip. "Damn it." He plucked it off and tossed it in the wastebasket with a grimace. "These cats get into everything. It's like living in Animal Kingdom."

"That ties in with what I'm about to suggest. It seems to me that you and Cara have some issues."

Yeah, like the fact that she couldn't stand him.

"So maybe it would be wise if we found other arrangements for Cara. Just because you turned her doesn't mean she has to live with you."

Seamus felt a tremor of alarm. Maybe things weren't going so hot, but he didn't want Cara to leave. It wasn't safe.

And he would miss her. Because he hadn't slept with her yet. "She can't be on her own yet. She doesn't know how to be discreet, she doesn't know our rules. And what if those guys from the alley come back around? These attacks don't make any sense, Ethan. What if she's in danger?"

"Relax. I don't mean leave our protection. I meant we could get her a suite of her own. I think she'd be happier that way."

"I don't want her to have a suite of her own." The very thought offended him. Why the hell couldn't she stay with him? What was so freaking awful about him?

"Look, I can see you're attracted to each other. But I think Cara is still confused and upset that her life has altered drastically. I think she might appreciate the space and the privacy." Ethan nudged the Chihuahua off his pants. "And she'd take her pets with her."

"No," Seamus said. He had no logical reason to say no, but it popped right out of his mouth with no hesitation whatsoever. "She stays with me."

Ethan studied him. "Then you might want to drop the master-and-servant routine. I don't think she enjoys being told what to do."

He had no idea what Ethan was talking about. He had been nothing but considerate of Cara in the forty-eight hours since he'd met her. He was living with a Chihuahua, for hell's sake. That was pretty freaking accommodating of him. He clicked to open his Internet browser. "I don't know what you're talking about."

Ethan snorted. "I don't think you do. You seem to have no clue you're falling for Cara."

That shocked him speechless. Seamus stared at his computer screen filled with the day's news, the TV lineup for that night, his daily horoscope, and the weather. Las Vegas. Sunny and eighty.

Seamus Fox. Stupid and three hundred seventy.

"I'm not falling for Cara." The minute he spoke the words, he knew he was lying. He was. The control he strove for, clung to, was already slipping away from him.

"Come on, Seamus. Maybe if you just let yourself have a relationship, you might enjoy it."

"I don't want a relationship, and you know why." The very thought of commitment to a woman made him sweat in unpleasant places.

"Because of Marie?" Ethan stood up and tossed the packet of papers onto Seamus's dining room table. "Come on, Fox. It's been two hundred years. Marie lied to you, betrayed you. But she's dead and Cara isn't Marie. You've got to learn to trust another woman sooner or later."

Later worked for him. "She didn't just betray me, Ethan. She had me sent to the guillotine. The only thing that saved me was a dull blade." It had gone only halfway through his neck. Assuming he was dead, they had tossed him in a pile of headless corpses, including two of his vampire comrades.

He touched his neck. His scar had never fully healed.

"I know that. I saw you that night afterward. Marie was a bitch. But you shouldn't judge Cara by Marie's betrayal."

"I just met Cara and you're a lousy shrink. Let it drop. We have more important things to worry about, like your campaign, and who the hell wanted me dead in that alley. I should have taken this more seriously. I should have questioned Kelsey more thoroughly."

Ethan just shook his head. "I'm not sure that would have mattered. And I trust you to be thorough, Seamus."

"I'm sorry about Cara," Seamus said, feeling guilt sit in his gut like a stone. "I shouldn't have turned her."

"But you did, and maybe you should ask yourself why. Maybe she's meant to be your mate."

"Marriage has made you obnoxious." Seamus headed to the fridge for a drink. "Not everyone wants your domestic bliss, you know. And I am sorry I ever met Cara in the first place." Maybe if he said it out loud, he'd actually believe it. "She's not happy, and I really don't want her to toss controversy onto your campaign."

"I'm sure it won't be a big deal. We'll just have to make sure her behavior is discreet. Keep her presence a secret."

Seamus had a suddenly horrible thought. "Then why the hell did we let her run off with *your* wife? Alexis wouldn't know discreet if it bit her in the ass."

Cara was so relieved to be out of Seamus's apartment, she would have done anything Alexis suggested for entertainment, whether she wanted to or not. But it was all the better that Alexis had suggested hitting the casino downstairs and gambling a little. They had gone and grabbed Kelsey, who had been reluctant, but wanted the company, and after changing clothes and doing one another's makeup, they had hit the casino floor.

"All I have is ten dollars," Cara said, digging in her purse. "Where is the money machine?" She needed something to distract her, and mindless gambling entertainment sounded like a perfect way to spend the night.

"Oh, we don't have to pay," Alexis scoffed and went up to the box office. "My husband owns this joint. Being married to Ethan has its privileges besides great sex. They can give us loaded cards to use."

"Okay. But if I win, I'll give back the original investment to Ethan." Growing up without a father, her mother dying when Cara was twelve, she was used to being poor but proud. She didn't like to take handouts.

"Fair enough."

Alexis went up to the box office, one of the two bodyguards trailing after her. The other stood at a discreet distance from Kelsey and Cara. Cara smiled encouragingly at Kelsey. "So, how do you know Ethan and Seamus?"

"I'm Mr. Carrick's secretary. I met him in New York in the sixties when I was a brand-new vampire, and he asked me to come to Vegas with him as his secretary. That's when I met Seamus."

Kelsey darted her eyes around the whole time she was talking, and she crossed her very thin arms over her flat chest. She had long black hair that tumbled over her sharp alabaster cheekbones. "Did you feel that?"

"Feel what?" Cara just felt aware, but content. Neither hot nor cold, nor hungry. Just . . . vampiric.

"That bad feeling. That fingers-on-my-spine feeling. There's someone here."

"There are lots of people here." The floor was packed, despite it being an average Thursday night in September. Time had no relevance in a casino. It could have been any day of the week, any month, any city, morning, noon, or night, and it didn't matter.

"There's someone bad here."

Cara didn't doubt that. If you had that many people in a room, there was bound to be someone nasty in the bunch. "Maybe you're picking up on someone's distress. Maybe someone lost a lot of money or something."

"No." Kelsey locked eyes with her. "Never mind." She gave a soft smile. "Seamus likes you a lot, you know."

"He could have fooled me."

"Well, men are stupid."

In that, Cara had to totally agree with Kelsey. Just thinking about how he'd ordered her to his room made her hot all over again. And bad hot, not good hot.

"But you can trust Seamus. He's a good man. He took care of me when I had my . . . accident."

"I'm sure he's responsible." He did what was expected of him, she could clearly see that. She just didn't want to be an obligation to Seamus Fox. She didn't want him to feel sorry for her. She didn't want him to control her life.

Alexis came back up to them, waving cash cards. "Where to first?"

"The Wheel of Fortune machine," Kelsey suggested, a spark of something other than fear in her eyes. The slots didn't appeal to Cara at all, but she felt compassion for Kelsey. She had obviously been through something traumatic and the rest of the vampires at the Ava cared about her, worried about her.

If the slots made Kelsey relax, Cara was all for it.

An hour later, Alexis was grumbling that she'd lost her shirt on the slots. "Well, Ethan's shirt," she said with a grin.

Kelsey was flushed pink in the cheeks and pressing buttons with enthusiasm. "I'm up eighty-seven dollars."

Cara had lost six dollars, then had contented herself with watching the other two. "Do you all mind if I hit the poker table?"

"No." Alexis hopped off her stool. "My ass is numb anyway."

As they walked across the floor, the lights blinking and the machines merrily beeping and chiming, Cara stuck her hands in the back pockets of her jeans and bit her lip. She sensed an ally in Alexis, but she didn't want to put her on the spot.

But she needed help or she was going to go insane. Or murder Seamus. "Alexis, can I ask you something?"

"Anything. I have a little sister who I raised, you know. I can give advice on anything, even shit I know nothing about."

Cara laughed. "I want to know how to get Seamus to toss me out. If I can't leave on my own, and I can't run away, I need to convince him he doesn't want me around. How do I do that?"

She'd been thinking about it while she'd mindlessly pushed slot machine buttons and it seemed to her the only course of action available to her. Being around him was too dangerous to her mental health and sexual stability. But she didn't think she could escape past six bodyguards. A glance back at Mutt and Jeff, as she'd silently named them, convinced her of that fact. They were big guys. They could probably snap a cactus in half and not think twice about it. Add four more like them and she was trapped.

"Annoy him until he doesn't want you around, huh? Very devious. I like it. How to lose a vampire in ten days . . . it just might work." Alexis frowned. "There are a lot of things that annoy Seamus. Breaking the rules being number one. Not to mention exhibitionism. Clinging women."

Kelsey shook her head, swiveling her tiny hips as she walked in three-inch heels. "He doesn't like clinging women, but he won't send you away for that. Like me. I drive him crazy, but he would never send me away. He takes care of me."

That seemed remarkably astute.

"Yikes, she's right," Alexis said with a grin. "Okay, so what is it you think Seamus likes about you? Because he obviously likes you."

Cara gave that a moment's thought. It wasn't hard to figure out. "He thinks I'm a sex goddess. He looks at me and sees a stripper. Sexual fantasy sprung to life. But I'm not a sex goddess at all. I can't even wear a bathing suit in public without feeling self-conscious. I dance only because I can do it behind a screen and pretend there's no one watching me." Except for that impromptu lap dance, which frankly hadn't gone all that well. "He looks at me and thinks sex."

"That makes sense. And it gives me an idea." Alexis stopped walking and glared at the bodyguards when they got too close. They immediately backed up. She dropped her voice down to a whisper. "They're not supposed to listen to my conversations but you never know. So what's the one thing that would really drive Seamus crazy?"

"What?" Cara whispered back.

"Commitment. A permanent relationship with a woman. Scares the shit out of him."

That made two of them. Cara felt a little deflated. "Well, I'm not going to offer him that."

"Why not? He won't take it. If you go all domestic on him, honey this, honey that, did you take out the garbage and why don't you ever buy me flowers... he'll have you out so fast your head will spin. Seamus doesn't do commitment. Period."

It made sense. "You may be on to something."

"I'm right. Vampire males are dominating and like to get their way. They're also terrified at the thought of being attached to one woman for eternity. Vampire marriage is forever, you know. It breeds relationship reticence."

"I'll give it some thought." Even pretending to be Seamus's girlfriend scared the blood out of her. What if it backfired and he actually *liked* it? They reached the poker room. "I'm not sure what to do. But first I'm going to win some money."

Seamus was a little confused. Somehow Cara, the feisty exotic dancer, the woman of his fantasies, who had orgasms while feeding from him, had morphed into a walking advertisement for *Better Homes and Undead Gardens*.

Opening his front door, he braced himself for what she might have done now. In seven days she'd managed to infuse a startling amount of pink into his apartment, from plump pillows in the living room to fluffy fuchsia towels in his bathroom. The woman was a menace with Internet access, shopping her way through half a dozen retailers online. Just tonight, after his shower, he'd found pink lint on his bollocks. It was an assault on his manhood. If his soldier friends from the First World War had ever seen him wrapped in pink, they'd have laughed their arses off.

But he couldn't begrudge Cara a few comforts since he was essentially holding her prisoner against her will for her own safety.

Stepping tentatively into the apartment, he spotted Cara up on a footstool. She glanced over her shoulder and smiled.

"Oh, good, you're home! I need help with these curtains." She waved a lot of fabric—pink fabric—toward him.

The devil help him, she was putting pink-and-orange striped curtains on his windows. "Uh . . . aren't those a little bright?" They were more painful than direct sunlight.

"What?" She looked puzzled. "They're cheerful. Day colors. Raspberry and Orange Crush."

"Well." Seamus threw his wallet on the dining room table, trying to find a tactful way to say those were the most god-awful curtains he'd ever seen. Then he decided he wasn't known for his tact. "Cara, I don't like those curtains."

Her eyes went wide, limpid pools swimming with hurt. "I'm just trying to make things more cozy."

"I understand. I appreciate your effort, honestly. But can't you make things cozy with curtains that aren't ugly?" And what was the matter with his desk? Everything looked rearranged.

"You don't think I have any taste." She flounced down off the footstool, hiking up her oversized sweatpants.

Seamus hated those sweatpants. They hid every inch of her body. For the last few days, she'd worn nothing but giant sweatpants and loose T-shirts. It was starting to irritate him. He sighed and reached for the pile of mail on the table, which had been tucked into a goddamn pink letter organizer.

"I never said you don't have taste." Everything he said lately was wrong. Just completely wrong. He could say snakes slithered and she'd take it as a personal insult. The only time she wasn't pouting was when she was feeding. But even then she wouldn't let him touch her anymore. It was like . . . it was like . . . they were *married.*

God, it was as horrible as he'd always imagined. No sex and nagging twenty-four/seven.

"You implied it." She defiantly shoved the curtain onto the rod she lifted up. "Did you remember to pick up the dog food?"

Shit. "No."

She made that sound, that pissy disapproval sound that said she was so unfortunate to be saddled with an unhelpful asshole like him. It was amazing she could convey all of that with one tiny sound through tightly pursed lips, but she managed it. Even though she'd mastered the technique of closing her thoughts to him, he didn't need to hear her thoughts to know she was pissed off at him.

"I guess I'll just run out tomorrow night then and get it myself. Fritz is on the verge of starvation."

Fritz was ten pounds overweight and sleeping on the couch at the moment, gut sagging toward the floor. "I'll get it tomorrow. Sorry I forgot." Seamus went to reach for a pen to write himself a reminder note and discovered all his writing utensils had been deposited into a hot pink, swirly container with a fluffy pink feather glued to the front. "What the hell is this? I can't find a damn thing!"

"That's because I organized everything for you. Once you get used to the system, you'll see it's so much more efficient."

Seamus supposed this was his fault. He had said no to giving Cara a suite of her own. He could be all alone in his bachelor contentment if he hadn't been stubborn. But he didn't want that. Despite the pink fuzzies on his man parts. He wanted Cara. In bed and out. Only she seemed to have lost any sexual interest in him, even while feeding.

If Ethan found out Seamus was guzzling twice his normal blood allotment for the sole purpose of self-feeding Cara, he was going to hit the roof. And blow right through it.

Cara seemed to take it as a matter of course that he was supposed to feed her. Only once had she asked how he ate, and he had told her the truth—from a refrigerated blood bag. She'd tried it twice, drinking a whole bag, before crinkling her nose. "I like it warm," she'd said.

Yeah, so did he.

"More efficient. Perfect." What would be perfect would be if she'd take off her clothes and let him spread her out on this table next to the fuzzy pen holder.

Maybe he should try again. Make another move, and let her know he wanted her desperately. Had the erection to prove it. She had been interested that night of the aborted lap dance, he was sure of it.

"Cara..." He snapped the pen in his hand in half. Damn, he was so pent up and confused and off-kilter. He had no clue what he was doing. "Cara..."

"Can you take out the garbage?" she asked as she clicked the rod and the hideous vomit-inducing curtains onto the wall.

"What?" Between his lust and the blinding pink and orange, he'd had a hallucinogenic moment and hadn't heard what she'd said.

"Take out the garbage, please. It's full."

No, he'd heard that. He'd just assumed he had misheard because he didn't give two shits about the garbage. He was horny, damn it. "Sure, I can take out the garbage."

"Oh, and when I was ordering the new comforter online for the bedroom, I noticed you have very boring checks to pay your bills. So I ordered you fun new ones. Betty Boop. They're adorable."

Seamus dropped the pen shards. Took a deep breath. It didn't matter if his name was printed on the same piece of paper as a cartoon bimbo. Really. It didn't. It's not like the opposition was going to get ahold of them. Oh, bloody hell. What if their political opponents got ahold of them? And why was she picking through his financial papers? Seamus rubbed his forehead.

"You know what? I'm going to bed." *Come with me,*

come with me, he projected. If he could just get Cara out of her clothes, it would make the curtains seem so much less horrible, he was sure.

"I'll come with you," she said. "Hanging these was harder than I thought."

And he'd just stood there and watched her finish the job. Nice. He went to her, took her hand. Lied through his teeth. "It looks good. Cheerful."

"You think so?"

No. "Yes. Definitely."

She leaned against his arm. "Thanks. It makes it so much easier to be a prisoner knowing I can decorate."

Was that guilt stabbing right through his heart?

"Just a little while longer, Cara, I promise. Until we figure out a few things."

"What things?"

"Don't worry about it." He didn't know where to start, and didn't want to scare her. "And you know a lot more now about vampires than you did a week ago."

"I know all about the laws, all about Ethan's political platform, all about half-blood vampires, but I don't know anything about you."

Cara had told him about her family, about her father leaving, about her blackjack-dealer mother dying. He felt compassion that her life hadn't been an easy one. But what was there to say about himself? His mortal family had only been his father, and he could barely even remember what his father looked like. "Yes, you do know about me. Irish farmer. Told you that." Seamus tugged her hand so they headed toward the bedroom. He didn't want to talk about himself. He wanted to take Cara to bed.

"What I don't know is who she was."

Seamus stopped walking. "What do you mean?"

"The woman who hurt you."

His fists clenched involuntarily and he squeezed Cara's hand. Was she reading his mind? He could have sworn all his thoughts had been closed to her. "I don't know what you're talking about. There was no woman."

"There had to be someone because you hold back."

This is where he really had no clue what women wanted. "Hold back?" She was the one who had nixed sex. "Come on, Cara, let's not do this. We're getting along here, things are fine. We were total strangers ten days ago and now we're living together and it's working out just fine. Don't make things complicated."

She studied him for a second, then shrugged. "Okay. Sorry."

Well, that was very unsatisfying. Seamus tugged off his shirt and pitched it toward the laundry hamper in his closet. It fell on the floor and he ignored it. He shucked his pants and went in to the bathroom in his boxers and brushed his teeth. When he came back into the room, Cara had picked up his clothes and deposited them in the hamper. She brushed past him into the bathroom, still wearing those damn sweatpants.

He got into bed, punched his pillow six or eight times, and flopped back. Something was wrong here, only he didn't know what it was. Fritz jumped up on the bed, turned three times, and lay down right next to Seamus. Right where he'd prefer Cara to lie.

"Get down, dog," he said in annoyance.

Fritz ignored him and stretched out his snout so that wet nose was touching the back of Seamus's shoulders. Seamus scooted over to the edge of the mattress to get away from the slimy touch. From the floor, Satan gave a frantic orchestra of yips and whines.

"What?" Seamus stared at him, willing him to lie down and die. It didn't work. Satan just turned up the volume.

"What's the matter with Mr. Spock?" Cara called from the bathroom.

"He wants on the bed."

"Can you pick him up, Seamus? He hates being left out."

Seamus counted to three. Thought about learning yoga. Decided it would be better to take up boxing. "Sure." Leaning over, he grabbed the fat Chihuahua with one hand and hauled him straight up. "It's not because I like you," he told Satan. "It's because I like Cara."

Satan wiggled free, scrambled over Fritz's back, and settled on Cara's pillow. Served her right. Seamus rolled onto his back.

One of the cats leapt onto the foot of the bed and sat on his right foot, crushing it. Seamus yanked his foot out from under cat ass. "Damn it."

The cat took advantage of the newfound space and curled up into a ball where Seamus's foot had been. Seamus turned on his side. The black cat jumped on the bed right where Seamus's face was. "Argh." He turned, but so did the cat, and he wound up with a furry tail in his mouth.

He pushed the cat's rump down until it lay on the sliver of bed between Seamus and the nightstand. "Stay."

Feeling squished and pissed off, Seamus flipped onto his back and watched Cara come out of the bathroom. Still wearing sweats. Still wearing a T-shirt, though it was a different one. An even baggier one.

"Aahhh, look how cute you all look," she said. "Where's Button? Button! Come here, baby."

The other Lab bounded into the room and leapt onto the bed. Cara slid in behind him. She lifted the Chihuahua off her pillow and cuddled him against her chest. The chest Seamus wanted to cuddle against.

The Labs grumbled at each other as they nudged and pushed for positioning.

"Cara, I'm not sure the bed is big enough for all these animals."

"Sure it is." She fixed the blankets over herself. "It's cozy and comforting."

Not the words he would have chosen.

"I'm going down to the casino with Kelsey and Alexis again tonight," she said, capping her words off with a yawn.

"That's fine." Even if it scared him, he couldn't see a legitimate reason to say no when she would have a bodyguard with her, and she'd be staying in Ethan's casino.

"I wasn't asking permission."

Seamus rolled his eyes and shifted, causing the black cat to shoot him a look of displeasure. He gritted his fangs. "Fine."

It was the only word he could manage, because this was a fine end to a long life. He was a vampire, for hell's sake. Strong. Bloodthirsty. Intelligent. And what else?

Whipped by a woman. A woman who lived with him, decorated his apartment, ordered him checks, and shared his bed, but who he had not had sex with.

She was silent for a minute. Then, "Do you think we need relationship counseling?"

"No!" He'd rather hack his own head off. And what kind of relationship did she think they had? Besides weird and asexual, that is.

"Well, you're very closed."

So was she. She'd yet to let him anywhere near her inner thighs in days. "Vampires don't go to counseling."

"Humph" was her opinion on that.

He wished he could read her mind and figure out what planet she was coming from, but her thoughts were shuttered.

"Good night," she said after a second.

That made him smile, just a little. "Actually, it's good day."

Brittany Baldizzi was still adjusting to the fact that she was half-vampire and her sister, Alexis, was now a full vampire, married to the president of the Vampire Nation. It was a big change, some of it a little unnerving. But she did appreciate that she could now call Alexis at all hours of the night.

She leaned her head on the edge of the bathtub to cool her flushed skin, and hit the button for Alexis on her cell phone. Even though Alex couldn't do anything to make the flu go away faster, it would make Brittany feel better to hear her sister's voice. Alexis had raised her when their mother had overdosed, and was Brittany's rock. Alexis would let her whine about how lousy she felt.

Actually, Alexis would probably come over and wipe her brow. Help her change her sweaty T-shirt. Tuck her into bed. Get her some ginger ale. All of which sounded very appealing from her hunched-over position on the cold bathroom floor.

She'd never been this sick in her life and it was awful.

Unfortunately, Alexis wasn't answering her cell phone.

When the voice mail came on, Brittany said, "Alex?" in a shaky, hopeful voice. But Alexis didn't pick up.

She dropped the cell phone and let a tear slip out of each eye and roll down her cheeks. She felt really damn awful. Like something had gone inside her intestines and started jackhammering through the interior walls. Not to mention she was light-headed and cold.

But other than her sister, she had no idea who she could call in the middle of the night on a Thursday for some sympathy and Pepto-Bismol.

Corbin popped into her head for some reason.

Brittany sighed and picked at her sweaty shirt, lifting it up and shivering when the cool air hit her wet skin underneath. Even if she knew how to call Corbin, she wouldn't. They didn't have a relationship or anything. He was just a vampire she had met in Ethan's hotel, and he had told her he was a scientist, researching a cure to vampirism. He had asked for a sample of her blood, and somehow, she wasn't really sure exactly how, but their clothes had fallen off and suddenly she'd been having amazing sex with him. But then, nothing. He had zipped on out of her apartment about a minute after he'd pulled it out, which had been fine with her because she'd been mortified at her behavior.

That should have been it.

It shouldn't matter. She really didn't even know him. But it still hurt, just a little, that he'd thought so poorly of either her or her sexual prowess that he hadn't bothered to call or anything.

And he was so cute. With his little Frenchie accent and his green eyes. Corbin Jean Michel Atelier.

Her stomach cramped convulsively again. She lurched for the toilet and gripped her way through another round of heaves. When she pulled back, shaking, eyes watering, hair in her face, stomach sour, she heard the front door to her apartment open.

Thank God. It was Alex. She must have heard her pitiful

voice mail and dashed over. Or somehow with her vampire senses she had detected Brittany's misery.

"Alex?" she whispered, eyes closed, hand fumbling for a towel to wipe her mouth.

"Brittany? What is the matter with you?" a voice asked from the doorway.

A voice with a French accent. Oh, shit. Brittany's eyes flew open. "Corbin?" she asked weakly.

He was standing in the doorway of her tiny bathroom, looking put together and suave in dress pants and a deep blue dress shirt that complemented his fair hair and green eyes. She hadn't seen him in four weeks, and he looked even cuter than she remembered.

There was no telling what she looked like, and the look of horror on his face wasn't encouraging.

He strode into the bathroom and bent down in front of her, pushing her hair back off her face and running his eyes over her. "What is wrong, Brittany?"

"The flu."

"Do you have a fever?" He pressed his cool palm onto her forehead. "It doesn't feel like one to me, but you are clammy. And you vomited, yes?"

"Yes." And forgot to flush the toilet. Mortified, she reached for the handle. He beat her to it and pushed it down forcefully. Lovely. Just lovely. The only man in her adult life she had ever mooned over and he showed up right when she'd puked her guts out. She probably had saliva on her cheek to complement the sweat-soaked sticking-up hair.

But he startled her by reaching out and lifting her into his arms. "Corbin! Stop, I'm all gross."

"Hush, Brittany. I'm taking you to bed."

Despite her queasy stomach, his word choice made her blush, remembering the last time they'd been in her bed.

His grip tightened on her. He felt good. Strong. Solid. She indulged in leaning against him, appreciating the fact that she wasn't alone. Her sister, Alexis, was the strong one, who liked solitude. Brittany craved company.

With one arm, he pulled back her white and pink bedsheets and deposited her gently on the bed. Brittany sighed in relief. The bed felt good to her sick body. Then he turned and rummaged through her dresser.

"What are you looking for?"

He came back to the bed with a T-shirt in his hand. "Getting you a fresh change of clothing. Your shirt is soaked."

It was also making her shiver. She held her hand out for the clean shirt. "Thanks."

But he didn't give it to her. Instead, he dropped it on the bed, grabbed the hem of the shirt she was wearing, and yanked it up.

"Corbin!" she shrieked. Hello. She wasn't wearing a bra. Before she even finished squawking out his name, he had the shirt completely off her. She was naked except for soft cotton sleep shorts.

Naked with Corbin and the flu. It was a cruel irony.

"I am not going to ravish you," he said in an offended tone, his French accent increasing. "I am a doctor, if you recall. I am trying to help."

She knew that. But it didn't make her feel any less of a doofus. She wanted to turn him on, not puke on him. "I know." Her arm sort of slid across her chest to cover her breasts. It was just too weird to be half-dressed. "Thank you."

He watched the arm movement. A small smile crossed his face as he bunched up the new T-shirt. "You do not need modesty around me."

Brittany didn't answer as he tugged the top on over her head. She helped get it down over her chest and then sank back into the pillow, exhausted. He got her a glass of water and a wet washcloth to wipe her face. He pulled the covers over her and patted everything in place. She still felt like hell, but it pleased her to have him cosseting her, taking care of her.

"Why are you here, Corbin?" she asked when he pulled a stray hair off her lip.

Now it was his turn to look embarrassed. He folded his arms and frowned. "I heard your distress so I came."

"You can hear my thoughts?" He had been able to do that before. That was how she had contacted him several times. Before they'd had sex and he'd run off.

"I did no such thing as running off." He looked indignant. "You told me to leave."

That answered her question on his mind-reading capabilities.

Brittany felt herself smiling. He did like her. He had just been embarrassed like she had. That made her feel so much better. "You're right. I did. But thanks for coming tonight."

Her eyes drifted closed. She was so tired all of a sudden. Exhausted.

"You are welcome, *chérie*," he whispered. Cool lips pressed against her forehead. "Sleep, Brittany."

So she did, feeling warm and protected.

Eight

Waking up with Cara next to him was Seamus's new favorite part of the night. In her sleep, Cara didn't roll her eyes at him or make prisoner cracks. When she was sleeping the hard, intense sleep of a fledgling vampire, she always sought him out. She moved her body over and over on the bed, until she was touching him. And she even snaked her arm across his waist or chest on a daily basis.

It gave Seamus immense satisfaction, a pure happiness to wake and have her embracing him, giving him her trust in her sleep.

When she woke up, usually thirty minutes to an hour after him, she liked to talk. He liked to listen.

"Mmmm," she said on a yawn, leg still thrown over his. She let her eyes open briefly then closed them again. "I was dreaming and it was nice, but weird. My grandmother barely spoke English, and now that she's sort of lost her grip on reality, she only speaks Korean, but in my dream she and I were shopping, like we used to do, every Sunday. We were on the bus going to the grocery store, and she was speaking English, like it was her first language. What do you think dreams mean, Seamus?"

"I think they're wishes and worries, churning through our unguarded brains while we sleep."

"I like that." She lifted her head and her hair fell over his chest as she smiled at him.

Seamus loved the feel of that satin cascade of hair tickling his bare skin. He loved Cara's femininity, the way she was all soft, everywhere, her skin, her body, her heart, her eyes.

"What did you dream about?"

Without hesitation, he told her the truth. "You." He'd been dreaming about her every night, drinking his blood, tasting hers, their bodies intertwined, their minds open to each other. It made him ache, and for more than the physical release his body craved. He ached to have Cara in a way that was fuller, more complete and permanent than what he had now. It felt like they were playacting at living together, and that it could all go away at any second.

"You dreamt about me?" She smiled, her eyes darting down to his lips. "Which one am I? A wish or a worry?"

"Both."

Cara was winning. She was up sixteen thousand dollars on an initial investment of two thousand. She felt the adrenaline surging through her as the dealer set her hand out facedown.

She was concentrating hard, ready to call it quits after this deal.

A small crowd had gathered around the table since she was winning heavily. Alexis and Kelsey flanked her, cheering her on.

Her opponents were three middle-aged men from Texas who were sure they could beat her. She was sure they were wrong.

"It's our game," one said in a slow drawl. "Texas Hold 'Em."

She ignored him and turned her card. Bets went around. The thickest of the three, who had to sit two feet out to accommodate his rounded belly, folded. The others met and raised.

It was going to be iffy. The one with the cowboy hat had to have three of a kind given the pair of jacks he was showing and the fact that he kept leaning forward eagerly.

She had a full house tens up.

And miraculously, the guy had nothing but the pair. When they showed their hands, the crowd burst into cheers and applause. Cara let out a victory yell. She had won twenty-two freaking thousand dollars. It was unbelievable. Just like that. When she gave Alexis Ethan's two grand back, she was going to have twenty thousand dollars.

"Oh, my God. You just killed him!" Alexis jumped up and down. "That was awesome."

Cara grabbed her chips from the dealer, heart racing, and stepped onto the rungs of her stool. "Yeehaw!" she yelled to the crowd gathered, grinning like crazy. Damn, this felt good. She'd been so cooped up in Seamus's apartment, doing nothing but decorating to annoy him, and while it was working, he didn't seem to have any intention of kicking her out. Because she had figured something out—Seamus was a really nice guy. He tolerated all her changes and demands with a stoic calm that amazed her.

It made her like him, damn it.

Meanwhile, she had discovered the horrible truth about herself. Not only did she like Seamus, but she liked being a housewife. It was just as she had always suspected, all those years of making dinner for her grandmother, and rearranging the furniture in their tiny apartment. She liked domestic tasks.

Which was scary. So she had run off to gamble, the perfect antidote to housekeeping urges. Winning was exhilarating. She gave Alexis a high five.

"Cara," Kelsey said.

"What?" Cara glanced over at Kelsey, who didn't sound nearly as excited as she should given that Cara had just won twenty thousand dollars.

"I think Seamus wants your attention. He's over there glaring at you."

Cara followed her finger and found Seamus and Ethan standing at the top of the casino floor stairs by the lobby. Ethan looked amused. Seamus looked pissed off.

Good. Alexis said Seamus didn't like exhibitionism. Since domestic nag wasn't working, maybe she'd gain her freedom this way. Which she was absolutely positive she still wanted. Truly, definitely positive. Staying with Seamus would be a bad, wrong, evil idea.

Cara stepped onto the seat of her stool and spoke to the crowd. "If you all catch me, I'll buy the next round of drinks."

And she swan-dived into the spectators, making a beautiful leaping arch. They caught her, though her right leg did torque a bit on the grab. She laughed. Hey, that had actually been kind of fun sailing through the air. She had two brawny guys with tattoos setting her back on her feet when Seamus moved in front of her.

"What the hell are you doing?" he said.

"Having fun." Pissing him off intentionally. "I don't want to spend eternity being bored."

"So you leap into crowds of gamblers?" he said in exasperation.

"Yes." She raised her chin. "Everyone, to the bar! This round's on me."

The crowd gave another cheer and the twenty or so people pushed forward to the bar. The woman next to Cara gave her a nudge. "Your boyfriend don't look all that excited for you."

"He's not my boyfriend, he's my jailer." That was what was so incredibly irritating, the real rub of what was bothering her. If Seamus would just let her make her own choices, she could say in all honesty she'd probably want to stay with him. At least long enough to explore the attraction between them. She liked Seamus, enjoyed his company, the way he was solid, reliable, loving with her pets. But knowing that she was trapped, knowing she couldn't leave, had to depend on Seamus, rubbed her wrong and then some. It was poisoning their potential relationship because she felt patronized.

What she really wanted was to go home to live in her own apartment, but date Seamus. Go to the movies, talk, get to know each other, fall in love. Like normal people. But he wouldn't let her go.

"Cara."

She ignored Seamus calling her and tossed a two-hundred-dollar chip at the bartender. "Something for my friends here."

Alexis grabbed her hand. "Let's dance. They're playing Madonna."

So she, Alexis, and Kelsey hit the dance floor and moved to the funky beat, laughing and having fun while Seamus parked his butt in a chair and watched. Just watched. With a ticked-off look on his face. Ethan was working the room, talking to the bartender, the DJ, the waitresses.

Cara was actually having a hell of a lot of fun, despite the chill coming from Seamus. She hadn't realized how tense she'd been until she'd starting acting silly with Alexis and Kelsey. They were lip-syncing and laughing and talking. Kelsey had loosened up as well, and Cara was glad to see she was enjoying herself. These vampire girls' nights out were going to have to become a weekly deal.

When a sensual song came on, Cara couldn't help but slide into a few of her regular, nonsexual dance moves. This song was part of her routine and it was like second nature to her. She did a shallow cradle rock just to limber up. Her jeans were a bit restrictive, but she felt her hips loosening up.

Alexis imitated her move, stiffly, and soon they were all laughing, until Seamus touched her arm. She jumped, startled at how fast he'd moved from his table to her side. He didn't look happy. He looked capable of biting through steel.

"Hey, cutie," she said with a smile, which wiped the anger right off his face.

"Are you drunk?" he asked in astonishment.

"Can we get drunk?" she asked. That possibility had never occurred to her. "How do we do that?"

"Never mind." He took her hand, tugged a little. "Can I talk to you, please?"

"Since you said please." She let him lead her off the dance floor and to the table he'd been sitting at. "What's up?"

"Cara." He cleared his throat. "I'm glad you're having fun."

"Good. I won twenty thousand dollars." She was still a little floored by that. It meant that she had a serious nest egg. If her educational program could be altered to online classes, she could probably push and take eighteen or twenty-one credit hours and finish the following spring. Then she could intern in an all-night animal hospital. Her dreams could still be realized if she did a little creative maneuvering.

"But you have to understand our goal is to remain under the radar. If we draw attention to ourselves, we run the risk of exposure."

"Oh." That did make sense. "So . . . you think I drew too much attention to myself tonight by winning?"

"That, and the diving into the crowd, and the sexy dance moves that had half a dozen guys salivating as they watched."

"Were you salivating?" She liked the thought of that. And she'd barely done anything out there on the floor. Wait until Seamus saw what she could do with water.

"Yes. I was definitely salivating." His hand fell on her knee.

"Okay."

He blinked. "Okay, what?"

"Okay, I'll try not to draw attention to myself. See,

when you discuss it with me rationally, explain to me the importance of discretion instead of ordering me around, I completely understand. I'll chill with the dancing." She stood up. Time to revert back to her domestic plan, which she had to admit was more her style than crowd diving. She actually liked organizing Seamus's apartment and putting color into his gunmetal gray life. She kissed his forehead. "I'm going to go cash out, then I'll go upstairs. It's been a long night. Will you walk the dogs for me?"

Seamus looked puzzled. But he nodded. "Sure. Okay."

"Thanks, baby. I'm going to say good night to Kelsey and Alexis."

She gave him a little wave and left him sitting there, frowning slightly.

Alexis pounced on her when she cruised past the edge of the dance floor. "Well? What did he want?"

"He wants me to stop drawing attention to myself. I told him I'd be happy to stop dancing inappropriately and then I called him baby, kissed his forehead, and told him I was going to bed. He has no idea what to think."

Alexis snorted. "Perfect. Confuse the hell out of him." She glanced back over Cara's shoulders. "He's actually leaving."

"I asked him to walk my dogs."

A grin split Alexis's face. "You are brilliant. He'll be kicking you out before you know it."

Great. She couldn't wait. Really. Cara clamped down on her confusion and reached out to hug Alexis. "Thanks for everything. I'm so glad I have someone to talk to."

"Me, too. It's nice to have another girl vampire running around. The testosterone level in this hotel is pretty high."

Cara hugged Kelsey. "It's been so nice hanging out with you, Kelsey. Say we'll do this again."

"That's a great idea, Cara," Kelsey said, hugging her back. "I'd like that."

"I think we're already starting a tradition. We'll have to do a girls' night out like once a week." Cara considered Seamus's reaction to that. "Only next time maybe we should pick a casino where no one knows us."

"Good plan," Alexis said, even as her eyes darted over to her husband, still talking to the bartender.

"See you all later."

Cara left the bar and headed down the hall. She realized almost immediately one of the bodyguards was following her. Considering she was about to collect twenty thousand dollars, she didn't mind having the muscle backing her up.

Because of the size of her winnings, she had to go to the main box office, and she started down the hall, high heels sinking into the plush gray carpet. It was a nice hotel and casino, very classy and understated, at least by Vegas standards. It was still over the top, with a shiny forties glamour, but a classy glitz. Lots of glass, lots of sharp silver accessories. Which made her wonder about the supposed vampire aversion to silver. Given the abundance of polished silver in her bathroom alone, it seemed unlikely that the legends were true.

It did smell funny in the hallway, though. Cara wrinkled her nose, wondering if someone had gotten sick in an obscure corner and the hotel staff wasn't aware of it. She glanced around a little, but didn't see anything obvious that could be causing the smell.

The only other person in the hallway was her bodyguard following behind, and a man coming in the opposite direction. The smell grew stronger and Cara felt her stomach churn. She glanced back at the guard, who seemed to be walking faster now, closing the distance between them. He spoke into his little earpiece microphone.

Cara slowed down. There was something about the man heading toward her, something about the way he lumbered, the way his body was thick on top, spindly from the thigh down, that tugged at her memory. He was closer now, close enough that she could see he was watching her, staring. His hand slid into the inside pocket of his jacket, and Cara felt the sense of danger explode over her, like she had that night in the alley.

"Seamus?" she whispered out loud, grinding to a halt, terrified. This was the man who had been there. This was the man Seamus had been fighting. The one she'd thought of as stupid because of the slackness of his features, the dullness in his eyes. This was the one who'd thought she was pretty.

A knife emerged from his pocket. A wicked, long, sharp, jagged knife, that looked like it could gut a deer with one swift slice. A deer, or her.

Cara panicked, feet rooted to the carpet, mind paralyzed with fear. She was considering what the hell she should do when the guy raised the knife. A whoosh of air went past Cara and she sucked in her breath, too frightened to scream. Her bodyguard was suddenly visible in front of her, and with one swift lift of his arm, he brought the other vampire to the ground.

A little shriek managed to escape her lips, and she clamped her hand over her mouth.

The bodyguard glanced over his shoulder. "You alright, miss?"

She nodded. He bent back down, handcuffed the vampire, tossed him over his shoulder, and started down the hall. "Come on," he said in a quiet, urgent voice.

"What... what was he going to do?"

"Kill you."

Just checking. She'd thought so, but she'd wanted to make sure. Her knees buckled. "Why?"

He paused long enough to glance over at her. "I don't know."

His tone indicated it was a stupid question.

"Where are we going?" She hurried to keep up with him, feeling like her Chihuahua must with the Labradors. Her legs moved back and forth at high speed, but she was still six paces behind him. And given the fear still thick in her throat, she did not want to be left behind.

"Mr. Carrick's office. We'll get you another escort to Mr. Fox's suite."

Cara wasn't sure what to say, so she shut up.

Maybe being with Seamus had more benefits than orgasmic feedings. It seemed she really did need protection.

These vampires were out for blood.

Who would have thought?

Seamus was watching Button, Cara's Lab, drop a bomb onto the sidewalk, and marveling that an undead Irish potato farmer turned soldier was now a glorified dog walker in Vegas.

It had been a mistake to take all three dogs out at the same time. They crisscrossed leashes, walked at different speeds, and in three different directions. Satan bit at Button's hind legs, which caused a lot of angry barking back and forth, and Fritz was obsessed with smelling every single bird dropping, piece of garbage, or dead insect they came across.

Seamus was rapidly concluding two things—that it was unnatural to domesticate dogs and bring them into human dwellings, and that he was a sucker. He'd fallen for that sweet forehead kiss and innocent smile from Cara and now he was whipped. Actually, he'd been whipped from the minute he met her. This was just visual confirmation.

Button finished doing his thing and bounded away, jerking back with a startled yelp when he reached the end of the leash's length. Meanwhile, Fritz and Satan enthusiastically ran over and sniffed Button's leavings.

"Aww, hell. Knock it off, guys. That's disgusting." He tugged them both back. They started down the sidewalk. At least it was a nice night. Clear and cool. There were the usual mobs of people out and about, and he'd chosen to stay on the Strip, though he was a half-block down from the serious crowds.

"Hey." A woman tapped his arm.

"Yes?"

Hostess for a restaurant with a nautical theme, the woman was wearing a mermaid-influenced skirt and breast shells. She crossed her arms over her shells. "You going to pick that up?"

"Pick what up?"

She pointed to Button's mess. "We have laws about that, you know."

Glancing down at it, Seamus could see why. That was really damn disgusting, and he suddenly felt guilty for letting Button do it in the first place. But hell, where was he supposed to take the dog? Drive him out to the suburbs and let him do his thing? They lived in a casino, and the dog had his choice of gravel, sidewalk, or the grass by the pool. Somehow Seamus didn't think that would go over big either.

"What am I supposed to do with it?"

Rolling her eyes, she bent over her hostess stand, just inside the door of the restaurant. She pulled out a blue plastic grocery bag. "Here. Pick it up and throw it away in one of the street trash containers so it doesn't stink up anybody's restaurant or bar."

He took the bag, feeling less than delighted at the prospect of cleaning up dog shit. "How do I get it in the bag?" He wasn't touching that.

"You use the bag to pick it up, then turn the bag inside out and tie it closed." She petted Fritz's head when the dog rushed over to wag his tail at her.

Seamus was half tempted to use vampire persuasion and get her to do it, but his conscience pricked him. He rearranged the bag over his hand and leaned down, holding his breath so he didn't have to smell it.

"Why are you walking your dogs at two in the morning anyway?" she asked.

"It's a favor for someone." Seamus gripped the mess and picked it up. A big favor. He quickly turned the bag around and tied it off. Now he had a warm plastic bag dangling from his fingers.

And his cell phone was ringing. He pitched the bag in the trash and wondered if Cara was worth this kind of aggravation. Maybe he should just let her leave like she wanted to.

The caller was Ethan. He pushed the on button. "What's up?"

"Come to my office, please. Cara had a little run-in with your friends from the alley."

Seamus went stone cold. "Is she okay?"

"She's fine. Just a little shook up. I have two guards with her at your place."

"I'll be right up." Seamus shoved the phone in his pocket and tugged on all three leashes. The dogs tumbled all over, turning left and right and nudging each other.

An emotion he didn't quite understand clogged his throat, and Seamus lost his patience. "Line up, boys. Now," he said in a low, firm voice.

Miraculously, they all snapped their heads up at his tone and untangled themselves.

He jogged them back to the casino as fast as he could, letting the Labs go full retriever speed, the Chihuahua traveling in his arms, yipping with excitement. Seamus blew right past the twenty-third floor, where Ethan's offices were. He needed to check on Cara first.

When he opened the door to his place, she was pacing in the living room, looking pale and frightened, but uninjured. "Are you okay?"

She nodded and held out her arms. Seamus was moved that she wanted his comfort. He walked toward her, feeling his heart rate return to normal. Damn, she'd scared the hell out of him. He needed to feel her in his arms, too.

But instead of walking into an embrace, she reached out and plucked the dog out of his arms. She buried her mouth in the Chihuahua's head and closed her eyes with a shudder.

Seamus stopped with his hand halfway to her shoulder. Okay, now he felt like an ass. She wanted the rat-faced dog, not him. And the bodyguards, Michael and Stanley, were unsuccessfully pretending they hadn't noticed. Wonderful.

They were standing on either side of the living room, one in front of the windows, the other by the door that led to the hotel hallway. They were busy studying the floor and ceiling respectively now.

"Can you wait outside, please?" he asked, jerking his thumb in that direction.

"Yes, Mr. Fox." They moved past him with a rustle of clothing and shoe squeaking.

Once they were gone, Seamus took a deep breath and tried to relax. Cara looked fine. That was what mattered. "What happened?"

She opened her eyes, and the fear there cut him deep. "I was just walking to cash out, and he was there in the hall. One of the guys from that night... the one who told me I was pretty. That I would taste good."

Seamus remembered that sick tone to the vampire's voice that night and how it had infuriated him at the time, but he'd been unable to help her since he was battling the other vamp. "Did he say something to you tonight?"

"No. He reached in his coat and pulled out a knife. The bodyguard came from behind..." She gestured with her arm behind her. "And then he knocked the guy down before I even realized what was happening. But the guard said the guy was going to kill me."

It took every conscious effort to keep from throwing his coffee table out through the back window. This seriously pissed him off. He wanted to know who the vampires were and what they wanted. And how he could kill them. No one was going to mess with Cara.

"Hi, Mr. Spockie-Wockie," Cara crooned to the dog. "I missed you." She looked over at Seamus, her expression troubled. "That guy... he smelled, Seamus. Like a sickly sweet sweat odor, but it was extreme. Like he hadn't bathed. It was almost a chemical scent."

She shuddered again and Seamus gave in to his urge and put his hands on her shoulders and drew her against his chest. She didn't resist. In fact, she sighed and laid her head on him, the dog resting between them.

"I'm damn glad you had a guard with you."

"Me, too." She glanced up at him. "I'm sorry I was so stubborn about wanting to leave and go home. I didn't understand."

Hugging her to him, Seamus ran his lips over the top of her hair. It was satin smooth. "It's my fault. I should have explained things better. I haven't exactly done a stellar job of initiating you to vampirism." Something about what she'd said pricked at him. "He smelled bad?"

"Yes. It was disgusting. Like . . . sick room. Like when my mother died of cancer." She gave another shudder and moved farther into his touch.

Then it hit him. "Drug blood. He's addicted to drugs. I've met a few over the centuries. Opium in the nineteenth century. Heroin and cocaine in the late twentieth century. I haven't met one in a while, but they all have that same medicinal smell to them." Seamus absently rubbed her back, wondering how hard it would be to track down information on this guy.

"That would definitely describe the way this guy smelled. So you mean he drinks blood that has drugs in it?"

"Yes. Now we just need to find him and see who sent him."

"Oh." Cara pulled away from him a little. "He's in Ethan's office. The guard handcuffed him and carried him in there."

"They have him now?" Seamus squeezed her waist and turned toward the door. He was looking forward to having a little talk with the man who had tried to harm Cara. His fists clenched in anticipation. "Stay inside. Michael and

Stanley are outside your door. Don't let anyone but them in until I get back."

She grabbed his arm. "What are you going to do?"

"Just what I said. Find out who sent him."

"Be careful. Don't talk to him alone."

Seamus studied her face, saw the fear written plainly there. He felt a smile tugging at his lips. "Why, Cara, I almost think you care what happens to me."

Her mouth pursed. "I just wouldn't want to live with the guilt if you got decapitated."

Seamus laughed. "We'll talk when I get back. I think it's important you understand what's going on with the election and what happened to Kelsey."

"Okay. I'll be here."

Both Labs nuzzled against her knees and she held Satan tightly. She looked vulnerable and beautiful. Seamus leaned forward and kissed her lightly, just brushing his lips over hers. He moved back immediately so he wouldn't be tempted to take more.

"Be safe."

Ringo stepped into the dancers' dressing room at the club.

"You can't be back here," a woman said, assessing him over her shoulder as she pulled on spiky shoes. She was wearing little else but the shoes, and Ringo allowed himself an appreciative glance up and down.

"I'm just looking for a woman, she dances behind the screen. Will she be here tonight?"

"What do you want to know for?" Her forehead wrinkled in a frown.

Ringo smiled, probing into her mind. He wasn't that skilled at mind control, but this woman had wide-open thoughts. He caught concern and caring for her friend, suspicion of him.

She was an attractive woman, lush, but still thin, her blood flowing steady and calm. Not a panicker, this one. And since he'd had such a delicious taste of Donatelli's Katie, Ringo had a sudden urge to repeat the experience with the stripper in front of him.

But first he had to get the information he needed. "I'm looking for someone to do a private party and I saw her dance, thought she might be interested."

"Cara? Nah." She turned to the mirror, swirled on more lipstick. "Cara's kind of a prude for a stripper. She likes to hide behind that screen. Besides, she just got hit by a car and she hasn't been working all this week. She should be back next week, but I doubt she'll do it. Like I said, she's funny about shit like that."

So Cara was expected back at work in a week.

Ringo stared at the stripper's backside, pointing enticingly toward him in a thong. Modesty didn't seem to be a concern for this woman. He stayed by the door, so the mirror wouldn't capture his lack of a reflection. "Know anyone else who might be interested? I'm offering five grand for two hours."

She dropped the lipstick. Her suspicion of him disappeared. "Five thousand for two hours? For just dancing or for other . . . stuff?"

"Just dancing."

"I'll do it. I'm Dawn, by the way."

"Pleasure to meet you, Dawn. Trust me, I'll make this worth your time." Ringo had no intention of hiring her for anything, but the offer had erased her reticence. "Though I'd offer triple if you and your friend Cara could dance together. Strip each other."

Her eyes lit up with greed in the mirror and, Ringo suspected, arousal. "I can call her. Won't hurt to ask."

"Not at all. Maybe if we stop over her house with a little cash advance, we can be even more persuasive." Staying to the left, away from the mirror, Ringo slid his hand over her bare ass displayed so prettily for him.

"We could do that."

He squeezed her flesh, attempted to exert control over her mentally. "But first, maybe we can do a little quick private viewing right now. Show me what you've got so I'm sure I want it."

To his amazement, it worked. She turned and, with a quick snap and pull, removed her panties and bra. Damn. Tear-aways. That's what he fucking liked to see. A stripper who was good at what she did. So many of these chicks in Vegas were sloppy amateurs.

Ringo bent down in front of her, taking in her smooth-shaven sex. "Very nice." He teased and petted her for a moment, then sank his teeth into her plump lips.

Given her shudder of ecstasy, she liked it as much as Katie had.

Ringo liked it, too. As her hot blood rushed into his mouth, he marveled that he'd been stripped down to nothing but lust and hunger. He was more animal than human now, a selfish base creature, and he'd do whatever he had to to stay in Donatelli's good graces, keep his flow of drug blood coming.

He couldn't go into Carrick's casino, the Ava, himself because he had been captured on their security cameras a month earlier when he'd shot Carrick in the chest.

Smith was incapacitated at the moment, probably sniveling in agonized hunger in his room, something Ringo never wanted to experience. But since Smith wasn't available, and

Ringo couldn't do surveillance, Williams had been left to head into the casino and watch Carrick and company.

Williams had the intelligence of bran flakes, but all he had to do was watch what was happening over there.

Ringo would find and take care of the girl.

He sucked harder, feeling the dancer's leg lock tighter around him, the first tremors of her orgasm rippling. Moving with vampire speed, he stood up and thrust inside her, setting her to screaming in pleasure.

He'd take care of Cara, but first he'd finish taking care of Dawn.

"Ethan, listen to this." Alexis stormed into her husband's office with her cell phone in hand. She had just listened to her voice mail and thick fear had wrapped around her stomach, her heart, her brain.

"Alexis, dearest, I'm in the middle of something." Ethan leaned back in his wide leather desk chair, giving the appearance of relaxation, but she could see the tension in his shoulders.

She was feeling pretty damn stressed herself, and she didn't really care that there were two bodyguards standing in front of Ethan. This was going to take two seconds.

"Just listen to this." She stuck the phone to his ear and pressed 4 to repeat the message. She knew what it said. Her sister, Brittany, uttering her name in a whispery raggedy voice. Then nothing.

Ethan's eyebrow went up. "Brittany? When did this message come in?"

Alexis yanked the phone back and listened to it again, just to further her torture. Brittany sounded so frightened, so unlike her. "An hour ago. My phone must have rung while I was in the bar. The music was loud and I guess I didn't hear the ring. But I'm going over there, Ethan. Something's not right."

She expected him to get up and accompany her to Brittany's apartment. But he just nodded. "Zeke will go with you."

One of the two guards immediately moved toward the door and stood beside her. "You're not coming with me?" That both surprised and hurt her.

Ethan shook his head. "A vampire tried to kill Cara as she left the casino tonight. We have him in custody and I need to turn him over to the proper authorities."

Alexis gasped. "Is Cara okay?"

"She's fine. Just shook up. But we need to get this taken care of."

She should freaking hope so. "Who do you turn him over to? I didn't know there were vampire cops."

"More like a tribunal. Please call me when you get to Brittany's so I know you're both all right."

Alexis recognized that look on his face. She stopped, walked over to the desk, and gave him a quick kiss. "It's damn hard to have to worry about someone other than yourself, isn't it?"

"Yes." He cupped her face and gave her a longer kiss. "Listen to Zeke."

Since Zeke never talked, that might be a problem, but Alexis had learned to compromise a little in her marriage. Sometimes it was easier to tell Ethan what he wanted to hear.

"Absolutely."

When Seamus walked in, Alexis was leaving, a worried look on her face. That didn't encourage Seamus. Alexis wasn't known to overreact.

"What's the matter with Alexis?" he asked Ethan the minute the office door closed behind him.

"She got a cryptic voice mail from Brittany and she's headed over to her sister's apartment to check on her. I know Alexis worries about Brittany quite a bit, but in this case I have to admit the message was odd. Brittany just said 'Alex,' then there was nothing."

"You're not going with her?"

"Zeke is. We have an issue in the other room that needs taking care of." He jerked his thumb to his windowless inner office. "We need to turn him over to the tribunal for attempted murder of a vampire."

The words made Seamus's temper flare. "Who is he? Did you recognize him?"

"No. But he's young, a half-century or so. Definitely American. He's not talking, but I suspect it's more because he doesn't know anything than due to loyalty. And he's an addict. Within a few hours I imagine he'll be going into withdrawal."

"Cara said he smelled medicinal. I was wondering if it was drugs."

"I'm almost positive it is. But what I don't understand is why they were targeting first you and Kelsey, now Cara."

Seamus had a bad feeling about the whole situation. "Do you think it has to do with the election?"

"It's possible."

"And how does Brittany fit into all of this?" Maybe it was time to head back to the club and see if he could find

Brittany's aunt. If he knew who Brittany's father was, then maybe they could find some answers to the entire ream of questions they had.

"I don't know, but I don't like it. Maybe I should follow Alexis after all."

"Maybe."

The door to the inner office crashed open and the handcuffed vampire came plowing through, growling in anger and desperation.

"Looks like our friend is awake," Ethan said.

"Good." Seamus moved forward, standing over him as the man flopped around on the floor, trying to regain his balance. "I have a few questions for our friend about the night we met."

He was starting to wonder about the young vampire, the one who had walked off with Kelsey blithely following.

"Starting with this one." Seamus rolled the guy onto his back with the toe of his boot. "Who the hell was the third vamp with you, the one with dark hair. And why did he want Kelsey?"

"Do you have a friend named Dawn?" Kelsey asked Cara, after the guards had let her into Seamus's apartment.

Cara was startled. "Yes. She works at the club with me. Why? How do you know Dawn? Did you meet her the night you were there with Seamus?"

"I'm not sure." Kelsey pushed her bottom lip out.

It was a marvel how the girl could work a pout. Cara would look like a bullfrog if she did that.

Kelsey hadn't changed out of her evening dress. It clung to her supermodel figure like a purple body sock. Cara wished she could exchange breasts with Kelsey for a night.

Just to feel what it was like to walk around with the ability to look down and actually see her feet.

"Well, she was there that night, in the dressing room with me. Maybe you met her after I went in the alley. Where did you go, anyway?" It had never occurred to Cara to wonder that before, but she did now. Kelsey had been with Seamus in the hallway when Dawn had been checking him out with Cara.

Then when she'd gone into the alley, Kelsey hadn't been there.

"*He* was there," Kelsey said. "The one from before."

Well, that was helpful. "Um . . ." Cara shoved her hands in the pockets of her jeans. She'd kicked off her heels and stepped into flip-flops. The lacy camisole top had been traded in for a comfy T-shirt. "Does *he* know Dawn?" Sometimes she had a hard time following Kelsey's train of thought. It was like talking to her grandmother. They weren't speaking the same language.

Kelsey nodded. "Yes. He does. Which isn't good. Dawn needs to stay away from him, Cara. He's dark. He lets me into his mind, and there are dark, evil things in there. He's lost in his own bad feelings, which is sad because he could be good."

The way Kelsey spoke, so calm, so matter-of-fact, sent chills tripping down Cara's spine. "Is he a vampire?"

"Yes. And I think Dawn is with him now."

"Who is he?" Cara whispered, scared for Dawn. Had she brought him to Dawn inadvertently?

But Kelsey just shook her head.

"Should I call Dawn?"

Kelsey tipped her head like she was listening to someone talk in her mind. It completely freaked Cara out. Especially when Kelsey nodded, like she was answering.

Cara knew Seamus could talk to her like that, but it was still damn unnerving to watch someone else doing it. "Kelsey? What do you hear?"

Kelsey's dark hair fell over her shoulder. Her black eyes met Cara's. "He says what happened with Dawn was an accident. He lost control of himself."

A sick taste of blood bile rose up in Cara's mouth. "Oh, my God. We have to go to her."

"Okay," Kelsey said with a shrug, like she hadn't just communed with a psychopathic vampire. "Can we stop for some blood on the way?"

Nine

If Alexis could wet her pants still, she would have done it in relief when she found her sister asleep in bed.

Pressing her hand to her heart, she allowed herself to relax a little. "Jesus," she whispered in the dark room. "Good thing I can't die because I think I had a heart attack tonight."

Assessing the situation, she realized Brittany had a puke pan next to her, a wet washcloth lying on her dresser—a normal no-no for fastidious Brittany—and a glass of water on the nightstand. Her sister must be sick.

Alexis reached over and smoothed Brittany's sweat-soaked hair off her forehead. No fever that she could tell, but she looked pale and in pain, even in her sleep.

Brittany stirred. "Alex?" Her eyes fluttered open.

"Yep, it's me. Are you sick, Brit?"

"I have the flu."

Alexis felt sympathy and guilt stab her simultaneously. Here she'd been out dancing in a bar and Brittany was sick in bed, calling her for help.

"Can I get you anything, baby?"

"No, I'm okay." Brittany turned on her side and pulled the blanket up farther. "After I called you and you didn't answer, Corbin came."

"Corbin? French vampire Corbin?" The dickhead who had slept with her sister then left without a word? The vampire scientist known to be researching a cure to immortality? That Corbin? Alexis didn't like the sound of that at all.

"Yeah. He found me in the bathroom and changed my wet clothes. He tucked me in." She sighed, her eyes drifting shut.

Alexis had a hard time picturing Corbin Atelier tucking Brittany into bed. "That sounds . . . nice. Are you sure you weren't dreaming, though?"

Brittany frowned. "I don't think so. He said he was taking me to bed. He took my clothes off."

Sex dream. The poor kid was conjuring up Corbin in her state of delirium.

"Okay, shhh. It was just a dream, sweetie." Alexis fussed with the covers, wanting to kick Corbin Atelier. He had gotten under Brittany's skin in a way Alexis had never seen another man, and she didn't like it. If she ever ran into the Frenchman, she'd give him a roundhouse kick to the crotch for hurting her sister's feelings.

"Just a dream?" Brittany sounded disappointed. "Maybe that's why his accent wasn't as strong as it normally is."

Alexis stroked her cheek. "I'm sure that's it. It was just a dream."

"What do you mean you don't know where she is?" Seamus stared at the bodyguard in front of his apartment, anger, disbelief, and fear rising together in him. "And what happened to the other guard?"

"He went with Miss Kim and Kelsey. We wouldn't let them leave alone, Mr. Fox." The jackass had the nerve to sound indignant.

"You weren't supposed to let them leave at all!" Seamus had no clue where they could have gone. Cara had just assured him she understood the dangers they were facing and would stay in the apartment. Why the hell would she leave?

"I . . . sorry."

"Never mind. Just call his fucking cell phone and tell me where they are." Seamus ran his fingers through his hair and tried not to worry. Ethan had gone to check on Alexis. Cara and Kelsey were missing. He had a bad, bad feeling about all of this.

The guard dialed on his cell phone and spoke in a low voice. Seamus resisted the urge to snatch the phone out of his hand.

"Sir, Daniel says they're at a club. A, uh, an exotic dance club called Some Like It Hot. Miss Kim wanted to pick up her paycheck."

That made no sense whatsoever. Why would Cara choose to pick up her paycheck on the same night she'd won twenty thousand dollars at Texas Hold 'Em and she'd nearly been killed by an assassin?

"Tell him to stay put and not to let Cara or Kelsey out of his sight for a second. I'll be there in five minutes."

The guard relayed the message as Seamus checked his pocket for his keys and wallet.

"Mr. Fox? Daniel says they went in the back and it's ladies only. He had to stay in the club."

Wonderful. "Tell him to find them and keep them with him or he'll be looking for a new place of employment."

And with that, Seamus ran for the elevator.

When Cara burst into the dressing room at the club, she found Dawn's boyfriend, Bryan, on the floor kneeling over her. He shot her a wild glance over his shoulder, his face leeched of all color, shock and horror glazing his eyes.

"Cara . . . Jesus. Look at her . . . God. We need help . . ." His voice trailed off in a sob, and Cara's stomach clenched.

Bryan was a 250-pound bouncer with more tattoos than fingers. Yet he looked like he was going to throw up. She tried to steel herself for what had happened to Dawn, but nothing could prepare her for the sight of her friend sprawled out naked on the dirty carpet, vicious bruises and angry red teeth marks all over her body. Everywhere. On her neck, shoulders, sprawling out over her breasts and stomach, her navel, and peppered over three-fourths of her legs. She was a pearly white color, her skin cool and damp, a sheen of perspiration glistening.

"Oh, Dawn. Oh, God." Cara swallowed her revulsion and fell to the ground beside Bryan.

"She's still alive," Kelsey said. "She's just lost too much blood."

"What?" She didn't look alive. Dawn lay very still. But when Cara glanced at Dawn's chest, she saw it was rising and falling in small, barely visible breaths. She burst into tears of relief and grabbed Dawn's hand. "Hang in there, sweetie, you're going to be fine. Bryan, did you call 911?"

"Yeah, like five minutes ago." He leaned forward, touched a tentative hand to Dawn's cheek. "Is she really alive?"

Miraculously, her eyes opened. Bryan let out a sob and a curse.

"The ambulance is pulling up," Kelsey said from the doorway.

"I'll go get them," Bryan said, swiping at his cheeks. He ran for the door.

"Cara?" Dawn whispered. "I'm cold."

"I'm sorry, honey." Cara grabbed a dressing robe off the clothes rack in the corner. She tucked it over Dawn as gently as possible. "What happened? What did he do to you?"

Dawn sighed. "I don't know why I did it . . . I cheated on Bryan. But it felt good, Cara. It felt so good, the best sex I've ever had. I begged him not to stop. I'm not sure what happened, but I think I passed out from pleasure." She wet her lips with her tongue. "Why do I feel like this . . . like there's an ice cube on my chest and I can't move?"

"You lost some blood but the ambulance is here now." Cara tried to sound reassuring. She gave Dawn a smile. "I think after tonight Bryan may be giving you that engagement ring you've been after. You scared the crap out of him. You didn't hear it from me, but he's out in the hallway crying right now."

"Really?" Dawn shivered, her teeth clattering together. "Maybe I don't deserve Bryan after what I did."

"It wasn't your fault. Trust me." Then Cara squeezed her hand and moved back to give the paramedics room as they maneuvered their gurney into the small room.

The first thing out of the one's mouth was, "What the . . . ? What happened to her? Did something bite her?"

Cara just shook her head. Bryan said, "I found her like this. I don't know what happened."

Ten minutes later, they had Dawn hooked up to an IV, settled on the gurney under a heated blanket, and were wheeling her back out to transport her to the hospital.

Cara stood in the doorway for a minute, watching them retreat. She rubbed her forehead and turned to Kelsey, who was in the back of the room sitting on a stool. "Kelsey, I guess we need to find our guard. I want to go to the hospital and make sure Dawn's going to be okay."

"She'll be fine."

The voice made her jump. It was a man, coming from behind her in the dressing room. Cara turned slowly and came face-to-face with a dark-haired man in an expensive suit, a cigarette burning in his hand. He wasn't good-looking so much as he was striking, and the smile on his lips was crooked, devious.

"Did you do this to Dawn?" This had to be him. The one Kelsey had been talking about. Cara could feel his coldness as he shrugged his shoulder.

"Yes." He took a drag off his cigarette and blew smoke in her direction. "And even though I lost it for a minute or two, I'm not going to apologize for it. We both enjoyed ourselves before she passed out. She'll be fine after they give her some blood back. I bet she even begs me for it again."

Cara's stomach roiled. She wasn't entirely sure what he had done to Dawn, but she found herself clenching her fists in disgust. "Who are you and what do you want?"

"I just want to talk to you for a minute." He turned to Kelsey, who was watching with wide eyes. "Come sit with me, Kelsey." He held out his hand.

She started to shake her head no, then frowned. "Kyle?"

His face relaxed, lip turning up in a smile. "You do remember."

Cara couldn't tell if Kelsey remembered anything or not, but she did walk right over to him and let the man take her hand. She sat down on the couch next to him, let his hand rest on her knee. It made Cara's stomach churn even more viciously. She wondered if he had done to Kelsey what he'd done to Dawn.

"I didn't expect you to be a vampire," he said to Cara. "Though I can understand why Fox wanted you. You're a nice package."

If he thought she was going to thank him for the compliment, he was insane. Of course, it seemed like he was a lunatic anyway. She wanted to just grab Kelsey and run like hell, but Kelsey was still holding his hand and didn't look particularly concerned. Cara didn't think Kelsey would follow her if she ran.

In fact, Kelsey was turning to him. Running her fingers over the nape of his neck to massage him. Patting the back of his hair down like he was a little kid instead of an evil vampire.

He didn't seem to mind her touch. He just said, "So, Cara, you belong to Seamus Fox. I wonder why he would break the law for you? Aside from the obvious, that is." He blew more smoke out. "I'm curious."

Kelsey brushed cigarette ash off his pant leg.

"You are incredibly annoying, you know that?" he told her, though without any malice.

"A lot of people say that about me," Kelsey said with a complete lack of guile.

The man laughed and moved his hand farther up her thigh. "I'm not surprised." He turned to Cara. "You can leave now and go visit your friend Dawn. Kelsey and I have some catching up to do."

Over her undead body. "I'm not leaving without Kelsey."

He looked amused. "Alright, fine. I have another appointment anyway. I'll leave. I'm very accommodating."

Somehow that's not the word Cara would have used to describe him.

Letting go of Kelsey's leg, he stood up. "I would never hurt Kelsey, you know." He moved in closer to Cara until his arm brushed hers and his dark, empty eyes locked with hers. Behind the cigarette odor, Cara caught a hint of the same sickly sweet smell the other vamp had. She stood still, determined not to show her fear, to not move away from him.

"You, on the other hand, are a different story."

Then he was gone and Cara released a whoosh of air. "Who the hell is that, Kelsey?"

Kelsey just stood up with a shrug and straightened the bottom of her dress. "That's Kyle."

"Bait," Seamus said with a grimace. "That's what your friend Dawn was. He wanted you there for some reason."

They were sitting in the back of the club, at the very table where Seamus had sat that first night with Kelsey, when he had watched Cara dancing behind the screen. Like that night, he ordered drinks for everyone at the table to assuage suspicion and to keep the waitress from losing out on tips. Four dancers were on the stage doing some routine with feather boas and nothing else.

"I don't understand, Seamus." Cara rubbed her eyes, looking tired and worried. She had just gotten off the phone with her friend's boyfriend. He had said that Dawn was asleep, having been given a blood transfusion and painkillers, and he had suggested she wait until the morning to visit.

Seamus hadn't seen Dawn's condition, but it sounded like she'd been bled too heavily by the vampire Cara had encountered.

"Why would anyone want me?" Cara asked.

"I don't know." Seamus kept thinking back to that night... *get Fox and his girlfriend.* At the time he'd assumed they meant Kelsey, but maybe they had meant Cara. But why? Who had a reason to kill him?

"Let's dance," Kelsey said suddenly to the bodyguard, grabbing his hand and pulling at him.

He looked horrified and shot a confused look at Seamus. "Mr. Fox?"

But Seamus decided it would be better if Kelsey weren't at the table when he told Cara about the night Alexis had found Kelsey, so he just smiled. "Go on and have a little fun, Daniel. Dance with Kelsey. I'll keep an eye on things."

That should be ample punishment for Daniel for taking Cara and Kelsey to the club in the first place.

Daniel dragged his feet, but Kelsey tugged and pulled until she had him out on the dance floor. It didn't block anyone's view of the nude dancers on stage, but was a free forum to bump and grind and imitate the dancers in whatever way club-goers might choose. Currently there were two sultry women dancing. Daniel stood like a stone statue, but Kelsey threw her arms around his neck and wiggled up and down the length of his brawny body.

Seamus almost felt like laughing.

"What's wrong with Kelsey?" Cara asked, watching her with the bodyguard. "What happened to her? She's like... I don't know."

"Missing a few cards in her deck?"

She nodded.

"Well, Kelsey was never exactly a genius. She was always a bit ditzy, but sweet. And a party girl. Always dancing and drinking and picking up men in the casino. Then after the presidential debate in early September, Alexis went up to Ethan's suite and found Kelsey drained of blood. The vampire who did it was still there and he stabbed Alexis, almost killing her. Ethan turned Alexis, and I gave Kelsey my blood and brought her back to life. Since then, she's been different." He watched her run her palms over Daniel's chest while her hips rocked against him. She wasn't smiling. "She doesn't laugh anymore. She's afraid to be alone. She seems more scattered than ever."

"She knows the guy, Seamus." Cara leaned closer to him. "I didn't want to say anything in front of her, but she knows him and he knows her. He seems almost . . . fond of her. And she calls him Kyle."

"Fond of her?" Seamus closed his eyes. Pictured that night Cara had been killed. Saw the thin man, the young vampire, saw how he had invited Kelsey to follow him and how she had, without hesitation.

"What does he look like? Is he thin, dressed well, dark hair, has sort of a quiet confidence?"

"Yes." Cara shifted in her chair restlessly, leaning in his direction. "Do you know him?"

Seamus shook his head. He took Cara's hand in his, wanting to touch her, to reassure himself she was alright. Safe. "No, but he was there the night we met. He was in the alley, and while I was dealing with the other two, he calmly told Kelsey to come with him and she did."

"So she knew him already. I tried to ask her how she

knew him, but she didn't really answer in any way that made sense."

"But he knows her, and he knew who I was, and he knew who you were tonight."

"Did she ever have any weird experiences before? Date a guy she was afraid of?"

"Wait a minute." Seamus sat straight up, squeezing Cara's hand as a thought came to him. "Wait a goddamn minute. Kelsey is the one who knew the guy who shot Ethan in the casino six weeks ago. She's the one who took him upstairs, then she left him alone up there because she read his mind and didn't like what she saw. Said he was dark and that he was going to kill Ethan. Ethan went up to investigate since she'd left the poor guy in a vampire glamour, but he was out of it by then, and he shot Ethan. He wasn't a vampire, though. We have it on tape. You can't see Kelsey, but you can see him." Seamus thought he'd recognize him if he was the same guy who'd been in the alley, but it would be nice to have a second set of eyes confirming all three were the same man. "If you saw him on tape, would you recognize him?"

"I think so." Cara looked out over the dance floor. "But why doesn't she remember? It's like when she was drained of blood, they took the memory with it."

"I don't know, Cara." Seamus studied Kelsey on the dance floor, moving sensually in that purple dress, her dark hair down her back. "I don't understand Kelsey's role in any of this."

The dancers moved their boas, used them as lassos on one another so the four were flush up against each other like naked bookends. Seamus watched absently, the lights moving from pink to blue to pink again.

"Cara, is Jodi Madsen here tonight?" Maybe it was time to see what Jodi might have to say about her niece Brittany Baldizzi and who her biological father might be.

"I'm sure she's in the back. She's usually here on the weekends. I can go get her."

Cara stood up. She was watching the dancers on stage, too. She had a deep frown on her face. "Is that what I look like, Seamus? When I'm dancing?"

Seamus couldn't read the expression on her face. This smacked of a trap. Any way he answered would be wrong, he was guessing. So he shook his head, determined not to trip himself up. "Absolutely not. You look way better than that."

"Well, I should hope so," she said, frown deepening. "They look sort of . . . ridiculous."

Oh, damn. He pulled her down onto his lap. She perched there stiffly but didn't pull away. "Trust me, Cara, you look amazing when you dance. In three hundred years you are the most beautiful woman I've ever met."

Eyes still on the foursome gyrating with the boas and each other, she said, "I thought you were three hundred and seventy. So there was a prettier woman in the first seventy years? Was she a dancer, too?"

Somehow he'd fallen in a hole anyway. "No, that's not what I meant. I was rounding down. Cara, in three hundred and seventy-one years you are the most beautiful woman I've ever known." Prettier than Marie, even, and she had been a stunning petite French beauty. Not that he was going to mention Marie.

She turned back to him. Looked at him, curious, studying. "What are we, Seamus? To each other? Is this the way it is for other vampires when they're turned? Do they feel for the vampire who turned them what I feel?"

"What do you feel, Cara?" Seamus felt the taut muscle of her backside and thighs against him, and he felt a strange, growing tingling sensation inside his chest. He also felt like he was dangling over the edge of a very high cliff, like the Cliffs of Moher, and he had no vampire flying skills. He was going to fall, and smack hard, if he didn't watch his step.

"I like you," she said softly. "That's what I feel." She kissed his forehead, her lips warm, then stood up. "I'll go get Jodi for you."

Seamus watched her walk away, her body a gorgeous work of art, all soft curves and contrasts. Her hair moved across her lacy lavender top, the black edges cut bluntly, long shaggy bangs framing her face when she glanced back at him over her shoulder, giving him a small, tense smile.

So she liked him. That should be good. But he suddenly felt like he'd just been delivered an "I'm glad we're friends" speech. And he was pretty damn positive he didn't want to be just friends.

So if he didn't want to be just friends, what did he want when it came to Cara?

He had no idea.

Not a fucking clue.

Ten

"Ethan, did you ever check in to that vampire slayers Internet loop?" Alexis paced back and forth in her husband's office, feeling frustrated and anxious.

"No." Ethan shrugged nonchalantly, though Alexis could tell he was braced for her response. He always held his hand out like a barrier when he was sure she was going to protest. "I'm sure that group who e-mailed you is just a bunch of thrill seekers. They don't really fancy themselves vampire slayers."

"How do you know?" Alexis opened the balcony door and stepped out into the rapidly disappearing night. Another hour, the sun would be up, and she'd be in bed for the day. There would be no one to watch over Brittany, make sure she was safe. Alexis scanned her eyes over the Vegas Strip, worried. She'd gotten the invitation to join the vampire slayers group, then was promptly kicked out the minute she'd been turned. Like they'd known.

Ethan came up behind her and rubbed her shoulders. "What's the matter, Alex?"

She wasn't sure exactly. "Something is going on. People want you and Seamus dead. Why? What haven't you told me?"

"I've told you everything," he said softly, his lips running over the tip of her ear. "I don't know why someone wants me dead. The guy we're holding isn't talking."

"Something is wrong. You know I'm not a worrier normally, but I just feel like something bad is going to happen." Alexis shivered.

Ethan gave a soft snort of laughter. "Actually, when it comes to the people you care about, you worry constantly. Before you only had to worry about Brittany, now you have to worry about me, too. But I promise, I will be fine. After nine hundred years, I've learned to defend myself fairly well."

Sometimes it still creeped Alexis out to think that her husband was as old as dirt, but he had a point. He hadn't lived that long by being stupid. "Maybe we should take a vacation . . . take Brittany and get out of Vegas for a few weeks."

Even as she said it, she knew he'd never agree to it. Not with the election looming.

"The timing is wrong, love. I can't leave now. Besides, security is best here in my own casino."

That wasn't very reassuring. "Then how is it you managed to get shot?" Just the memory made her uncomfortable. Made her glance right and left, even though they couldn't possibly be at risk from anything other than rain out on their thirty-second-floor balcony. Or a vampire.

"That was unfortunate. I was distracted and overconfident. I won't be caught off guard again."

The hardness in his voice made her feel a little better. He was taking this seriously.

"And I won't let anyone harm you or Brittany. I have a guard watching Brittany twenty-four/seven. He should already be in place."

"Thank you." Alexis held on to his hands as he wrapped his arms around her middle. She leaned against his chest. "How did you meet Kelsey? You both told me it was in New York in the sixties, but I mean specifically."

"I went to a party at an artist's loft and saw Kelsey. I knew she was a vampire immediately. And it was also clear she was doing a steady diet of drugs. I put her in rehab and gave her a job. I don't think she ever knew who turned her vampire—too much LSD running through her."

That probably explained a lot. "I think Kelsey is a sweetheart, I really do, but I also think maybe she lost a few brain cells too many during the sixties. Then a few more when she was drained of blood six weeks ago. She says the weirdest things sometimes. Tonight in the casino she asked me if I've ever been to the Venetian. She said she heard the blood is better there, but that she won't go there because that's where they took her. When I asked her what she meant, she wouldn't answer."

Ethan stiffened. "Donatelli lives at the Venetian."

Alexis jerked around, started. Her husband's face was filled with fury. "Ethan? You mean . . . oh, shit."

Cara had never really liked Jodi. She thought she was a bit crass, but then Cara could readily admit she was a prude. Now, however, she decided she'd been right all along.

Jodi sat guzzling down a scotch and leering at Seamus. He appeared oblivious to the sultry looks and the cleavage, but it still irritated Cara.

"I remember you," Jodi said to Seamus. "You were at Alexis's wedding. I'm sure you noticed me. I was the one who was ignored by the bride. My own niece, the ungrateful little bitch, didn't even invite me. I had to invite myself."

"So you don't keep in touch with Alexis and Brittany?"

"No." Jodi tossed back what was left of her drink. "They don't want anything to do with me. They both think they're too good to associate with their aunt, the ex-stripper. But they're no better than me. They're just dishonest about it. I mean, come on, what did Alexis do to get that rich guy to marry her? That requires some oral skill, and I don't mean conversation."

Cara couldn't help but curl her lip in distaste. Unfortunately, Jodi saw her do it.

"You know what I'm talking about, don't you, Cara? Some people look at a stripper and they think whore. I mean, when you first met Seamus, it wasn't like he thought to himself, hey, there's a smart girl. I bet we could have some interesting talks over wine."

She should interrupt with some cutting remark, but Cara just found herself sitting there at the table in the back of the club, while the dancers moved on stage, and her face went hot. Jodi was saying exactly what she had told herself.

"No, he was thinking about your body, about hot, sweaty, nasty sex. And that's fine, because sex makes the world go round, and we get paid damn good for what we do. But some snooty bitches will look down their noses at you. The same ones who sleep their way to the top. Me, I'd rather be up front and honest about it." Jodi glanced up and down at Cara.

"By the way, when are you coming back to work? You don't look hurt to me, and now with Dawn being gone, we're really shorthanded."

"I'm not sure," she managed to spit out. "Seamus?" Cheeks still hot, feeling like she'd been slapped and intentionally humiliated, Cara turned to him. "When can I go back to work?"

Part of her wanted him to say never. That it wasn't safe. That between him and her twenty grand in winnings, she should quit her job as a dancer. That he didn't like men looking at her and thinking of hot, sweaty, nasty sex.

He didn't even come remotely close to doing that. He just said, "Whenever you feel ready. It's up to you."

What happened to her supposed safety? And why, when he was finally respecting her independence, did she feel so annoyed?

"I guess I can start back tomorrow night. If that's okay with Seamus."

"That's fine," Seamus said with apparent unconcern.

Jodi laughed, gesturing for the waitress to bring her another drink. "Money and sex, Cara. That's what it's all about."

Then her laugh died out and she looked puzzled, head cocked to the side. Her fingers trembled on her empty scotch glass.

"Who was Brittany's father?" Seamus asked in a soothing, even voice.

Jodi made an indistinguishable sound from her mouth, her lips working, eyes glassy. Cara suddenly realized what was going on. Seamus was probing her mind.

It was disconcerting to watch. Jodi looked paralyzed, like a stroke victim, trapped in her own mind, spittle forming in the corner of her mouth.

"You don't remember his name? He was dark haired, dark eyed, foreign, rich . . . and you were jealous of your sister because she was married and didn't need a sugar daddy. He should have been yours." Seamus stopped speaking and sat back. He turned to Cara. "Damn. She doesn't remember his name. There's nothing there."

He released Jodi, who looked confused for a second. She wiped her mouth, then narrowed her eyes at Cara. "So be here tomorrow ready to shake your shit. I have to get back to work." A little unsteady, she stood up and nodded to Seamus. "Thanks for the drink."

Cara watched Jodi leave, her retreat in haste, no effort made to sway her hips and display her still firm backside the way she usually did.

"Well, that's disappointing," Seamus said. "I had hoped she'd know more identifying information. There were lots of foreign vamps running around Vegas twenty-eight years ago. It's a good town to hide in."

Only half-listening, Cara looked from Jodi to the dancers on stage. Was this all there was for her? She had always taken pride in who and what she was. At the moment, she felt nothing but a sick burning pit in her stomach that wasn't hunger. It was anger. Despite all her efforts to be independent, liberated, and totally on her own, she felt two emotions that made her squirm. Embarrassment that men watched her dance and got aroused. And love, for Seamus.

Two traps she said she'd never fall into, and yet she was sitting there caught by both ankles, strapped helpless to her emotions, conventions, and nature.

She had become a stripper to pay for school, and to prove she wasn't repressed. She was a virgin to prove she wasn't a slut. And she didn't date because she knew that if she loved a man, she would love with all of herself, and that was damn scary.

Her mother had been like that, and her mother had wound up alone.

Cara had loved Marcus and had thought he respected her, when in truth he had been having sex with everything that walked, everyone but her.

Obviously the man she had loved hadn't been the man Marcus really was.

So clearly she was just bad at relationships, and didn't *know* what she felt, because honestly, how the hell could she love Seamus? He had made her a vampire without consulting her, held her prisoner, and didn't like her choice of draperies. She shouldn't even like him, let alone love him. It didn't make any sense.

But he was also the most amazingly kind, patient, and generous man she'd ever met. He took care of Ethan's political campaign, he soothed Kelsey's nerves, from day one he had tried to make her comfortable in his apartment, and he walked her dogs without complaint.

Seeing Dawn on the floor like that, having her own brief run-in with a killer vampire, she realized she wanted nothing more than to stay with Seamus. Permanently.

Maybe it was shock. It had to be shock, because why else would she be thinking she loved Seamus and that she didn't want to dance anymore? It didn't make any sense to feel either one of those convictions. Yet she did.

While her entire sense of self was buckling and heaving like asphalt above an earthquake, Seamus paid their bill and patted his pocket for his car keys.

"Ready?" he asked, oblivious to her shocking revelations.

She thought she loved him. Wasn't it written on her forehead? Throbbing across her chest? How could he just stand there and not notice?

Drowning in confusion, she reached for a life jacket. Anger. "What happened to my safety? Don't you care that if I dance here tomorrow night the assassin will try to kill me again? I would be totally exposed and vulnerable."

He stared at her blankly for a second, then gave one of those male sighs that indicated he was willing to blame her behavior on PMS. "Can we talk about this in the car?"

Wrong move. She felt indignation rise with volcanic fury. "We'll talk about it now."

Seamus sat back down, eyes wary. "I figured you could have a guard—me. I don't want you to dance, but if you have to, then I'll watch you."

That slightly mollified her irrational anger. She knew she was being unreasonable, but she couldn't stop herself. She felt that if she didn't cling to her fury, she would burst into tears. "Why would you tell me to go back to work if you don't want me to?"

"Because if I told you no, you'd get mad at me. I was trying to let you make your own choice."

"By telling me to dance naked for strange men?" Maybe she did have PMS. She wasn't sure about vampiric physiology but wasn't it possible she could be having a hormonal surge of some kind? She felt on the verge of cracking, borderline hysterical.

Seamus just sat there. He didn't say a word, just sat in the chair with his hands on the table, his blue shirt turning an orangish color when the pink lights reflected off it. She couldn't read his expression.

"Well? Aren't you going to say something?"

He shook his head. "No."

"What do you mean, no? I asked you if you want me to dance naked for strange men."

His jaw twitched but he remained silent.

"Seamus!"

"I'm not answering anything because no matter what I say it will be wrong. We've done this before and this time I opt out."

Cara was stunned to realize he was right. She was being a shrew because she had decided she loved him. That made no sense.

The corner of her mouth tilted up involuntarily. "Okay, let's go home."

"Really?" He looked immeasurably relieved. He stood up and reached for her hand.

"Really." Everything suddenly made much more sense to Cara. Independence wasn't achieved by dancing naked in defiance. It was reached through respect, and Seamus respected her enough to refuse to argue with her. Enough to never press his advantage after feeding and have sex with her. Enough to let her dance, despite his concerns.

"Let's go home." So she could tell him she intended to dance only in private from then on. And show him exactly how she felt about him and those sexy blue eyes of his.

Seamus was getting good at bullet dodging. One minute Cara had been furious with him, the next she had been chattering away in the car as if nothing had happened. He wasn't sure why he was even bothering to stay standing. Maybe he should just let a bullet hit him and take him down. Hadn't he always said he wasn't going to cater to another woman's irrational whims?

Yet something made him stick to Cara. Something kept telling him that once they got solid ground beneath them, their relationship could be amazing. It already was amazing.

So when they got into the apartment, he decided they needed to be clear about what they were, what they were doing, where the future was headed. Not that Seamus knew how to approach the subject, or even how to articulate what he felt. He just did it the way that made the most sense to him. While Cara kicked off her sandals by the front door, he squared his shoulders and faced her.

"Ethan suggested you could have your own apartment. I told him no, because I don't want you to move out. Really don't want you to. But if you want to move out, I'll understand that, and I'll let you move out. I mean I won't protest or pull vampire rank or be a jerk. If you move out. If you want to."

Yeah, that was clearing things up. He sounded like a vampiric Rain Man.

She just looked at him, her hair falling over her shoulder, the dogs running around her, licking at her fingers. "I don't want to move out."

"Oh, okay. Good." Seamus cleared his throat. Now what?

"Can I be honest with you?"

That was a scary thought. God only knew what would come out of her mouth. But he knew what was expected of him. He'd gleaned that much from twentieth-century chick flicks. "Of course. You can always be honest with me."

Even if she ripped his heart out of his chest and flung it against the wall with her words. Sure, he was cool with the whole honesty thing. He was a modern vampire, with pink lint on his nuts. He could talk about his feelings. A stake to the heart might be more pleasant, but he could do this. Honesty. Sure. He was on it.

"I really am a virgin."

That wasn't what he expected her to say. It didn't make sense to him and he blurted out, "Are... are you sure?"

Her cheeks bloomed pink. "Yes, I'm sure! I ought to know something like that, don't you think?"

Okay, so it had been a stupid thing to say. But... she danced with no clothes on. She had a vibrator. She'd had orgasms while feeding from him. Cara was sexy, sensual. Not a virgin. Damn. A virgin?

His brain hurt. Along with another part farther south.

"Of course. But... you..." Where the hell was a speechwriter when he needed one?

"Look, I know it seems kind of ridiculous, but I never wanted to give that up to anyone, you know what I mean? I'm a control freak. I dance because I can hide behind the screen. It doesn't feel like anyone is watching me. I dance for the money, not the audience."

"But the vibrator..." Seamus wondered if that counted toward nonvirgin status, or was that a technical loophole? He was seriously intrigued by the thought that she'd gone there alone, with a battery-operated toy, never having experienced that with a man. Though why in hell had he mentioned the vibrator out loud? Way to sound like a perv.

She folded her arms across her chest and looked around nervously. "Well, I just use it, um, externally. I don't think I would know how to actually do, well, anything else."

They were a train wreck. They both sounded like a couple of twelve-year-olds looking at porn.

"I haven't had sex in two hundred years," he said, because it seemed like an appropriate time for a confession.

Also, if they ever got to the sticking point—sex—he wanted her to know he was a bit out of practice.

Cara looked startled. She rubbed her toes on her opposite ankle, and pulled her T-shirt down over the waist of her jeans. "Oh, well, uh... wow. Any reason?"

"The last woman I slept with betrayed me. She had me sent to the guillotine." Seamus touched the scar on his neck.

Her eyes softened. "Oh, baby, that's horrible."

He would have thought her compassion would be embarrassing, but he kind of liked the way her fingers reached out for him. He let her touch him, run her thumb over his puckered scar. "I was her lapdog, though I didn't know it at the time. I swore I wouldn't give up control to another woman ever again. I am a control freak, too."

"My last boyfriend... he said he was cool with waiting until we got married to have sex. And later I found out why he was so willing to be chivalrous—he was having sex with a handful of other women."

"Oh, sweetie, what a bastard. I'm sorry." He didn't understand a dog like that. One who turned sex into selfish rutting. "And if it makes you feel better, the woman I thought loved me was sleeping with another man, and together they had plotted my death from the beginning."

"Uh! What a bitch," Cara said, looking indignant on his behalf.

"Vampire slayer," he said.

"Oh. Yikes." She stared up at him, her body lithe and lush against his, her dark eyes wide with desire. "Since we're being honest... I want to sleep with you, but I'm afraid to give up control."

"Me, too." He wasn't sure he could trust her not to kick him in the teeth. It wasn't Cara, it was him. Ethan had told him he had trust issues, which was probably true.

"So what do we do about it?"

Seamus wrapped his arms around her waist, tensely. It felt like they were circling each other, waiting for the other to make the first move. "I don't know."

"Also since we're being honest," she said in a husky whisper. "How do you really feel about my dancing naked for other men?"

That was easy. Jealousy exploded in his gut, sick and hot. "I hate it. That's how I really feel. I want to rip every one of their faces off and shove them up their arses. I feel like knocking their damn skulls together and covering you from head to toe in fleece."

She opened her mouth.

And Seamus kissed her. He leaned down and took her mouth with determination. The hell with this. They were going to do what they both wanted to do. And if he was going to have to sit in that club and watch her—guard her—while she danced behind that screen, he was going to be damn sure he was her first. He wanted to take her, brand her, hold her to him, make Cara and everyone else understand that she belonged at his side.

They were mates already, living together. Now he wanted to seal that, put his scent on her.

So he kissed her hard and fast and deep, sliding his tongue between her surprised lips. When they both came up for air, he said, "Did I mention that I hate the dancing naked for other men?"

Without waiting for her response, he covered her lips with his again, his hands trailing down her back onto her tight, firm ass. She felt perfect beneath his hands, and she tasted delicious, like rich, fine wine, her lips soft and pliable, juicy. After a long, hot minute, Seamus pulled back with a suppressed groan.

"Well," Cara said, breathing hard. "Don't hold back. Tell me how you really feel."

Desire, hot and hard, ripped through him, and he made no effort to control it. "Tell you how I feel? This is how I feel."

Seamus yanked his shirt off with vampire speed and pulled her against him. He licked along her bottom lip, then kissed her feverishly, kneading her backside beneath his fingers. It was perfect, this was right, it was everything, and he wondered what the hell he'd been waiting for. Cara was kissing him back, eagerly, her hands racing across his chest, gripping him.

He wanted to feel her flesh against his, touch the body that had been teasing and taunting him since the first minute he'd seen her. He wanted to be the only man who had ever been allowed to taste her, run his hands over those curves. He wanted to fill her with his hard body and make her scream in pleasure. But first he had to get those clothes off.

The T-shirt went with one tug. And she wasn't wearing a bra. A very beautiful, full chest was right in front of him, gloriously naked.

Cara jerked back, startled. "Did you just rip my shirt off?"

"Yes." He threw it on the floor, where Button promptly buried his nose in it, kicked it up with his snout, and wound up with the T-shirt on the top of his head.

Seamus had to admit he was starting to like the dogs. They were such total idiots, he felt better about himself just watching them.

"Oh, okay." Cara blinked, her hands snaking over her bare chest to cross and cover.

She was hiding her breasts from him. Seamus couldn't believe it. It was so damn cute and sexy that she was self-conscious, shy, whatever you wanted to call it, in front of him. It made him feel a notch above the club-goers. Like him and his opinion mattered to her.

He started to grin, even as he tried to prevent it. "Drop your arms, Cara."

"No." She looked squeamish at the very thought. Her grip on her elbows tightened.

"Drop them or I'll do it."

That made her flush with indignation. "Screw you."

"That's the plan." Seamus took a step toward her as she backed up a foot. "Trust me, Cara."

"Do I have to?" she asked, now hunched over a little at the shoulders.

"Yes." He put his hands on her wrists and ripped her arms apart, off her chest, and held them out at her sides. "I trust you. I do. Give me the same thing." He stared down at her, his breath hot and thick, his erection pressing into her thigh, his fangs down and ready. Her chest heaved, and she jerked her head to toss her bangs out of her eyes.

No words came out of her mouth, but her eyes pleaded with him, told him to take the risk. Seamus let go of her arms and stood still to wait for her reaction. If she covered herself back up, they had problems.

But Cara didn't do that. Instead she fit her index fingers through two loops on his jeans left and right and stepped in close, pressing her bare chest against his. Her lips ran along his shoulder and neck, while every muscle in his body tensed with pleasure, anticipation.

"I trust you," she whispered in his ear. "Now let's do this."

She made it sound like they were about to leap off a building or charge into battle.

Maybe they were.

Seamus turned his head so he could brush his lips over

her cheek, feel her soft skin beneath his. He took her chin, tilted her head up, and kissed her gently, then frantically, then fiercely. He bit her lip, let a drop of blood bead and meander into his mouth. Her hands were on his chest, then his back, then his arse, gripping and grinding and tugging.

When she sped up, he slowed down, when she eased back, he stepped it up, so that they were both building and breaking down, ebbing and flowing, frustrated and hot. Seamus was doing it intentionally, conscious of her virginity, aware that he had only one chance to do this right, to make it good for Cara. And he wanted to draw it out for himself, enjoy Cara at length, to make a two-hundred-year celibacy end in ecstasy, not a quick three-minute explosion.

"Seamus," she murmured, trying to undo his belt.

If she was ready to move to the next stage, it was time to move to the bedroom. Seamus lifted her up into his arms and started down the hall.

"Whoa," she said. "I still can't get used to vampire strength."

"Wait until you see my endurance."

"Don't scare me," she said with a small laugh.

The Labs leaped around Seamus, barking, like this was a game. Satan sat in the doorway of the bedroom, looking like he'd tear Seamus's ankle off if he attempted entry.

"If you guys trip me, you're going to the pound," he told them.

Cara made a sound of horror. "Don't say that! Daddy didn't mean it, sweeties. And if he did, Mommy wouldn't let him do such a horrible, nasty thing."

She made ushy, gushy, shushing sounds while Seamus contemplated fatherhood to Cara's furry brood. It wasn't a horrifying thought. He had raised dogs for years in England.

But they'd stayed in the kennel, like dogs should. They hadn't lived in the house with him, sleeping in his bed, and he had never once thought of himself as their daddy.

While he couldn't imagine he'd ever think of any four-legged creature as his baby, he liked that Cara was placing him in that role. She didn't want to move out. She wanted to stay with him, with her dogs. For now, anyway. And that was good enough for him.

He stepped into the bedroom. When the dogs would have bounded in after them, he put out his finger and commanded, "Sit."

Button and Fritz plopped their rumps down in the hall, their tails swishing back and forth. "Good boys."

Satan, who had been sitting, stood up at the command to sit. Seamus used his foot to encourage Satan to run out into the hallway.

Then he slammed the door shut on all of them.

"That was mean," Cara reprimanded.

"I don't need an audience, I'm sorry. They'll get over it." Seamus laid Cara down on his bed—their bed—and stepped back to undo his belt buckle.

She bent her knees so her legs were up in the air, but she didn't cover her chest. In fact, she thrust it toward him in a sexy little pose. Her skin was pale, milky white, the moonlight streaming through the wood blinds onto the bed, onto Cara's beauty.

Seamus just about stopped breathing. "You're so beautiful," he said, fingers freezing on his zipper. "Damn, Cara, I just can't tell you how gorgeous I think you are. That night . . . the night I met you. It was like you just drew me in. Like you are now."

Man, he needed to just stop talking around her. Instead of the Irish gift of the gab, he had the gift of the gag.

"You're not just saying that, are you? You're not playing me?" she asked with a saucy grin, fingertips sliding across the ends of her black silky hair.

"No. If I was being a player, I'd sound better than this." He shook his head as he unzipped his black pants. "I sound like a potato farmer around you. Nothing like a man who spends his night strategizing politics and putting a spin on words and policies."

"I like you both ways. When you talk shop with Ethan, you sound commanding and in charge. It's sexy. But when you're with me, you're more real and that's sexy, too."

He couldn't see how a bumbling idiot would be sexy, but he wasn't about to talk her out of it. Instead he ditched his shoes, socks, and pants and leaned over the bed, running the gristle of his unshaven chin over the smooth denim covering Cara's knees. He stroked one hand down her calf and used the other to undo her pants. Her breathing had changed, her eyes widening, and he knew she was as aroused as he was.

Before taking her pants off, he bent over and ran his lips along her nipples, closing his eyes, breathing in her scent. Goose bumps rose on her warm flesh and she shifted, lifting her chest.

"Do you want this?" he asked, pulling one tight nipple into his mouth and sucking, reveling in the feel, the texture, the moan she gave. It had been so long since he'd made love to a woman, he'd nearly forgotten the torturous pleasure, the slow cadence of sex, the teasing anticipation, the discovery of a woman's erogenous areas.

He had touched Cara several times now when she had been feeding from him—he already knew the way her moist inner flesh felt, and how she arched her back when she came. He had had several sleepless days that could be attributed to experiencing that. But he hadn't tasted her until now, hadn't had her hands on his bare chest before, hadn't experienced her interest in his pleasure, too.

It was better than he ever could have imagined. She scratched at his skin, harder when he pulled faster, fiercer on her nipple, and her drive drove him on, until her chest was slick from his mouth, her nipples peaked, her moans agonized and high.

"Take my pants off," she begged.

That was the beauty of being a vampire. He had them off before she was even finished speaking.

Cara blinked up at him. "Show-off."

"You haven't seen anything yet."

A sly little smile crossed her face. "I can't wait."

Neither could Seamus. He moved his hands over her abdomen, between her thighs, parting them. Cara spread her legs willingly for him, which made his tongue thicken and his desire boil hotter still. He bent down and put his mouth on her moistness. And tasted.

Cara had thought she was turned on, thought she was close to the edge, since Seamus had been kissing, petting, and sucking on her mouth and breasts for a solid twenty minutes, but when he put his tongue between her thighs, she broke the bed.

Literally. She jerked back so hard in ecstasy, the headboard cracked where her shoulders and head made impact.

"Oh, shit," she said, more stunned than hurt.

"Are you okay?" he managed to ask between licks, clearly with no intention of stopping.

Thank you.

"Yes, I'm fine. Seamus..." Cara squirmed, trying to turn sideways so she could lie down and enjoy the full effect. Not that half the effect was bad—amazing, actually—

but full would be better. But she was having a hard time concentrating on what she was doing because every two seconds he slid up, then trailed back down in a delicious, torturous, warm, wet motion.

Two hundred years of celibacy hadn't negatively affected his technique.

Wow. As she gripped the duvet cover, eyes rolling back in her head as she tried not to explode just yet, Cara realized she was picking up on Seamus's thoughts.

It wasn't complete sentences or a message sent directly to her, it was more just random words and impressions. His desire, his sexual want, his urgency and taut muscles.

Delicious... hot... fucking gorgeous... all floated over to her from him. Heat, throbbing, pulsing want that spiked each time his tongue connected with her flesh. That he was turned on turning her on made her moan louder, which made him grip her thighs tighter in a sexy, arousing circle.

Seamus drew his mouth back suddenly and she gave a cry of frustration, knowing that she was about two seconds away from having an orgasm. "Don't stop!" she begged. "Seamus, please."

Don't come yet, he said in her head, thumb sliding over her swollen clitoris. Then he opened up his thoughts fully to her.

It was like a tidal wave of emotion, desire, pleasure, crashing over her, into her, above her. Cara sucked in a breath, overwhelmed. She lifted her hand, for what she wasn't sure, but Seamus took it, laced his fingers with hers.

Their thoughts mingled, their pleasure collided as he took her mouth in a hard, passionate kiss. It was amazing, stunning, to feel him everywhere, inside and out of her. She felt his appreciation for her curves at the same time she projected back her interest in his hard, male body.

Running her fingers over his chest, she kept going until she reached his erection, letting him hear, feel, see, know that she was ready for him. He wanted to be inside her, thrusting, that feeling, urge, loud and drumming into her skull.

Stroking his warm flesh, she hoped he could hear that she wanted him, too, that she was ready, that their connection was so whole and total and exhilarating, that she had to experience what the rest was like. What it would feel like with him buried deep inside her.

"Are you sure?" he asked out loud, pulling back to study her face.

Cara traced his jaw with her finger, loving the way he felt, chiseled and rough, and waited for the panic to engulf her, the vice to close around her emotions, making her feel trapped and helpless. But none of those feelings were anywhere in her. What she felt, besides the total mind-melding arousal, was freedom. To feel and do whatever she wanted, no worry for the future, no pressure to be something she wasn't. Just freedom to be with a man she cared about for now in a sexy, uncontrollable way.

"Yes, I'm sure."

His fingers were stroking, stroking, stroking, pushing in deeper each time while he waited for her response, and Cara moved restlessly beneath him, eager to have what she'd denied herself for years. "Do you have a condom?"

"No." He moved in between her legs, his erection pressing against her, hard and demanding.

Fifteen years of safe sex mantras had her pushing on his chest. "Stop. You need a condom."

"For what?" Seamus asked, nuzzling along her ear, while his fingers pried apart her... oh, whoa.

He was just resting there, big and wet and intriguing,

leaving her feeling empty and unsatisfied. Wanting what came next. Wanting more. What had she been saying? "For . . . protection," she managed, her entire body tingling in anticipation.

"You can't get pregnant and you can't catch anything from me. You're a vampire."

"Right." Cara lifted her hips just a little, distracted by the way he was just hanging around down there. He needed to do . . . something. "I'm an immortal vampire." On the edge of an orgasm.

"My vampire," Seamus said as he pushed at her, hard.

Cara winced as a sharp pain tore through her. "Ow. Ow. Ow. Get out, get out."

"Shh. Just relax. I'm only half in. It will feel better when I'm all there."

What the hell kind of logic was that? Here, if your ear hurts, stick that cotton swab in even farther. Hot stove burning your hand? Just leave it there longer.

Cara tried to back up. "There is no way. It hurts too much." She felt intense pressure, and a damn uncomfortable burning sensation. Game over. She wanted out.

Seamus pinned her with his weight. "Don't move, Cara. Let me finish. Trust me." *You have to trust me,* he added in her head.

Oh, now he was going to make her feel guilty. Like if she shoved him off, he was going to be hurt. Well, she was hurting right now, with his big vampire you-know-what impaling her. "I trust you. But I've changed my mind. I don't see the point if we can just do other stuff."

She'd give him oral sex if he would just get out.

"Appealing as that sounds, I'd rather do it this way," he said.

Ugh. He was reading her mind.

"Just one time in, and then if you still say no, I'm gone, okay?"

This was ridiculous. They were bargaining for penetration rights. "Just one. Then you owe me big-time."

"Deal." He kissed her forehead, her temple, her lips softly.

Mouth over hers, Seamus pushed into her, and everything sort of clung and pinched and stung, then suddenly he was fully embedded in her and the pressure was gone. It was snug, but slick, pleasant, his pelvis bumping an interesting spot.

Not nearly as bad as before. Cara relaxed a little. Her shoulders had been almost up to her ears from tension and discomfort. She was about to open her mouth and mention that she'd done her part and he could use the nearest exit, when he pulled back on his own. And pushed into her again, his tongue mimicking the movement in her mouth.

Hey, now. This wasn't bad at all. He did it again and then again, slow and easy. Um, actually, this was kind of nice, the way her body sort of wrapped around him. He was past his one-thrust allowance, but she wasn't sure she minded.

Seamus gave a tight, low groan. "Cara... oh, yes, baby, this feels good."

That was a sexy sound. She was having *that* kind of effect on Seamus, and that was hot. She touched his firm butt. He had a great one, all tight and hard and manly. It seemed like a good time to really get a grip on it.

It made them collide together a little harder, sending a jolt of desire through her. Okay, now she was understanding how and why this worked. A gasp slipped out as a delicious shiver rippled up and over her. That little thing he was doing, faster now, this made sense, this was hot.

"This *is* good."

"Told you. You need to listen to me more often. I'm always right."

As long as he was wasn't being smug about it. Pinching his butt to show what she thought of his words, she wrapped her legs around his thighs and rocked up to greet him. They both grunted in delight at the impact.

"You're not right about the curtains," she managed to say between gasps, groans, and thrusts.

Seamus wrapped an arm around her and tumbled them in a one-eighty, so that he wound up on his back and Cara was splayed out on his chest, amazed that he was still inside her. Intrigued by the possibilities, she wiggled a little to adjust her position.

He said, "I am definitely right about the ugly curtains. And I'm right when I say you're going to enjoy being on top."

"I disagree about the curtains." She gripped the bed on either side of Seamus and let her hair fall over his chest. Experimenting, she swiveled her hips and marveled at how there was no pressure, just an incredible tingling arousal. "But I have to admit you're definitely right about this."

Not really knowing what she was doing, she just starting moving, adjusting as needed, trying different rhythms, angles, and motions, startled at how just a tiny shift could move her from nice to eye rolling. Seamus lay still and let her work it all out, though he couldn't seem to resist pinching and licking her nipples and interjecting words of encouragement.

"That's it, baby, take what you want."

She had found a damn good position, one that allowed her breasts to brush against his chest, and her body to grind together with his, hitting a perfect spot. Cara closed her eyes, dropped her head down alongside his shoulder, and picked up the pace, driven to pump harder, more frantically.

"Yes, Cara, go, you're doing it, you're so fucking hot." Seamus's voice was rough, excited, and she felt his thoughts cloud over her and in her again, wrapping his desire around her own and spurring her on.

"Should I stop?" she said, hoping like hell he didn't say yes, but figuring it was polite to ask. "I think I'm going to come."

"Don't stop. Hell no. Come on me, Cara."

He didn't have to tell her twice. She wasn't sure she could stop any longer, anyway. Snapping up her head, she rocked down on him, and exploded. The orgasm snapped up through her, forcing her back to arch, and her teeth to clamp down on her lip in a violent clench.

Her amazement, her exhilaration, her thoughts, all poured out, spilling like honey and running quickly down over Seamus. He groaned at the intensity of her emotion, her delight as she rode out her orgasm, thighs spread over him, body fitted down onto him like a hot, wet glove.

Shit... hello... damn... Seamus... all rolled through her thoughts, like random words her brain grabbed on to, her body singing with physical stimulation. It was arousing, a little slap to his already racing libido, and Seamus started to thrust up inside her, drawing a startled gasp from Cara.

Love him... love Seamus fell out of her head right into his and Seamus paused for a split second, wondering if he had heard that right. She loved him? That wasn't possible.

But he loved her, he knew, fiercely and desperately. Cara groaned, like she had heard him.

I love you came loud and clear, like she'd whispered it right into his ear.

Seamus swallowed hard, then grabbed Cara and flipped her onto her back. As he thrust, her legs fell farther apart, her arms slack against the sheets, her eyes half closed, expression rapturous. She was his, his, his. His woman, his vampire, his lover, his fledgling. He wanted all of her, hard and fast, he wanted her to understand who and what he was to her, that no man, mortal or immortal, was ever going to touch her flesh the way he could.

Reaching down, he cupped her cheek, using his elbow for stability as he pushed into her again and again. With his thumb, he traced her smooth skin, her pert rosy lips. Her tongue came out and wet his skin before she bit him. Just sank her fangs on the backside of the fingernail and drew blood. It was so unexpected, so erotic, that Seamus lost his rhythm for a second.

But when she sucked, making little sounds of approval, he went at her with renewed energy, wanting in her deeper, everywhere. He bent over and plunged his own fangs into her creamy shoulder, pinning her still when she jerked in surprise. He drew hard, quickly, pulling back with a mouthful of her hot blood rushing all over his tongue.

She looked up at him with dilated eyes, thick black pupils glassy and unfocused. "Oh, Seamus. More, more! Harder."

He could do that. Shifting up higher on his knees, he went harder, rushing on, spiraling out of control in a way that felt better than good, more than ecstasy. It was consuming, all there was, just Cara and just him buried deep inside her. She ran her lips over his bicep, then slipped her teeth into him. She sucked frantically with lots of sound and jarring movement as his thrusts bounced her around.

The tug of blood pulled at his body, his legs, his groin, his lungs, blending him with her completely and totally. He clamped on to her neck, and he heard in his head, felt through her emotions, her scream of utter ecstasy. Rolling them, locked together, they grappled and gripped and pulled and sucked while Cara had a second orgasm, then a third nipping at the heels of the second, her mind a delicious jumble of nothing but frantic delight, urges for more.

They had kicked most of the bedding off and had traveled the whole length of the bed. Squashed against the headboard, Seamus found the barrier he was looking for. Wedged like this, Cara couldn't scoot away from him by the sheer power of his thrusts. The headboard and wall kept her still, made her body take the full length of him. Somehow she had turned sideways, her bottom nestled in the crack between the mattress and board. But her chest was still front facing, and while the whole thing was probably spine breaking, Seamus buried a hand in her glossy thick hair, wrapped his fingers around and around, and pounded himself to a finish.

He licked her blood off his bottom lip as she swatted at his arse and tried to shift, to move away from him or to bite him, he wasn't sure. Either one he wasn't going to tolerate. He locked her arms above her head, crushed her with his weight, and exploded, two hundred years of sexual restraint hurling out with a massive yell. It went on and on, until he was nothing but a shuddering mass of spent muscle, sweat on his forehead, throat raw.

"Damn," he managed, before he collapsed on her.

Cara was taking deep, uneven breaths and pushing her hair off her face, her eyes wide. Seamus knew he should get off her. Her thighs were going to be sore, not to mention more delicate parts, but he didn't want to let her go.

So easing out of her body, he rolled onto his back and took her with him. She lay limply on his chest, though her fingers softly stroked his shoulder.

"Seamus?"

"Yeah?" He swallowed the excessive saliva in his mouth and wrapped his arms solidly around her back and bottom.

"Wow." She sighed. "I'll think of something better to say later, but for right now just . . . wow."

"That's good enough for me," he said, though Cara was asleep before he even finished speaking.

Seamus closed his eyes and did the same.

When they stepped off the elevator, Alexis ran into Ethan's back. "Why did you stop? Who's in the hall?"

She was starting to get a little unnerved. Given that every time she turned around and blinked lately someone was being attacked, she was feeling a little cautious. "Get back in the elevator!"

Yanking on her husband's arm and turning around to find the down button, it took her a second to realize Ethan was laughing.

"What's so funny?" She let go of him, disgusted with both his reaction and hers. When had she become so quick to panic? She'd always prided herself on keeping her cool in all situations. Marriage had made her a wimp.

"I think we'll have to wait to discuss the current situation with Seamus. Listen." Ethan jerked his head down the hall toward Seamus's apartment. They were a good twenty feet away from the door, two other suites between the elevators and Seamus's.

"I don't hear anything." Alexis moved around Ethan, annoyed with her husband, annoyed that she couldn't seem to stop worrying about her sister, annoyed that maybe Ethan's political opponent wanted him dead. It was stressing her out. She just wanted a bag of blood and bed.

"You don't hear that?" Ethan asked in amazement, rooted to the gray carpet in the hallway.

"No, Mr. Super-Cool-So-Much-Older-Than-Me Vampire. I don't have your hearing skills." But now that she thought about it, she did hear something. "What is that? It sounds like . . . pounding."

Ethan's lip twitched. "You could call it that, I suppose."

Frowning, Alexis concentrated on listening. That pounding sound was accompanied by moans. Well. She was starting to get a clearer picture of what was happening down the hall.

Especially when Cara's voice rang out, sharp as glass, "Oh, Seamus! More, more. Harder."

"She wants more," Alexis said to Ethan.

"And harder."

The male grunts joined in chorus with the female moans, the pounding increasing. Alexis started to feel a little jealous. They were rocking the casino down there. "Should we tell them that everyone on the thirty-second floor can hear them?"

"I doubt they care." Ethan was grinning.

"I guess not." Alexis headed toward their own apartment. "Though I have to admit I'm kind of surprised. I didn't really think Cara liked Seamus all that much. Maybe it's the high from winning all that money. Or maybe it's the fear of almost being killed again tonight. Staring death in the face makes people do weird things."

"Having sex is a weird thing?" Ethan looked baffled.

"Why wouldn't they be sleeping with each other? They live together. They spend a great deal of time together. It seems perfectly natural that they would be, and I'm pleased for Seamus. He's about a century past due for a girlfriend."

It didn't seem that simple to Alexis. Cara had talked about wanting to escape. Have Seamus kick her out. It didn't make sense to Alexis that she would suddenly change her mind. It made her start to wonder if Cara was actually a spy.

Alexis gave herself a mental eye roll. Geez, she was losing it. Cara was an exotic dancer, not a spy for Donatelli.

"I don't think I'd like to date another vampire. What happens when you break up? You'd spend the next four hundred years avoiding each other. No thanks." Alexis opened their door and went inside, kicking off her sandals. She hated wearing shoes in the apartment.

"Sometimes the things you say make no sense, given that you're married to a vampire," Ethan told her. "But I love you anyway."

That made her bristle. "Are you trying to start something with me?"

Ethan gave a lecherous smile. "Yes. Listening to Cara reminds me how I'd like to spend the rest of the night."

Alexis threw her purse up on the kitchen countertop. "How? Begging Seamus for more?"

He made a face. "Very funny. No, I want to make love to you, my beautiful wife."

Even though she felt tense, Alexis let him pull her into his arms.

"Ethan?" she asked, even as he kissed her neck and started to undo the buttons on her thin sweater.

"Hmm?"

"If Donatelli has a hit out on you, I'm going to rip his testicles off and make him eat them. Just to warn you."

Her husband pulled back, his blue eyes burning with desire. "Alexis, my love, you are hot when you get violent."

Alexis trailed her fingers over his crotch, suddenly feeling much better. "I'm going to have to teach Cara karate. She needs to know how to protect herself. Same with Kelsey."

"The three of you training together?" Ethan finished with her buttons and tossed her sweater to the floor. "That sounds brilliant, yet absolutely frightening. Now be quiet and let me make you scream."

She could do that.

Eleven

"She's a vampire," Ringo told Donatelli. "Fox must have turned her the night she got hit by the car."

"Interesting." Donatelli sat back in his wrought-iron chair at a café inside the Venetian's shopping complex.

Ringo wished his employer would have chosen a more private location. Generally speaking, Ringo liked to stay quietly in the shadows, a good habit for an assassin, and this hotel was always crammed with people rubbernecking at the fake sky and indoor gondola ride.

"It's just beautiful," he heard one woman say to her plump companion as they stared at the ceiling mural.

Ringo had to disagree. He also had to swallow hard and force himself to ignore the pounding rush of blood in the women's bodies. Always, always hungry. He fed, he just wanted more. Now that he had taken from both Katie and Dawn, the stripper, he was no longer satisfied with bagged blood. He yearned and ached to hold warm flesh close to him, to feel their shudder of pleasure when he sank into their veins and drew hot juicy blood up and out.

Both those feedings had been paired with sex, making it all that much more addictive. These tourist women didn't inspire sexual feelings in him, but the blood did. He was hard at the thought of feeding again. And on the other hand, the women were not unattractive. Even the curvier one was pretty, and big breasted. It would be damn satisfying to give them pleasure like they'd never known, to make them scream like Dawn had. He could take one then the other, back and forth...

"Did you know Williams never came back?" Donatelli asked, stirring sugar into his coffee.

Ringo looked at him blankly, the women still stealing his attention as they bent over to inspect a vase in a shop window. He wondered briefly if Donatelli was going to drink the coffee, why older vampires could drink liquids besides blood, and how the Italian had gotten his status as major vampire player in the first place, before he became fully aware of what Donatelli had even said.

"He didn't come back? Where did he go? Is he dead?" Ringo was having a hard time concentrating on their conversation. It felt like he was under water, with everything trailing and cloudy.

"I don't know where he is. He went to Carrick's casino and never returned. I can only assume he is dead or allowed himself to be caught by Carrick. With Smith still out of commission, I need you to retrieve Williams and bring him back to us."

"And the girl?"

"No need to do anything about her. We'll just let it be known in the Nation that Fox has a fledgling. His first ever,

I believe. Excellent timing for me that he'd choose now to be a hypocrite." Donatelli smiled, but there was no warmth to it. "Maybe I should send him a thank-you gift."

Ringo's eyes wandered over to the women again. The petite one met his gaze. Her smile fell off her face and she shivered, gave a sharp intake of breath. The soccer mom was afraid of him. Ringo turned back to Donatelli. "A fruit basket?" he asked, letting his sarcastic thought slide out before he could debate whether that was wise or not.

But Donatelli actually laughed. "That's amusing. I like that."

Ringo lit up a cigarette, and couldn't prevent a grin. He hadn't been serious, but why the hell not? It might be funny. "I can have one sent around right about the time I'm hauling Williams's ass out of there."

"Perfect." Donatelli tilted his head slightly to the left. "Now you're free to go. And I don't mind if you take a few minutes first and enjoy the desperate housewives over there."

His eyes locked on the two women, and Ringo knew Donatelli had picked up on his arousal, his desire to feed. Humiliation washed over him, stronger than the blood lust. Every step he took into vampirism, he walked further and further from himself. Not that he'd been a man of upstanding character before, but he had answered to no one but himself. Now he did whatever Donatelli and the blood lust wanted him to do. He wanted to rail against that, stand tall, and remind himself that he was still his own man, even as he swam frantically in the warm waters of addiction.

"I'm fine, but thanks," he said. "I'll go straight over to the Ava."

"Suit yourself." Donatelli ran a finger over the rim of his coffee cup. He gazed out over at the mall area.

Suddenly the two women stopped in front of the chocolate shop. Both turned around and smiled in their direction. The one bent down and whispered to the other and they gave girlish giggles.

"You're certain? It appears the ladies are coming in this direction."

They were. They were strolling back toward where Ringo and Donatelli sat, their hips swaying, their bags carried artfully, their hair tossed back playfully. Ringo's mouth watered, his muscles tensed, his foot tapped, tapped, tapped under the table.

"No, I'm fine," he managed even as a sweat broke out all over his body.

Donatelli stood up and tossed some money on the table. "Then I'll just go and enjoy them solo. Have a good evening."

The Italian walked over to the women and said something. They stopped, smiled, pointed, and were soon deep in conversation, all three walking away together.

And Ringo realized this was how Donatelli had gotten to his position of importance in the Vampire Nation.

He was a ruthless bastard.

Seamus was half asleep, listening to the sound of the water as Cara took a shower, a dog on either side of him, a cat sitting behind his head. He felt delirious with pleasure, carefree and in love. Yep. The big L. He'd gone and done it.

Somewhere between that first moment he'd laid eyes on Cara and the first time they'd had sex, he'd fallen in love with her. It felt right, good, strong. He was in love and nothing could ruin his mood.

His cell phone rang and he dragged it out of his pants

pocket and checked caller ID. It was Ethan, so he answered it. "Yeah?"

"Are you guys done yet?"

"What do you mean?" Seamus propped himself against the headboard, disturbing Mimi, the black cat. She gave him a dirty look and pushed her paws into his gut, kneading him like dough. In his mellow mood he let her.

"I mean, are you and Cara *done*? I need to talk to you about this whole mess."

Seamus didn't even want to know how or why Ethan knew what he and Cara were doing. Nor did he really want to talk about the political climate. But it wasn't going to disappear, and he and Cara *were* done, for at least the next hour or so. After that invigorating nap, he might be ready to go again, but he should let Cara recover. "Alright, why don't you come to my place in ten minutes? And can you have security send up that tape of the night you were shot? I think Cara and I have seen your assassin friend."

"Really? Interesting. By the way, I have a thought or two I want to discuss with you."

"See you in ten." Seamus hung up the phone and dropped it on his stomach next to the cat. Not even assassins and frustrating mysteries that seemed to dance around him and dart away before he could solve them could ruin his sense of bliss. He was one slap-happy vampire.

The water was off and Cara was softly humming in the bathroom. It was a song Seamus didn't recognize, cheerful and upbeat. She made a twang sound, and he picked up on the fact that it was a country tune. Unable to resist, he got out of bed and went to the bathroom naked.

Pushing the door open, he saw Cara drying herself off with one of the new pink towels, steam rising all around her. Her soft black hair was clinging to her head and back, and her skin was dewy, flushed a subtle red in the spots where the hot spray had hit repeatedly. When the towel slipped and Seamus caught a glimpse of her perky round backside, he slipped in behind her and wrapped his arms around her.

She jerked a little, then relaxed. "Hey. You move so damn quietly, like a mouse."

"Like a vampire." He nuzzled the back of her ear, her hot skin warming him up, her backside pressed against his rapidly growing erection. Running his palms over her abdomen, he asked, "Are you okay? Not too sore?"

She leaned back and kissed his cheek. "I'm fine. Good. You are... mmm." Turning, she wrapped her arms around his neck. "Beyond my wildest dreams."

That was a compliment worth recording. Seamus kissed her forehead, pulled her body in close to his. "I thought it was amazing, too, but I was, well, rougher than I intended to be."

It didn't seem like she'd minded at the time, but he still felt a twinge of guilt now. He could have proceeded with a little more caution and finesse, but once he had let the horse out, he'd gone for a full gallop.

"Just remember paybacks are hell." She gave him a saucy look, a secret womanly smile that told him she was pleased, satisfied.

Which made him satisfied. And turned on. "Cara..." He bent to kiss her.

The doorbell rang.

"Shit."

"We can ignore it," she said, pressing her hips into his.

Seamus groaned in frustration. "No, it's Ethan. He's bringing up the tape of the would-be assassin."

Cara sighed and pulled back. "Which one?" she asked

dryly. "The one who tried to kill him or the one who tried to kill me?"

That made Seamus ill just thinking about Cara being in danger. "The one who tried to kill him. The asshole who went after you is still in lock-up, detoxing. Once he's clean, we'll transport him for a trial by his vampire peers."

Cara shivered and reached for her clothes. "I guess we should get dressed."

"Ethan might prefer that." He went back into the bedroom for a pair of jeans, forgoing the boxer shorts.

Two minutes later he left Cara in the bedroom to call the hospital to see about Dawn's condition, and he went to let in Ethan, who was grinning.

"Hey, Fox."

"Carrick." Seamus didn't like the look on Ethan's face or the way he clapped him on the shoulder a little too hard.

"We'll try to make this quick. I know it's late. You're probably ready for bed." The grin grew wider. "Again."

Ethan was about as subtle as a jalapeño. "Where's Alexis?"

"She's really worried about Brittany. She wanted to pop in on her again before she retires for the day."

"I thought Brittany just has the flu."

Ethan shrugged. "You know how Alexis is with Brittany." He glanced around Seamus. "Hello, Cara, interesting night, wasn't it?"

Seamus turned and took her hand, worried about the somber look on Cara's face. "How's Dawn, babe?"

"They said she's fine. She'll be going home this afternoon then after a few days of rest and proper nutrition she'll be completely recovered." She rubbed Seamus's palm restlessly. "I talked to Bryan. He says she doesn't really understand what happened to her. That she doesn't remember anything. But she told me she had sex, with that vampire. Why would he do that? Leave her like that?" Cara visibly shuddered.

Ethan tapped the tape in his hand. "Young vampires lose control. Conscienceless vampires enjoy the power, the thrill. If we can catch him, we could censure him, put him under a no-travel restriction. He would have to stay here so we could monitor him, sort of like the Frenchman."

"But first we have to figure out who he is, and what he has to do with Ethan. And you and I." Seamus held his hand out for the tape. "Let's see who this bastard is."

"I have to tell you what Alexis told me."

Ethan surrendered the tape, but his words gave Seamus pause. "What did she say?"

"That Kelsey told her the blood was better at the Venetian, but she won't go there because that's where they took her the night she was attacked."

"The Venetian? The only vampire I know who hangs out at the Venetian is . . ." Seamus swore. "Donatelli. Shit. You don't think he's responsible for all of this?" Anything was possible, but Seamus didn't really see the motivation. Why kill him? Cara?

"It's possible. Let's see this tape, then we need to have another conversation with Kelsey."

Donatelli. It boggled the mind. Was he so desperate to take office that he would kill his opponent?

The tape went into the machine sitting in a cabinet under Seamus's plasma TV. A man was stepping off the elevator, bent over talking to someone, presumably Kelsey, since they couldn't see her.

"That's him," Cara said before Seamus could really even get a good look at him. "The guy who was in Dawn's dressing room."

"You're sure?" Ethan asked.

"Positive." Cara shifted closer to Seamus. "What is he doing? Why is he unzipping . . . oh, geez."

"He was with Kelsey, babe." Seamus curled his lip as the assassin's eyes closed in ecstasy. Seamus really could have done without this one-sided oral sex clip. He grabbed the remote and turned it off before he tossed up his blood breakfast. "That's the guy who was in the alley, too. The one who walked off with Kelsey. Do you think he works for Donatelli?"

"Let's get Kelsey down here and find out." Ethan pulled out his cell phone. "Yes, this is Mr. Carrick. Find my secretary, Kelsey, and send her to Mr. Fox's suite. Thank you."

Ethan turned back to them. "Security will find her and get her here in a few minutes. Sorry for interrupting your morning, Cara."

Cara waved her hand and sat down on the leather sofa. "No, it's fine. I want to know what the hell is going on. Why this happened to Dawn. I feel so bad . . . he wouldn't have approached her if it wasn't for me, I'm sure of it."

"It's not your fault, Cara." Seamus sat next to her, stroked her knee. "It's mine. You know Donatelli and Ethan are in the middle of a heated presidential election. If this is the Italian's doing, then I led them right to you and to Dawn. Regardless of whether or not Donatelli called out a hit on any of us, we have to be prepared for him to use you against Ethan. He's going to point you out to the Nation as a sign of my hypocrisy, and Ethan's. You'll be scrutinized, questioned." Seamus sighed and turned to Ethan, his friend and mentor. "It's time for me to come clean. I should hold a press conference and explain about Cara, then resign."

Ethan had the unnerving ability to stand completely still, hand in pocket, and say nothing. He could just stare at someone, until they started babbling again out of nerves. He did that now and Seamus found himself blurting out an extended explanation. "I should have done that from the start. Damage control. I need to distance myself from you so it doesn't cloud the election."

"Don't be stupid," Ethan said.

Seamus would have called it smart. "Come on, you know I'm right. And since this is my fault, I should be the one to fix it."

Ethan looked prepared to argue when the door opened.

"Seamus? Do you need me for something?" Kelsey walked in, wearing a red bikini and a shawl-type thing that covered a one-inch strip across her pelvis. "I was just going for a swim before bed."

"I see that." Though Seamus had a hard time picturing Kelsey doing hard laps in the hotel pool at 5 a.m. in that decorative little bit-of-nothing bathing suit. Yet it wasn't like she'd be sunbathing. Which left him to conclude that Kelsey was never going to make sense to him and it wasn't worth it to try.

"Mr. Carrick. Cara. Hi." Kelsey smiled, lifting her arms to adjust her ponytail.

Seamus had never seen her wear her hair up like that. It made her look like she was sixteen, instead of a sixty-year-old vampire. "Come sit down, Kelsey. Mr. Carrick wants to talk to you."

Her face fell. "You're going to fire me, aren't you?"

It was tempting to laugh. Kelsey was always Kelsey, no concept of the bigger picture.

"No," Ethan said. "We just need to know everything you know about the man who shot me. The man who bled Cara's friend Dawn tonight at the club."

"Kyle?" she said nervously, like there might be more

than one guy running around attacking them. "What about him?"

"How do you know him?" Seamus asked.

"I met him here, in the casino. He was playing blackjack and chain smoking. I talked to him and we went upstairs to . . ." She bit her lip. "Talk. And then I left because he was going to kill Mr. Carrick."

"What happened the night you were drained of blood, Kelsey? Was Kyle there?"

Her eyes shuttered for a second. "I don't remember."

"You don't remember anything from that night?"

"Well . . ." She wiggled her toes in her sandals. Worked her fingers through the holes in her cover-up. Bit her lip. "I was waiting for Kyle, to tell him that you had fallen off the roof of the building—remember that day?—and that he could use that as an out with the Italian. That he could tell him he'd pushed you and the job was over, so he would let Kyle go. But when I followed Kyle to the Venetian, they grabbed me and then there was noise and pain, and when I woke up, Kyle made this horrible gurgling sound . . . then I don't remember anything after that. Honest."

If she crossed her heart, Seamus was going to shake her. They could have used this info a little sooner. "So the Italian hired Kyle to kill Mr. Carrick?"

"Yes." She nodded. "He's not a nice man."

"Kyle?"

"The Italian." Kelsey rubbed her wrist. "He likes to hurt people." Her legs crossed and her arms wrapped around her nearly naked chest, like she could protect herself.

Ethan rubbed her upper arm. "It's okay, Kelsey. We won't let him hurt you again. Do you know if he is the one who turned Kyle?"

"I'm not sure, but I think Kyle works for him now. And I really didn't remember anything before, I swear, Mr. Carrick."

"Alright, then," Ethan said, with a patience Seamus admired. Kelsey could turn a saint into a raging alcoholic. "But if you remember anything else make sure you tell us."

She nodded. "Okay."

"Do you know where we could find Kyle? Does he live at the Venetian?"

"I'm not sure." Kelsey looked away from Ethan and Seamus and back again. "But he's here at the Ava if you want to talk to him."

Seamus started, instinctively moving Cara behind him. "He's here? Now? In the casino?"

"Yes." Kelsey shrugged. "He's here for the big ugly guy."

Ethan glanced over at him. "The addict who went after Cara."

"How do you know, Kelsey?" Seamus asked.

"I can hear his thoughts. I'm good at that with him. He's here."

Right here, in their casino, the whole damn time she'd been talking. And Kelsey just strolling off for a dip in the pool.

"By the way," Kelsey added. "His name isn't really Kyle. It's Ringo. He just likes to be called Kyle."

Twelve

Ringo had determined where Williams was in the casino. He could smell him when he got to the twenty-third floor, where Carrick's offices were. Wearing a dumb-ass-looking floral delivery disguise, Ringo had gone up in the elevator, disgusted that he had reached this low point in his life.

He wasn't anybody's delivery boy. He had done his hits fast and clean: walk in, plug them, walk out. Or better yet, a nice clean shot from a roof or an open window. This sneaking-around shit, worrying, wondering, begging, was getting old. Fast.

The minute he'd stepped into the office area, he knew Williams was on the same floor. The sick, sweet odor of a drug-addicted vampire drying out clung everywhere, like raw sewage. At least he knew Williams wasn't dead.

"Hey, where do you think you're going?" a security

guard asked him as he stepped toward the glass doors that led to the reception desk.

"I have a delivery."

"At five in the morning? What the hell you delivering?" The guard was skeptical, and he was also mortal, which always worked in a vampire's favor. Ringo could blow past him if he needed to.

But Ringo just smiled and pulled the door handle. The offices were locked. "It's a special delivery, you know what I'm saying. For a . . ." He glanced down. "Kelsey. The secretary." It was a risk, using Kelsey's name, but if she was around, he wanted to talk to her, and hers was the only name he knew besides Carrick's and his wife's, and he didn't want either of them seeing him.

"Kelsey doesn't come in until the afternoon. I'll take whatever it is for her."

"You want what I'm supposed to give her?" Ringo feigned amusement.

"Yeah, I can keep it for her. What's the big freaking deal?" The guard was starting to get pissed. He shifted restlessly.

"Do I have to spell it out for you? It's not just flowers, it's a Strip-o-Gram. I'm supposed to entertain her. Let her touch whatever she wants to touch, got it?"

"A what?" The guard looked shocked. "Man, that just ain't right. Guys stripping for girls . . . shit."

"Hey, this is Vegas. Guess her friends got together and wanted to surprise her for her birthday."

"It's Kelsey's birthday? No kidding. Yeah, that sounds like something Mrs. Carrick would do, give Kelsey a Strip-o-Gram. Jesus. You want to take it to Kelsey's room? She's on the next floor. Twenty-four-oh-two. It's probably better if you do that weird crap away from the offices anyway."

"Great idea. Thanks, man." Ringo clapped him on the arm.

"Hey, don't touch me," the guard said, lip curling.

"Sorry." Ringo backed up, reached the elevator, and turned. Step one accomplished.

When he got to Kelsey's room, he took a chance and knocked, hoping his luck would hold out. He leaned against the door frame and smiled winningly at the peephole. Thirty seconds later the door opened.

"Kyle."

"Kelsey." He held out the bouquet of flowers he'd been hauling around. "These are for you."

She was wearing a very small bikini and nothing else. Her feet were bare, one foot crossed over the other. "Thank you." She took the flowers, sniffed them. "Lilies. Pretty, but you really shouldn't buy a girl lilies, Kyle. They're funeral flowers. I might get the wrong idea."

There was something so wonderfully simplistic about Kelsey, yet amazingly complex. Ringo kind of liked the unexpected randomness of how she spoke, what she said. She annoyed the crap out of him, but she was growing on him. Like mold.

"How was I supposed to know they were funeral flowers? I'm just a dumb guy. I just saw them and thought they were beautiful, like you." He stepped in and put his hand on her cheek, caressed her cool flesh. "I'd never hurt you, you know that."

"I know." She closed the door behind him. "But you can't hurt Cara either. Or Seamus or Mr. Carrick."

"I'm just here for Williams, the Italian's security guard. I'm not here to hurt anyone." He could say that with total honesty. "I just need to get Williams out and you can help me."

"I don't want to go near him. He's the one who shot me, isn't he?"

"Yes. But you don't have to be near him. You just have to get me into his room. If I can get him out, then nobody has to get hurt, babe. We can keep this simple, just between you and me."

She worked her lip over with pearly white teeth. "You have to get away from him. He'll ruin you."

The thing was, he was already ruined. But he knew what Kelsey meant. Hell, he had been thinking, feeling, for days that he had to get away from Donatelli, get back to being his own man. But he wasn't sure how to do that. Wasn't sure it was even possible. Yet, the idea nagged and itched him.

"I know that, Kels. But he's one seriously powerful vampire. What am I supposed to do?" He didn't like her implication that he was just staying with Donatelli for the hell of it. Putting a hand on her bare waist, he pulled her to him. "I don't like it any more than you do."

"Kyle..." she said in a plaintive voice, snuggling up against his chest, lacing her fingers through his.

"Why do you call me Kyle?" he asked, amusement soothing his annoyance. "You know that's not my name."

Her lips brushed his jaw. "But I call you Kyle because you like it."

She was right. For being such a ditz, she was so perceptive sometimes it was scary. When her mouth covered his, Ringo kissed her back with frustration, desire, and an odd sort of tenderness that came out of nowhere, nosing the other feelings aside and winning the race.

It startled the crap out of him. Any emotion surprised him, but this one...he didn't know where it came from or where to put it. It sat there, on his chest, like a goddamn boulder.

Kelsey was wrapping her leg around his, digging into his back with her clawlike nails. Her bikini bottoms bumped against his dick and it would be easy to peel the nylon back and plunge into her. She wouldn't stop him. Would probably welcome it.

But Ringo settled for kissing her, for tasting her mouth, lips, tongue, for holding her in his arms like normal people did, with normal lives, and normal pleasures.

When they came up for air, Kelsey whispered in his ear, "I care about you, Ringo. So did Kyle."

Kyle. His kid brother. His mistake had been in caring for Ringo. It had only gotten him killed. Kelsey was making the same mistake.

"You're fucking crazy, you know that?" he told her, lowering his hold so he was touching her ass, gripping hard to emphasize his point. "You shouldn't care about me."

"But I do." Her voice was a soft, sensual whisper, confident and pretty, flowing over him like sweet, rich blood, reminding him of everything he wasn't and everything he couldn't have.

"Then be a good girl for once and do what I tell you." Ringo figured he had one chance, and he was going to take it. "Listen to me carefully, because I have a plan."

Cara didn't like where this was going. "Seamus, maybe this isn't a good idea."

But he barely even glanced at her as he laced up thick combat boots. "We have to take care of this, Cara. This guy is a serious threat to us as individuals but also to the Nation. He's out of control, and I want to know once and for all if Donatelli is giving him his orders."

Hair still damp from her shower, Cara twisted it into a rope, let it go, and shook it so it would unwind. She was nervous. Really on edge. It did not seem like a good idea to let the man she loved charge off into battle the morning after taking her virginity. It was all too medieval.

"But what are you going to do with him?" She'd seen that dagger Seamus had stuck in his belt. That was one ugly-looking knife. And how did Seamus even know how to use it? She didn't think he was a wimp or anything, but come on. He was a campaign manager, not a crocodile hunter. Could he really handle himself with a lunatic vampire?

"You don't think I can handle myself?" Seamus asked in shock, glancing over at her, bent over, one foot on the coffee table as he tied. "You think I'm some kind of pansy who can't protect myself or my woman?"

Damn. She hated the whole mind-reading thing sometimes. She hadn't completely mastered closing him out.

"I don't think you're a pansy! Not after last night. Not before last night either. I'm sure you're perfectly capable of protecting yourself and me, it's just that I'm a woman, and I care about you, and I'm going to worry. I can't help it."

The eloquent response she received for all her efforts was just a grunt.

Geez, Alexis had been right when she'd said these male vampires were sensitive about their masculinity and territory.

"I heard that," he said, dropping his foot to the carpet and standing up.

Oops. Cara said, "Heard what?" Then took him in. He was wearing black pants, a black T-shirt that showed off some serious muscle, and the boots. It made her forget to worry for a second. "You look hot."

"Nice try," he said.

"What? It's true." Cara looked at Seamus, visions of the night before dancing through her head, and suddenly she felt deluged and overwhelmed by emotion. Tears materialized from nowhere and dribbled out of her eyes. She launched herself at Seamus right as his expression turned from annoyed to alarmed.

"Hey, hey, what's the matter?" He caught her up in his arms. "Shh. Come on now. Everything is fine. We'll get this cleared up and we can go back to things being normal."

"What if you get hurt?" she said into his chest, embarrassed by her reaction but unable to stop herself.

"I'm a vampire. I'll heal." He kissed the top of her head. "I have to go."

She clung tighter. "No."

He gave a soft laugh. "Cara. I'm going ten flights down, not to Zimbabwe. I'll be back in an hour."

"Let me go with you." Not that she could really be of any assistance, but at least she could watch his back.

"Hell no. You're staying with Alexis." He gave her a squeeze, then tried to set her away from him.

Cara hung on. She was terrified and she wasn't sure why. It was just a feeling . . . just the lingering horror of seeing what had been done to Dawn, remembering the fear in Kelsey's eyes, and the way they had ganged up three on one on Seamus that first night she'd met him.

"I love you," she said, in case she never got a chance to tell him. She wanted him to know, spoken out loud, of her own free will, instead of plucked from her thoughts.

Seamus stared down at her, his face relaxing. "I love you, too, Cara. When this is all settled and everything is safe . . . I'm hoping . . . I want . . . I'm asking you to stay with me. Here, in our apartment."

"Yes." There was no other answer. It was what Cara wanted deep down inside of her. She couldn't imagine going back to her old apartment, alone. She and Seamus both managed to lure out the best qualities in each other, and they had an amazing friendship paired with explosive passion.

With the rough backside of his thumb, he wiped a tear off her cheek. Then he kissed her, a hard, possessive, claiming kiss.

"I'll take you down to Ethan's now."

"Okay." She held his hand and let him lead her down the hall, trying damn hard to trust him.

When they got to Ethan and Alexis's, the president was arguing with the First Lady. Or rather, he was arguing and she was agreeing.

"Alexis. I'm serious. You have to stay here."

"Okay," she said, sitting at their dining room table and flipping through a magazine.

"I'm serious," Ethan said from the doorway, while Cara still held on to Seamus's hand.

Cara saw Alexis pause in turning a page. "I heard you. I agreed."

Ethan marched back over to his wife, face grim. "Alexis. You understand how important this is."

"Yes."

"You have to stay here with Cara."

Alexis slapped her magazine shut and glared at Ethan. "I said *okay.* What the hell do you want from me? A pint of blood?"

Ethan relaxed and gave her a grin. "Not in front of our friends."

"Ha, ha," she said, but she gave him a small smile. "Be careful."

"Always."

Seamus extracted his hand from Cara's as Ethan gave Alexis a kiss. Cara forced herself to keep her mouth shut and not give Seamus any warnings or advice he wouldn't appreciate. If she weren't careful, she'd be nagging him to wear a hat in winter and telling him not to run with a stake in his hands.

The minute the door closed behind them, Alexis stood up. "You need to change your shoes."

Cara glanced down at her flip-flops. "Why?"

"Because we're going to follow them."

"But you just told Ethan you'd stay here." Cara stared at Alexis, heart starting to race. She would feel so much better if she could just keep an eye on Seamus.

"Screw that. This keeping the home fires burning shit just isn't for me, and Ethan knew that when he married me. He fully expects me to follow him. I think he'd be disappointed if I didn't."

"I don't think Seamus expects me to follow him."

"And you wouldn't have if I didn't, right?"

"True."

"But you want to, don't you?"

"Yes."

"Then let's go." Alexis opened up a drawer in the buffet and pulled out a rather serious-looking sword.

Cara must have made an involuntary sound of horror because Alexis glanced over at her. "Don't worry. I'm trained to use it."

"It's almost as big as you are," Cara said.

Alexis swung it up in one deft move and sliced through the six taper candles gracing a candelabra on the dining room table. The cut was swift and clean, and each candle toppled off in a silent death fall. The sword remained completely in Alexis's control and she gave it a few swirls before resting the tip on the floor in front of her.

"Not a problem, though, I see," Cara amended.

"Nope. And I feel like Ninja vampire when I use it. It's very cool. If you want, I can train you."

"Sure." Maybe it wouldn't be a bad idea to know how to defend herself. It seemed vampire politics created enemies and she was now the girlfriend of a powerful conservative party vampire.

"Could you teach me how to pole dance?" Alexis asked, tucking her blond hair behind one ear. "Ethan would love that."

"I could do that." And it gave her an idea for that night. She could surprise Seamus with a little routine.

"So are you in love with Seamus?"

"Yes," Cara admitted, feeling her cheeks go hot. She laughed. "Isn't that just crazy? I always said I wouldn't do this, fall head over heels, but I tell you . . . I feel as sappy as a greeting card."

"I understand. Totally. I felt the same way." Alexis shook her head. "They have no idea how lucky they really are. Now let's go save their asses."

Cara swallowed hard and decided that if she didn't get killed by an assassin, Seamus would do it with his bare hands when he saw her.

But she just wanted a peek, just enough of a look to see that he was alright. Then she'd retreat and everything would be just fine.

She was almost sure of it.

"It used to be a lot easier to do this kind of stuff, didn't it?" Seamus asked as he and Ethan headed down the hall. He couldn't believe the way Cara had clung to him. It pleased him at the same time it made him feel guilty for worrying her. But hell, he could take care of himself. Had been doing it for almost four hundred years. "We used to just sign up for every war that came our way. Now it's harder."

"Very true. Now we have responsibilities. People relying on us. We have to exercise caution." Ethan touched the frame of a painting hanging in the hallway and straightened it. "We're civilized. We own property. And we have women waiting for us at home."

"It's not so bad, is it?" Seamus pictured Cara in his bed, the way her eyes had darkened when she said she loved him. "Not so bad at all."

"Nope. Different phases in life, that's all. And meeting Alexis was just what I needed."

Seamus thought the same could be said for him and Cara. He'd been so discontent, so frustrated, so uptight. Cara had changed all that, forced him to relax. But he didn't like that she had cried when he'd left. That made him feel lousy, guilty. "Hey, do you remember Hutchins? The captain who was at Waterloo with us? Remember how his wife used to follow the drum?"

Ethan laughed as they got on the elevator. "Shit, I'd forgotten about him. Every time we were ready to head out to the front lines, she would grab on to him and wail and scream for him not to leave her."

Seamus could still picture it, her skirts flying, bonnet askew, head lifted toward the sky like she was begging God for intercession. "He was always so embarrassed, but he couldn't bring himself to toss her off. He'd pat her and try to reassure her until the cook would finally pull her off.

The one time she got him around the knees and they both went down in the mud."

They laughed. "We used to cut him up over that," Ethan said. "But now I have to sympathize with the poor chap. I find my wife is a little hard to control sometimes."

"At least you understand Alexis. I have no clue what Cara is going to do half the time."

"Will she follow us?" Ethan asked.

"No. Of course not," Seamus scoffed. At least he didn't think so. "Will Alexis?"

"Absolutely."

"You probably should have put some clothes on," Ringo said to Kelsey when they left her room and got on the elevator. It didn't seem to occur to her it was a little odd for her to be strolling along in a bikini while he was wearing a suit. But hell, maybe it wasn't. He had ditched the delivery jacket in Kelsey's room.

"There's no time. Mr. Carrick will be down here in like five minutes."

Ringo questioned that Kelsey would be able to pull this off, but he didn't see that he had a whole lot of options. He just had to make sure any fallout didn't land on her.

They stepped out on the twenty-third floor, the office level. The office doors were unlocked and a receptionist was typing on a computer.

"Hey Kelsey," the receptionist said, barely glancing up. "What are you doing?"

"I just forgot something in Mr. Carrick's office. I'll be in later like normal."

"Okay." The woman didn't even seem to notice Ringo

or the fact that Kelsey was wearing a bikini. "Happy Birthday," she added.

"Thanks," Kelsey said, without missing a beat.

Ringo couldn't prevent a small smile as they went down the hall. Damn, she was cool under pressure. He never would have guessed it.

She didn't even balk when there was a mortal guard outside the room Williams was in. "Hi, James," she said with a smile.

"Kelsey." His eyebrow went up. "If you're going swimming, the pool is on the first floor."

"Ha, ha. Very funny." She smiled at him. "Can you go get me a cup of coffee?"

"Sure." The guy went down the hall.

Just like that. "Very smooth," Ringo told her.

"I'm working on the mind-control thing. Now go in there," she said, shoving him. "I'll keep watch."

Opening the door, he braced himself, not sure what in the hell he was going to find on the other side. It wasn't as gruesome as he imagined, though Williams looked like hell. He was lying on a couch watching TV, handcuffed to the furniture leg. Ringo wasn't sure if the restraints could actually secure a fifty-year-old vampire but Williams looked too sick to give a shit.

"Hey." He stepped in front of him.

Williams struggled to sit up. "Blood. I need blood. They're giving me blood that is bad or something... I'm dying, Ringo. You've got to help me."

Using his foot, Ringo stepped on the handcuffs and snapped them in two pieces. "Get up."

"How we going to get out?" Williams took a deep breath, his normally pale pallor nearly translucent. "Fuck,

I'm going to be sick." He leaned over and puked while Ringo turned away in disgust.

He did not want to end up like Williams. Yet he knew he was already there. He was only one missed feeding away from the shakes and sweats Williams had.

The door opened and Kelsey ran in. "Guard is back, and Seamus and Mr. Carrick are coming down the hall."

"Alright." There was no time to screw around. Ringo hauled Williams up by his shirt and dragged him over to the window.

"What are you doing?" Williams sputtered and whacked at Ringo with weak, unfocused punches. "Let me go."

"I'm saving your ass. The entry is blocked. We're going out the window." Ringo took a hard-backed chair and swung. The glass shattered upon impact, shards flying everywhere.

"We're in a high-rise. We can't." Williams stopped to hurl again.

"You want to get back to Donatelli and his drug blood or what? I can leave you here to dry out." Ringo shoved him toward the open window, the sun just starting to appear in the east, their shoes crunching and sliding on the beads of burst glass. "Or you can go out my way."

"No . . . the fall will kill us."

Nothing could kill them except decapitation, lack of blood, or a stake through the heart. "What's a few broken bones when they'll heal?" Ringo got a hand on Williams's pants at the waist, another on his shirt at the shoulder. He jerked him up onto the window ledge. "Withdrawal didn't do anything for your weight, man. You're fucking heavy."

Williams shot him a panicked look, his hair matted to his head, dark circles ringing his watery eyes. The door opened and Ringo heard voices, shouts. He shoved, hard, while Williams scrambled with his feet, trying to find a hold on the wall, the ledge, anything. His arms flailed toward Ringo, desperate to grab on, his hand clasping Ringo's jacket. Ringo locked eyes with him, broke Williams's weak hold, and sent him winging out into open air. The guy dropped before Ringo could even blink.

Carrick and Fox were coming at him. He could sense their shock, their malice, but he was ready. Turning around, he reached out and grabbed Kelsey by her thin arm, jerking her in front of him and snaking his arm around her throat. "Back off!" he yelled.

"What the hell are you doing?" Fox demanded as he and Carrick jerked to a halt five feet in front of him. "Let her go."

"No. She's coming with me." Ringo bent over without breaking his hold on Kelsey and pulled a knife out of his boot. He put it in front of her throat.

"I don't think so," Carrick said, his voice arrogant and disdainful. "Neither of you is leaving."

Ringo wanted to kick him just to hear him whelp. Bastard. "You can let us leave by the door or we'll go out the window. Doesn't matter to me, but we're leaving."

Kelsey whimpered. Ringo wasn't sure if it was for effect or if she was really scared. He stroked her back with his free hand so she would remember this was what they had to do.

"Look." Fox held out his hand. "Let Kelsey go. Then we'll let you leave out the window like your friend did."

Ringo wasn't about to wind up on the ground vulnerable, bones cracked, lying by himself. He was going to let Williams crawl back to Donatelli, and Ringo was going to ease himself off the drug blood, somehow or another. Kelsey was meant to serve as a way for him to get out of the building standing. They had worked it out, and he was not about to let these assholes get a hand on him.

He started to walk Kelsey around Fox and Carrick when Alexis and the other woman, Fox's girlfriend, burst into the room.

Thirteen

Seamus thought he might have an aneurysm when he saw Alexis running into the room, brandishing a sword, for Christ's sake. Cara was behind her, at least, but it wasn't at all reassuring.

"Stop!" he yelled at Alexis. She careened to a halt, Cara nearly plowing into her from behind.

"Oh, my God, Kelsey," Cara cried.

"Let her go." Alexis went into her kick-ass sword-swinging stance.

Next to Seamus, Ethan gave a sigh. "She said she'd cut Donatelli's testicles off. I thought she was kidding, but clearly she wasn't."

"Get out of my way," the assassin Kelsey called Ringo said, in a low, calm voice that disturbed Seamus more than anything he'd seen so far. This was a dangerous man.

Seamus stepped in front of Cara, eased her back into a corner. He'd let Ethan disarm his wife. But this guy was serious, and for Kelsey, they needed to play it safe.

"Alright, just let Kelsey go and you can walk out." They'd catch up with him later and get some answers.

Cara tried to move around him, but he held her back. She grappled with him, desperately grabbing and clawing to get free, so he wound up stumbling forward. "Cara, what the hell are you doing? Knock it off, babe."

"Get out of my way, Seamus," she said, her voice growing hysterical. "Look at Kelsey."

The fear in her voice made him turn. Kelsey had been holding the guy's wrist where he was pressing the dagger to her throat. It had seemed natural, instinctive, for her to try to shield herself, pull the weapon away. Now Ethan realized that she was actually *pushing* the knife into her flesh. She was bleeding, torrents of red starting to stream down over her bare skin, racing to her bikini top.

"Kelsey," he said in confusion, as Alexis let out a scream.

Kelsey's eyes were rolling back, gliding shut, her knees giving out, but she pushed harder, hitting her jugular.

Ringo finally seemed to realize something was wrong and he jerked the dagger back and let it clatter to the floor. Seamus figured he'd bolt, and at the moment he didn't really give a shit. His concern was Kelsey and all that blood. It was everywhere, arching in a violent spray.

But the guy didn't leave. He gave an agonized groan. "Kelsey . . . what . . . why . . ." He held on to her even as she went down like a thin rag doll, cradling her in his arms. The look he wore was blank, stunned, confused, as they all saw the blood spilling down the entire length of her. Ringo had blood on his face, chest, arms.

Cara pushed around Seamus, yanking her T-shirt off as she fell to her knees. She pressed the fabric on Kelsey's neck in a futile effort to stem the flow. "She'll heal, won't she, Seamus?"

Her action propelled him forward. "Yes, she'll heal." Though he couldn't imagine why the hell she'd done what she did. He took off his own shirt and laid it over Cara's back. He didn't like her sitting there in her bra, regardless of the circumstances. "There is blood in the fridge. She'll need to drink to replace all this lost blood."

"Got it," Ethan said.

Seamus eased Kelsey out of Ringo's arms and put her on Cara's lap, where Cara petted her hair and murmured to her. Kelsey had passed out, her fair skin taking on a bluish purple tint. Ethan popped open a blood bag and poured it between her lips.

Which left Seamus to deal with Ringo. The guy sat back, his lips pressed tightly together. Absently, he wiped blood off his cheek.

"If we're going to throw punches, can we move to the other side of the room?" Seamus asked cautiously. "Away from Kelsey." He was on the balls of his feet, but he was ready for a fight if this guy wanted one. It had to be his fault Kelsey had sliced herself, and that pissed Seamus off.

Ringo just shook his head, expression unreadable. "No." He held out his hands. "Shit. Just cuff me. That's what Kelsey wants."

That threw Seamus off. He wasn't sure how to respond. "How do you know what the hell Kelsey wants?"

"She has a hard time staying out of my head. She wants me to detox. Says you'll take care of me. That's why she did it." A finger went across his neck in a slitting motion. "Her way of forcing me to stay." He held out his hands again. "Come on. I only have another hour or so before I'm going to be desperate for some drug blood. If I leave here, it doesn't matter what I tell myself, I'll go right back to him, right back for another fix. Lock me up now before I change my mind."

Seamus hauled him to his feet by his outstretched wrists. "Who do you work for?"

"You know who." Ringo shook Seamus off and fixed his suit jacket, his expression scornful. "Donatelli. And by now the whole Nation knows that you have a fledgling who is a stripper. Just a little election gossip."

Glancing over at Cara, Seamus shifted uneasily. He had seen this coming. All his goddamn fault. He should have turned Cara and just resigned right then and there. He should have taken her and gone back to Ireland to let things blow over.

Cara was stroking Kelsey's hair, whispering to her while Ethan popped open a second bag of blood, tossing the empty one onto the carpet. Kelsey's neck was covered in thick, clotted blood, but Seamus could see it was healing. Her skin was a more normal tint, and her breathing had evened out. Cara hadn't bothered to pull on the T-shirt, but didn't seem aware of the fact that she was sitting there in a red lace bra.

She was beautiful.

And Seamus realized he had done the same thing all over again. He had fallen in lust with Cara initially, which had clouded his judgment. It had been the same with Marie, and like then, others had paid the price for his weakness. Cara, Ethan, and even Kelsey were paying for his lack of self-control, and he felt the guilt crushing him all over again.

He loved Cara. But sometimes that wasn't good enough.

Cara was aware that Seamus was watching her, a strange pained look on his face. It made her uncomfortable, but her main concern was Kelsey, who was starting to shift uneasily. "Are you sure she's going to be okay, Ethan?"

"I'm sure. But I'll have the Frenchman check on her just to be sure."

"The Frenchman?" Alexis said, stopping her anxious pacing. "You mean Corbin?"

"Yes," Ethan said.

"Is he in town?"

"Yes."

"And you knew?"

"Yes. He has been detoxing the vampire who went out the window and who is right now probably on his way back to his drug pusher. We'll need Atelier to help Ringo through his withdrawal."

Cara winced, thinking there wasn't going to be any easy way to break an addiction. Yet she found she was having a hard time dredging up sympathy for the man who had bitten Dawn two dozen times and left her almost drained of blood, naked on the dressing room floor. Maybe it was the drugs that had caused Ringo's behavior, but it was going to take her a long time to get over what he had done.

Alexis glared at her husband. "How long has Corbin been here?"

"A week."

"You could have mentioned that to me."

"I suppose I could have." Ethan was impassive. "But it's not relevant."

Alexis gasped. "I would have liked to talk to him."

"You still can. He's right outside the door."

Cara watched a tall, debonair man enter the room. He smiled charmingly.

"Good day to all of you. Did you require something, Mr. Carrick?"

"We have another patient for you." Ethan pointed to Ringo, who had been tied into a chair by Seamus. A cigarette dangled artfully from his lips.

Corbin made a sympathetic sound. "Of course." He walked past Alexis, bowing his head. "How are you, Alexis? And your sister, Brittany? I trust she is recovering from the flu?"

Alexis narrowed her eyes. "How did you know she has the flu?"

His steps faltered. "She told me." Then he knelt down beside Kelsey. "Miss Kelsey has had an accident, yes?"

"You could call it that," Ringo said sarcastically.

Cara pulled her T-shirt off Kelsey's rippled wound. "Her throat was cut, but I think it's healing."

Corbin examined the laceration, his long fingers moving with precision and gentleness. "Yes, she will heal. You, however," he said to Ringo. "You are in for a difficult time."

"Bring it on," Ringo said, tossing his hair out of his eyes.

Kelsey's eyes snapped open. She sat up in Cara's lap. "Kyle? Where's Kyle?"

"Right here, Kels."

She turned and sighed in relief when she saw Ringo. "I had to, you know. For you."

"I know. But you could have warned me."

"No," Kelsey said. "I couldn't."

"I know." Ringo shrugged.

Cara felt Seamus's shirt slip off her back. She realized

she was still sitting there in her bra, so she dragged the black T-shirt on over her head. Seamus's scent enveloped her. It made her feel comforted. *I love you,* she told him, needing to hear his voice.

But he didn't answer. In fact, he didn't even look at her. Cara realized he must not have heard her. She wasn't exactly an expert on the whole thought-projection thing.

"Why don't we go get you into the shower, Kelsey." The sight of so much blood all over Kelsey's body was incredibly gruesome.

"Good idea," Seamus said, inspecting the shattered window, knocking out a few remaining shards. "Why don't you ladies go to bed for the day? I think everyone could use some rest." He leaned over and looked down. "No body on the street."

Cara realized she had been dismissed. He was talking to Ethan with that last pronouncement, not her. It was puzzling, but she reassured herself that the night had been completely overwhelming. Seamus was obviously distracted, thinking, strategizing. Obviously.

"I could use a shower," Kelsey said, standing up, using Cara's shirt to swipe at her chest. "Cara, oh, my gosh, I ruined your shirt. I'm sorry."

That almost made her laugh. "It's okay. It can be replaced." She wasn't sure why Kelsey had slit her own throat, but she knew it had something to do with Ringo. Which was just astounding. Cara wondered if she could make herself rip open her flesh for Seamus. That seemed a little drastic.

Alexis didn't put up an argument about leaving, nor did she say good-bye to her husband. Their only contact was when she started toward the door, and Ethan yanked her back by the sword she was carrying.

"Leave the sword, Baldizzi. And quit watching *Highlander* reruns."

Alexis surrendered the sword without a word and the three women went into the hall, Cara nervously holding on to Kelsey's arm. She didn't want Kelsey to suddenly drop or anything.

"I am so angry I could spit," Alexis hissed. "Why the hell didn't he tell me Corbin was here?"

Cara was feeling a little uneasy herself. Seamus hadn't exactly been Joe Affectionate in there. "They feel like they have to protect us from everything. Maybe it's because they were raised in earlier centuries, when women were considered the weaker sex."

"I don't know. I think that may be true for Seamus, but when Ethan was a kid, women were pretty tough. They had to be to survive." Alexis narrowed her eyes. "I think Ethan is just being an asshole, that's all."

"Yeah, they do that, too, sometimes." Cara sighed. Something was wrong with Seamus. She could sense it. He hadn't even *looked* at her when she left.

They got on the elevator and three women gasped in horror when they looked at Kelsey.

"Actress," Alexis said, pointing to Kelsey. "They're filming a movie here in the casino. *Vampires in Vegas*."

"Really? That's exciting," the one wearing a Margaritaville T-shirt said.

"And that blood is so realistic," her friend added.

"Thanks," Alexis said. "I'll tell the special effects guys. They always need ego stroking."

They got out at the twenty-fourth floor, waving to the women.

Kelsey shook her head. "I don't think Mr. Carrick

would like you telling people they're filming a vampire movie here."

"Fuck him," Alexis snarled.

"I'll leave that to you," Cara murmured, and they all grinned, glad to have the somber mood broken. "Did you see their faces when we walked in? I thought they were going to wet themselves. I guess we should have been more discreet."

Kelsey unlocked her door.

"Where the hell were you hiding that key card?" Alexis asked.

Cara was wondering that same thing. Kelsey's bikini could have been bought at babyGap.

"I'll never tell," Kelsey said, then promptly told them. "Here, in the front of my bottoms. I never lose it that way."

Guess not.

"I used to lose it all the time and the front desk people were getting bitchy with me. So I try to be better about it now."

They stepped into Kelsey's hotel room, which was just a standard room with a king-size bed, sitting area, and bath. There were clothes, makeup, and books over every surface. Cara wandered over to the dresser and spotted *The Secret Life of Bees*, *Gossip Girls*, *The Complete Works of Shakespeare*, *The Origins of Islam*, and *Why Do Men Have Nipples?*, all crowded together in a precarious tower.

"Wow, this is quite a selection."

"I like to read," Kelsey said.

Who would have thought?

Alexis shoved a black cocktail dress over and sat on the bed. "Okay, Kels, maybe this is rude to ask, but why the hell did you slit your throat?"

Cara would never have had the guts to ask, but she was glad Alexis had. She was morbidly curious to know what had inspired that drastic action.

Kelsey didn't look offended. She took her hair out of its now messy ponytail and shook it free. "Because Kyle is addicted to drug blood. That's why he stays with the Italian and why he does things he shouldn't. He's a good man in there, but he's been lost. I knew if he left today, he'd be lost for good, and I knew that if I hurt myself, he'd pass on his chance to escape so he could help me. So I slit my throat, and now he's going to be okay, I'm sure of it."

"I'm impressed," Alexis said.

"That was a very compassionate thing to do," Cara added, a lump in her throat. There was something that was bothering her, buzzing around the edges of her consciousness, irritating and nagging.

"I had to," Kelsey said, slipping out of the bloody bikini, no concern for modesty. "I had to make it right for him. It was scary when my memories were all messed up, it was like everything was scrambled in the dark, but now I think I remember everything, and I know that Kyle can be saved."

Alexis looked skeptical, kicking her feet back and forth on the side of the bed. "Holy shit, you've got a thing for him, don't you?"

"Yes," Kelsey said, and walked into the bathroom, her very long legs pale with streaks of rusted blood. She didn't bother to shut the door, but the shower came on.

"She's falling in love with a sicko murderer for hire. I can't believe this," Alexis said, shaking her head.

"Maybe once he's off the drugs, he'll be alright." Kelsey certainly believed that. Maybe they should, too, for her sake. And maybe Cara could learn from Kelsey how to trust people, learn that caring for someone, showing compassion, didn't make you vulnerable. That at some point you had to take a leap of faith and love. Cara had done that with Seamus the night before and she wanted to be as confident as Kelsey that she'd done the right thing.

"Drug addicts don't just get better. And nasty people don't do one-eighties and become suddenly good." Alexis held up one of Kelsey's very, uh, suggestive panties. "What is this thing? It looks like she put it through the paper shredder."

Pressing her lips together, Cara tried not to laugh. "They're panties... the back is crisscross strings."

"So all you have on your ass are these stripes?" Alexis shuddered. "I'm sorry, that's just ridiculous. I mean, how totally uncomfortable. And it would make crisscross lines in your pants. And I really, really find it hard to believe that men are attracted to women's ass cracks."

"I've never taken a survey." Cara rubbed her stomach. "Damn, I'm hungry. But I don't think we should leave until Kelsey is safely in bed. And I don't know where Seamus is."

"What does he have to do with anything? I'm sure Kelsey has blood in her fridge. Just snag a bag. I could feed, too."

Alexis was already up and opening Kelsey's minifridge. "We should make sure Kelsey has another bag before she goes to bed."

Cara debated if she was hungry enough to drink it cold from a bag, and decided she was. "I usually hate it in the bag, but for some reason I'm starving."

"Do you need a glass or something?" Alexis asked, pulling out three bags of blood and tossing them back and forth in her hands.

"No, I like it from Seamus." Cara was kind of embarrassed to admit that, though she wasn't sure why.

"What do you mean, from Seamus?" Alexis looked at her blankly.

"I drink blood from him. You know, his blood." Cara could feel her face starting to burn. Damn, she was blushing and Alexis's reaction wasn't helping. Her friend's eyes went wide.

"You mean, like when you're having sex, you take a little nip here and there? Just a taste?"

"Well, yeah, that, too. But I mean, even when we're not having sex, when I need to feed, I drink straight from Seamus." Even as she said it, she realized something sounded strange about that. It had never once occurred to her to wonder why she fed from him but Seamus fed from a bag. She had liked it too much to wonder about the logistics.

"He feeds you?" Alexis asked in astonishment. "All the time?"

"Well, not every time. I have had it from the bag, but I didn't really like that. So usually Seamus just, you know, lets me at his wrist..." Cara trailed off as Alexis gaped at her like a hooked trout. "What? Is there something wrong with that?"

"Yeah. You know all those unwritten vampire laws? Well, that is one of them. No feeding from other vampires."

"Why not?" Cara pressed her hand to her forehead. This didn't make sense.

"Because one, you are usually taking blood from a more powerful vampire, increasing your own power. Two, you are draining them, meaning they have to drink double their normal quantity. Three, most important of all, it can be used as a means of control, a way for an older vampire to create a submissive fledgling because it's addictive. Essentially, it's illegal so we can protect the rights of fledglings." Alexis shook her head. "Holy shit. I can not even fathom why Seamus, of all vampires, would do this."

"Addictive? It's addictive? I'm *addicted* to Seamus?" It wasn't love she was experiencing, it was chemical dependency? Cara felt hot everywhere, a sick churning in her stomach, panic rising up into her throat. "You mean I'm like Ringo? I have to check into rehab or what?"

"I don't think that's a good comparison," Alexis said quickly. "He's chemically addicted to drugs. I think what vamp feeding does is more like an association of extreme pleasure with feeding."

"Oh, that sounds so much better," Cara choked out. She was stunned, humiliated, devastated. "I have to talk to Seamus." Murder him.

"Okay, okay." Alexis shoved the bag of blood at her. "Here, if you want it. And Cara, I'm sorry, I didn't mean to just blurt it out like that... I'm sure it's not a big deal."

"Of course it is, and you know it. I'm glad you told me." Cara glanced disdainfully at the blood bag, knowing it was going to be cold and tinny. Then anger propelled her to grab it. She would drink it and she would like it. She was not going to be addicted to Seamus Fox, slimy lying pervert that he was.

Tossing her head back, she drank the whole thing, trying not to gag. She managed to keep it all in, and shuddered, crushing the empty bag in her hand like a frat boy with a beer can.

"Hungry?" Kelsey asked as she came into the room wearing a fluffy white towel.

"I'm going to kill Seamus," Cara told her.

"I hear ya," Alexis said. "I'm pretty pissed at my own man right now."

"I'm very very grateful I am not married to Seamus," Cara said, locating a trash can and dropping the bag into it. "If I was, we'd be heading to vampire divorce court."

Anger felt good. It was better than the alternative, which was bursting into tears. For a second, she had almost succumbed to crying, but this was better. Anger could be stoked, flung at the source of the problem, used as a shield to protect yourself from embarrassing displays of vulnerability.

"A vampire divorce isn't easy to get. I think Ethan's sister Gwenna is only one of a handful who have managed to do it."

Cara wiped her hands on her jeans. She hadn't even known Ethan had a sister. "Who was she married to?"

"Donatelli."

"No kidding? That guy gets around." She turned to Kelsey. "Are you sure you're okay?"

"I'm fine." Kelsey was rooting around in the pile of clothes on the bed.

"Okay, then I'm leaving. Seamus has some squirming—I mean explaining—to do." She patted her pockets to make sure she had her room key. "Too bad Ethan has your sword, Alexis. I could use it right about now."

"Maybe it's good that you don't. You don't want to cut off anything you may regret not having later."

"Hah. I would die—*again*—before I ever have sex with Seamus Fox." It was the thought of the night before, the way he had made love to her, that sent her careening out the door, the tears refusing to be held back any longer.

Seamus glanced absently at his cell phone. Damn. It was Cara. He and Ethan were strategizing how to approach

Donatelli, if at all. They were weighing their options and hadn't yet come to any conclusions.

He knew Cara had picked up on his discomfort earlier. She had looked hurt when he hadn't said good-bye. But he hadn't trusted himself to speak, not after she had spoken into his head that she loved him. He hadn't answered because he hadn't known what to say. He did love her. He loved her immensely, with a richness and depth he hadn't even dreamt was possible. But that very love was clouding his judgment, and he had made grave mistakes. Again.

If he was avoiding her, it was because he didn't know how to explain that, how to make it clear he wanted to marry her more than anything, but that he didn't trust himself.

"You can answer that," Ethan said, relaxing back in the leather chair behind his desk.

"Thanks." Seamus cleared his throat and stood up. It wasn't the time to tell Cara anything, especially since he didn't know how to articulate what he was feeling, but he still felt nervous. Like she knew he was having unexplainable doubts.

"Hello?" he said cautiously.

Even as he answered, Ethan's cell phone rang. "Shit, it's Alexis. Pissed off at me, I'm sure."

"Seamus, I need to talk to you," Cara said. "When will you be back?"

Her voice sounded funny, like other people were around and she was trying to be discreet.

"I'm not sure, babe. Half an hour?"

"How about now. This can't wait."

Uh-oh. That was anger. He knew that tone. That was the pissy, you've totally screwed up voice. He glanced at Ethan, who was grimacing and saying into his own cell phone, "Fine. I said okay. Fine. No, I didn't. Alexis . . ."

His conversation didn't sound any more promising than Seamus's so he figured they were both going to have to take a break from politics and do a little relationship damage control.

Seamus sighed. "Okay. I'll be home in five minutes."

"Good." She disconnected without saying good-bye.

He had no clue what could have possibly made her angry. But maybe that was a positive thing. She wouldn't be so hurt, so sideswiped when he told her he had made a mistake and that he wasn't sure if they were going in the right direction. That he needed to think about his future and assess why he couldn't have a relationship without adversely affecting other people in his life.

Ethan dropped his phone on his desk. "It is not the least bit satisfying to hang up a cell phone. You can't even get a proper slamming action when you're mad as hell."

"Alexis giving you a hard time?"

"Yes. As if she has a right to be irritated about me not rushing to tell her Corbin was in the casino. What am I, the man's bloody secretary? And then she shows up with a sword this morning and can't possibly see why I'm angry. Bugger." He reached out and bent a ballpoint pen in half. "That feels better. Do you need to leave, too? Alexis said Cara is steaming about something herself."

"Did she say why?" It might be nice to know what he was walking into.

"No." Ethan shrugged and stood up. "Just that she totally supports Cara in the fact that you're a lying, manipulative asshole."

"Great." It was better than he'd thought. Hell.

"We're in the proverbial doghouse, aren't we?"

"I think we're actually in the sewers. They've been discussing us with each other. That is not a good thing, Carrick." The more he thought about it, the more Seamus started to sweat. Cara had not sounded happy.

A flash of fear crossed Ethan's face. "What have they got up to?"

"Let's find out," he said with way more bravado than he felt.

Fourteen

Somehow Seamus had beat her back to the apartment, which only served to irritate Cara further. She had wanted time to brush her teeth and her hair, change out of his shirt, and stroll out feeling powerful when he came in the door. Instead, she was forced to look at him lounging on the couch with Fritz while she came in the door knowing both mentally and physically she was wrecked.

"Hey, babe," he said. "How's Kelsey?"

"She's fine." So he was going to play it casual, like he had no idea she was ticked at him. Schmuck. "But when I was talking to Alexis it became obvious that there are a few things you have failed to mention to me."

"Like what?" he asked cautiously, his hand stroking the back of Fritz's head.

"Like that it's against the rules for a vampire to feed from another vampire."

His jaw worked. He didn't say anything for a long, long moment. Then it was only, "This was different."

"Really? How?" Cara wasn't sure what she had expected him to say, but this wasn't it. He wasn't denying it. He just looked obstinate.

"You didn't like blood at first. I had to force you to drink the night you died. I was concerned you'd starve if I didn't keep feeding you myself."

"And the orgasms I had didn't motivate you at all?" Running her hand through her hair, she grabbed a pillow off the overstuffed chair because she needed to squeeze something besides his throat.

"Of course not." But he looked and sounded like he was lying and they both knew it.

"You knew that the more you fed me, the harder it would be for me to get used to bagged blood. You let me *get off* on you, knew you were making me dependent on you, while you kept me here locked up, so no one would know that I existed."

"Yes."

It was like a slap, right across the face, one side to the other, ringing her ears and blurring her vision. He wasn't going to explain, put a spin on it, make it sound less disgusting? And why the hell was he still just reclining on the fucking couch like the minute she shut up he could just drop off into a nap? Cara took the pillow in her hands and threw it at him as hard as she could.

Fritz yelped and jumped to the floor, but Seamus just caught it before it collided with his face.

"Arrrgghh!" she shrieked and stomped to the bedroom. She was tossing things into her suitcase when he managed to rouse his lazy ass off the couch long enough to amble in.

"Cara, come on, don't overreact. I just wanted you safe, and I wanted you out of the public eye for political reasons, that's true, and I wanted you strictly because I wanted you. But I didn't lie about any of that. And you were dependent on me because you're a fledgling and I needed to initiate you into vampirism, not because I wanted to make you dependent."

"Initiate? That's what you call last night?" She glanced wildly around the room, making sure there was nothing she absolutely couldn't live without, because she was never coming back to this apartment again.

Screw her toiletries in the bathroom. Those were all replaceable. She wanted out of there immediately. God, how could he say it like that?

"No, that's not what I meant. Stop, babe." He reached for her. "You know that's not true. I made mistakes and I'm sorry for them. But last night was not a mistake. It wasn't about anything but you and me, and my love for you."

Cara darted out of his touch. She didn't want to feel his hands on her skin, she didn't want to notice he looked damned attractive standing there still shirtless, eyes pleading with her. She was so humiliated. She had given her virginity to him, and he had been playing her all along.

He'd admitted to her that he'd been interested in her for sex right from the get-go, and it seemed that's what had motivated him every step of the way. He must have known a good thing had dropped in his lap—the chance to glue a hot stripper to his side for the next century or so. Sex whenever he wanted it, for the low price of a little blood. It must have been too tempting to pass up.

Rushing past him, she dragged her suitcase when it fell sideways off the wheels from her violent yanking. She had a big handbag that she'd unearthed out of the closet and she scooped up Mimi and set her in the bag. Mr. Spock tried to wiggle away, but she clipped his leash on him and wrapped it around her wrist. Button was lying on the air-conditioning vent and she called to him, "Come on, Button, come on, sweetie."

He bounded over to her and she bent down for a hug, burying her face in his fur for a second, throat tight. "That's my boy."

Rascal, her orange tabby, was sleeping in a basket in the dining room and she put him in the bag along with Mimi. They both gave mewls of protest, but she stuck it on her arm anyway. They weren't going very far.

"Cara..."

She ignored Seamus and went for the door. Going back to her apartment wasn't an option right this minute since it was daylight and there were killer vampires running around. She was pissed, not stupid. But she figured she could get a room on a different floor.

"Come on, Fritz." She held out her hand for her other Lab, but Fritz just wagged his tail at her and stayed next to Seamus.

"Fritz! Here." Desperate to get out, she slapped her leg to get him to come to her. He just gave a friendly bark, then licked Seamus's hand.

Wonderful. Seamus had seduced her dog, too.

"Cara. Just take a deep breath and let's talk about this. We can work this out. We both want the same thing here, I know it."

"We both want you dead?"

"No. We want to be together. I know we do. Let's go to counseling. Remember you wanted to do that? Let's try that."

"Vampires don't go to counseling." She threw his words back at him, gathered all her animals minus Fritz, and marched out the door, eyes blurry from threatening tears. Over her shoulder she called, "And I'll be back for my dog when you're not here to manipulate him the way you have me."

Seamus watched Cara storm out, bags hanging and banging against her leg, dogs tangled together, cats meowing in protest.

He looked down at Fritz, stunned. "What the hell just happened?"

Fritz barked and sat down.

That seemed like a good idea, so Seamus sat down, too. "Holy shit."

He'd just had his heart ripped out of his chest and, he had to say, it didn't feel all that great.

Cara knew she must look like a psycho with her clothes a mismatched mess, her hair going in twelve directions, swollen eyes and red cheeks from crying, animals and luggage hanging off her. But it never occurred to her that she would be denied a room.

"I can't give you a room without an ID or a credit card, miss," the desk clerk said like this was totally obvious, which normally it would be to Cara.

At the moment, though, she was feeling just a hair shy of hysterical. "But I left my purse in Mr. Fox's room and I just can't go back up there. I just can't!"

"Okay," the man said carefully, like he was afraid to argue with her. "Is there a friend you could call?"

"A friend? Yes." She nodded in relief. "I'll just call Alexis. Can I borrow your phone?"

He hesitated, then lifted the receiver, finger posed over the touchpad. "What's the number?"

"It's here in the hotel. Room thirty-two-twenty, Mrs. Carrick's room."

Now his eyes went wide. "Your friend is Mrs. Carrick?"

"Yes." She held her hand out. "Give me the phone!"

Except Ethan answered, so she hung up on him. She couldn't face him, not even on the phone, knowing he probably knew about Seamus and their argument. Knew that Seamus was feeding her like a . . . like a . . . sex slave. She shuddered.

The desk phone rang immediately and the clerk answered, looking relieved to be diverted from Cara. But two seconds later he was shaking his head in alarm. "No, Mr. Carrick, I absolutely did not hang up on you. There is this . . . this woman here and she's insisting she knows your wife and she wants a room but she doesn't have any ID and she has these dogs with her . . . I don't know." He shifted the phone and asked Cara, "What's your name?"

"Cara Kim."

"Cara Kim." He listened. "Uh-huh. Alright. Okay. Definitely, yes, sir. Thank you. Have a nice day, sir." There was a sweat breaking out on the guy's forehead, and when he hung up, he let out a sigh before glaring at Cara. "I can't believe you hung up on Mr. Carrick!"

"Sorry, but I didn't want to talk to Ethan because he'll talk to Seamus and then Seamus will come looking for me, and . . . and . . ." She tried to stifle a sob, but it slipped out. "What did Ethan say? Can I have a room or not? I'm just so tired." Now she was crying full force and Button was starting to rub against her leg in sympathy.

"Oh, God, it's okay," the guy said, adjusting his tie. "Don't cry, God." He darted a nervous look left and right.

"Mr. Carrick said to give you a room and charge it to the business expense account. He said you're Mr. Fox's girlfriend and to give you whatever you want. So, I'm really sorry, but I didn't know, you didn't have any ID or a credit card or anything and I was just doing my job, so . . . what do you want? Mr. Carrick said to give you whatever you want."

"I want a room!" Cara spoke so frantically the woman checking in with the desk clerk to the right glanced over in alarm. "And I am no longer Mr. Fox's girlfriend as of ten minutes ago. So I would like a bellman to go to Mr. Fox's apartment and get my belongings and bring them to my new room. I have some clothes and toiletries, plus all the pet supplies, and I want the raspberry and orange drapes hanging in the living room. And the pink towels in his bathroom."

He had never wanted them in the first place, so she'd be damned if she'd leave them there. They had been expensive, and when she'd ordered them online she'd put them on her credit card.

The desk clerk, whose name badge read HARRY, was scrambling around, yanking a piece of paper out of the printer and quickly writing. "Clothes, pet supplies, drapes, pink towels. Anything else? Turn-down service in your new room? A robe or something?"

Turn-down service for a vampire. That struck Cara as funny. "No thanks, I'm not big on chocolates on my pillow. I just want a place to sleep for a little while. I'm really, really tired."

"Got it." He typed with manic speed and produced a key card for her. "Fourteenth floor. Far enough away from the noise of the casino and the pool, but plenty far enough away from him, too."

Cara took the card. "Thanks."

"Hey, I understand. I just went through a nasty breakup myself. The last thing in the world you want is to run into the shit by the ice machine, you know what I'm saying?"

"Yeah. I know exactly what you're saying." Cara turned.

"You can leave the bags. I'll have them sent up," said suddenly helpful Harry.

"Thanks." Cara trudged over to the elevator, made it up to the room, got inside, and collapsed on the bed.

She was sobbing before her head even hit the pillow.

Seamus was trying to sleep, with zero luck, when the doorbell rang. He sprang out of bed and headed for the door with vampire speed, hoping it was Cara. She'd only been gone for an hour. Maybe she had taken a walk in the casino, cooled off, and now they could talk rationally about the situation.

He yanked the door open. "Cara."

It was a bellman.

"Can I help you?" Seamus asked, incredibly, sickeningly disappointed.

"Good morning, Mr. Fox. I'm here to, uh, collect Miss Kim's things." He looked at the list in his hand. "Her clothes and some other things."

"You're kidding." Just drive the stake farther into his chest. Damn. It hadn't taken her long to act on her anger. She was really and truly moving out.

The chunky middle-aged man shook his head. "No. I'm sorry, sir."

Seamus started to get angry. She could have at least given him time to explain. She could have come back herself and said good-bye. "Fine." He swung the door open wide. "Come in."

In the bedroom, Seamus jerked Cara's dirty jeans out of the hamper and threw them on the bed along with her hairbrush and nine thousand hair bands, which had been cluttering up his dresser top. From the bathroom, he scavenged all her face and body junk and threw it into two plastic bags. He had to shove the expensive smelly shit out of the way every time he brushed his teeth. It would be nice to have all his counter space back.

The bellman hovered in the doorway. "And the pink towels, too, sir."

"The towels?" Seamus asked in outrage. "She wants the fucking towels?"

"Yes, sir."

Now that took some kind of nerve. "Fine." He ripped them off the towel bar. "Hot pink isn't really my color anyway."

The bellman took them and headed for the front door with the other plastic bags. "Can you get the pet supplies out while I put these on the cart?"

"Sure. Absolutely." Seamus opened the hall closet and pulled out the crates, the leashes. In the kitchen he gathered bowls and cat and dog food. Fritz danced around behind him, playing with a rag rope. "But she can't have this dog. He stays with me until she comes and gets him herself."

"The dog isn't on the list." The bellman deposited the crates on the luggage rack in the hall and came back for the food. "But the drapes are."

"The drapes?" Seamus ran a hand through his hair, appalled.

"Yes. I'm sorry, sir. You know women just get a little, well, emotional when you have a fight." The bellman shifted back and forth uneasily.

"Isn't that the truth." Seamus clapped the poor guy on the shoulder. "Sorry you got stuck with this detail." Then he shoved a dining room chair over to the windows and lifted the curtain rod down. "She can take these ugly-ass things. Won't break my heart. They look like the circus puked on my windows."

The bellman let out a snort.

"Do me a favor. Grab all that pink crap off my desk, too. She can take her pencil holder and mail slots and organize the hell out of her new pink room."

"There's stuff in these organizers," the bellman said as he picked over the desk.

"Just dump it all out and get rid of anything pink." Seamus moved on to the second window. "What's her new room number anyway?"

"Sorry, sir, I was told not to say."

Seamus made a rude sound. What, did she think he was going to come after her? Stalk her? Please. He was way too proud to come begging after her. He stared at the stripe in the drape, the pattern blurring together as his heart splintered into a thousand pieces, his skin feeling like a denizen of wasps were stinging simultaneously. He wanted to beg. He wanted her back. He wanted her drapes.

He was fondling the silk material when Ethan walked into the room.

"What the hell happened, Seamus?"

"I have no idea. What about you?"

"Alexis isn't speaking to me. She went to Brittany's with an overnight bag."

"Shit." They stared at each other, confused and hapless. Seamus climbed off the chair. "Let's get drunk."

"That is a beautiful idea."

The idea seemed decidedly less brilliant twelve hours later when Seamus was tied up alongside Ethan on the rooftop of the Venetian, alcohol buzz wearing off.

"So," he said to Ethan, staring up at the sky ablaze with the orange aftereffects of a sunset, his head pounding and his lower back aching. "Maybe confronting Donatelli dead drunk wasn't the best idea we've ever had."

"I don't think so," Ethan agreed. "And I have to say I wasn't aware how much tolerance for liquor I've lost in the last eighty years. If I had known, I might have stopped at nine gin and bloody tonics. The tenth was·the one that did me in."

Seamus's mouth was thick and thirsty. He shifted, trying to get his wrists out from under his back, but was unsuccessful. "When I was a mortal lad, I could drink my age in ale. Age sixteen, sixteen mugs of ale. Got me quite a bit of attention."

"I didn't know that about you. Seems astonishing that after nearly four hundred years there is actually still something I don't know about you."

"There's something else you don't know." Seamus gave up trying to get comfortable and lay still on the hard poured concrete. "Since the night I turned her, I've been feeding Cara myself." He wasn't sure why he told Ethan, other than maybe he needed someone to understand, to recognize that he hadn't meant to be a sick bastard. He'd just wanted to please Cara. And keep her with him.

"Ah. And she found out that isn't the usual way of things?"

"Yes."

"Why were you?" Ethan didn't sound judgmental, just curious.

"At first, she didn't want to feed, so I didn't want her to starve. She wasn't ready for cold, bagged blood. Then, she got so much pleasure from feeding from me, and I admit, I enjoyed it... well, it didn't seem like a big deal. It felt right, not wrong." Seamus closed his eyes. "The bottom line is I didn't have a good reason. I just wanted to. I wanted her, that's all."

"I could see the temptation. But you should have given her a choice."

"I know. And now she's never going to speak to me again." He groaned. "I've screwed everything up and now I've dragged you down with me."

"No, I dragged myself down with you. I pissed Alexis off all on my own." Ethan gave a snort. "I bet Donatelli is downstairs just laughing his scrawny ass off. We must have sounded like absolute idiots down there."

Seamus could only imagine because truthfully he didn't remember a whole lot after the seventh shot in the fourth bar. Then it was a blank until they were being shackled with industrial-strength chains and Donatelli was threatening them. "*Total* idiots. Do you think he meant it about leaving us out here to starve while the sun drains us of our strength?"

"Oh, yes. He meant it."

"You don't sound worried. Have you called Alexis?" Seamus had already tried to mentally contact Cara. She had him completely blocked out.

"No. I'm too drunk still. I can't focus." Ethan laughed. "I can't feel my feet."

"And that's funny?"

"Yes."

Seamus managed to move his foot far enough to kick Ethan. "Feel that?"

"Yes, you asshole."

Seamus grinned at him. "Well, if I have to starve and be drained of my energy by the sun, I'm honored to do it with you, Carrick."

"We're not going to die. It would take three weeks for me to starve. I am a Master Vampire. I do not die easily."

"Ooohh. Bad ass."

"Fuck off, Fox. I'm trying to die with dignity."

Seamus laughed so hard he made his gut ache. "Maybe I am still drunk."

"And maybe you're ugly, too."

That cracked them both up all over again.

"Try to call Cara," Ethan suggested when they could breathe.

"Doesn't work. She's got her Call Block on for me."

"Who else do you have a mental connection with? You're less drunk than me. You should be able to contact someone."

"I don't make it a habit of mentally hooking up with people. The only person I talk to that way is Cara." Seamus rolled up on his side. His arse was going numb. "When we get out of here, I'm going to apologize to Cara. I'm going to make this right. I love her, man. I want to marry her and move back to Ireland. She can be a country vet."

"You really want to leave politics?"

"You know I have to. People will demand that I resign. I'm okay with that. I just want you in office for another term. I don't have to be there." Though it made him feel a little solemn to imagine Ethan working without him, getting another advisor. They had worked together for a long time, and Seamus had tried to have a positive impact on the

Vampire Nation. But he had broken the law and it was time to step back.

"We'll see, Fox. It might blow over. It might be nothing. And I'm going to apologize to Alexis, too. I should have told her the Frenchman was here. I didn't because I thought she'd give him hell for sleeping with her sister. I just didn't want to deal with the drama, but that wasn't fair of me."

Seamus glanced over at Ethan in amazement. "Brittany slept with the Frenchman?"

"Oops," Ethan said. "Probably wasn't supposed to tell you that."

They both laughed, then fell silent. Seamus studied the sky. Brittany and Corbin. Hell. Everyone had been having sex but him. And given the morning's events, he wouldn't be having sex again anytime soon either.

"What about Kelsey?" Ethan asked.

"What about her?"

"You've spent a lot of time with her. She has your blood now. Maybe you could contact her."

Seamus hadn't thought about Kelsey. "It's worth a try. You never know what you're getting with Kelsey, but maybe she would tell someone where we are."

He closed his eyes and tried to concentrate, visualize Kelsey, pick through time and space and reach her. *Kelsey,* he called. *Can you hear me?*

Seamus? Her voice came back to him just a few seconds later, suspicious and hesitant. *Why are you in my head?*

Ethan and I need your help. We're trapped at the Venetian hotel. Send the security team. Seamus was about to elaborate when Kelsey slammed her thoughts shut.

"Shit. She just closed me out. I told her we were trapped and needed help and she shut me out."

"She's the worst goddamn secretary," Ethan complained. "She names computer files shit like 'Things I don't know what to do with' and she puts rainbow-colored sticky notes all over my desk. I hate that."

"Cara ordered me Betty Boop checks."

That set Ethan off all over again.

"And she bought these pink fluffy towels so that after I showered I had pink lint on my balls."

"Stop," he said, laughing so hard he was doubled over wheezing. "I can't take it."

It felt better to get it all out there, to make Ethan laugh. If it was someone else, he'd laugh himself, and it was better than sobbing into more alcoholic blood. That had only gotten him tied onto Donatelli's roof.

"Then today, after she left and got a new room, she sent the bellman to get her stuff. Including the towels."

Ethan made a choking sound. "No fucking way." His laughter sent him rolling over to the left.

It took Seamus a second to realize that Ethan had rolled right off the side of the building. "Carrick?" He tried to sit up, to see what had happened. He could see the shackle attached to the wall, and snaking off the roof where Ethan had disappeared. "Carrick, you okay?"

Great. Now Ethan was dangling over the side of the building drunk. Very presidential.

"I'm fine," Ethan called. "And I broke the chain. I should have done that an hour ago." He leaped up onto the roof, hands still locked behind his back in steel cuffs.

Seamus nodded, suddenly feeling very prosaic. "Cool. Now get me out, too, and we can be on our way."

Fifteen

By sunset, Cara was sobbing again. She had taken a break from wailing to let the bellman in with her belongings earlier and had caught a few hours' sleep. But now she was awake and she was right back to bawling her eyes out, clinging to Seamus's T-shirt.

It smelled like him, musky and masculine.

And she had reached a new low, cuddling up on the bed with the cotton shirt cradled in her arms. Knowing it was pathetic didn't make her stop. She was actually dragging it across her face for another whiff when there was a knock on the door.

Maybe it was Seamus. She didn't think her instructions to keep her room number from him would be an obstacle to a man like Seamus. He could probably hunt her down like a bloodhound, for all she knew. Obviously there was a lot about being a vampire he had failed to mention in the weeks she had lived with him.

She thought about opening the door. She really did want to see him. She missed him. The night before had been so intimate, so tender, so hot, those feelings of love couldn't have been her imagination. Maybe if she just gave Seamus a chance to explain. Plus she was hungry. She hadn't fed since the bagged blood that morning with Kelsey and Alexis. Seamus's blood tasted so much better...

Cara flung the shirt completely over her face, wiped her tears with it, and breathed in deeply. She was losing it. And she was not going to answer the door.

The pounding came harder. Her dogs lifted their snouts in disapproval.

"Cara, it's Alexis and Kelsey. Open up."

Damn. She supposed she couldn't ignore them.

Still holding the now soggy T-shirt, she got up and answered the door. "Hey."

Alexis's jaw dropped. "Whoa. Things didn't go well with Seamus, I take it."

"No."

"What happened to your hair?" Kelsey asked. Despite her early morning adventures in self-mutilation, Kelsey looked fresh and perky, dressed in sexy skinny jeans, a silk camisole, and a sparkly shrug.

Cara touched her head. "I don't know. What does it look like?" She hadn't really brushed it since her postsex shower some fifteen hours earlier. She had pulled shirts on and off over her hair, cried into it, slept on it, and chewed the ends at one point. Chances were it wasn't looking all that great, but she wasn't sure she cared.

"It looks like you've been electrocuted," Alexis said.

"But that's irrelevant." She paced back and forth in front of the bed, while Kelsey sat down.

Cara flopped on the row of hotel pillows lining the headboard and wished more than anything she could still eat chocolate.

"We're here because Ethan and Seamus are missing."

"Missing? How could they be missing?"

"I don't know. But none of the guards know where they are, which is insane. They don't go anywhere without at least two bodyguards. I haven't seen Ethan since this morning when we had a little bit of an argument. He's not answering his cell phone. And when I try to call Ethan mentally all I get is this fuzzy sort of static."

"Maybe they're avoiding us. Maybe they're somewhere together bitching about us." It had only been twelve hours. They were grown vampires. Cara couldn't work up the energy to worry.

"But Seamus called Kelsey and said they were trapped at the Venetian and that they needed help."

"He called Kelsey?" Okay, that ticked her off. "Why would he call you instead of me?" Like Kelsey could possibly know the answer to that, but she was asking rhetorically.

"I don't know. Maybe he was afraid you wouldn't answer. But he sounded really urgent, Cara. They need our help. I think the Italian has them."

"Donatelli?" A shiver went through Cara. In her mind, he had been elevated to the status of a monster. "Why do you think that?"

"Because he lives at the Venetian," Alexis said. "I think they went there to confront him about everything that has been going on."

"Why would they do that without guards?" That didn't sound at all logical.

"Because they're stupid."

Cara wasn't going to argue with that. "So what do you think we should do?"

"I think we should go check out the poker play at the Venetian. You are the Ava's Texas Hold 'Em champ. Maybe you want to see what the play is like at the Venetian."

That reminded her that she'd never cashed in on her winnings, and she had left the chips in Seamus's room. They weren't going to do her any good there. "I'm not sure about this. What good is it going to do to go over there? We don't know that Ethan and Seamus are even there, and there is no way we're going to be able to search private rooms."

"But we can flush Donatelli out of his suite and have a little chat with him. If he's hurt my husband I will do unspeakably painful things to him."

The venom in Alexis's eyes was a little scary. "I thought you were mad at Ethan."

"I am. But he's still my husband. The only one who can slap him around is me. And after he apologizes for being an idiot, we're going to have really great makeup sex. The bottom line is, we all make mistakes, including me, and I love him."

That hit Cara hard. She loved Seamus. She knew she did. He was a good man, loyal and responsible and always, always willing to take care of others. He had made a mistake, because he had wanted her. Was that such a terrible thing?

She wasn't sure. It was really damn hard to trust. "Do you think I'm making a mistake leaving Seamus?"

Alexis shrugged. "I don't know, Cara. Only you can know that. It's possible to love someone and not be able to live with him." She pulled Kelsey off the bed by grabbing her hand. "But right now I have this urgent awful feeling something is wrong and I need to go after my husband and bring him home. You can come with us or you can stay. It's totally up to you."

There were two choices. One, she could stay in the hotel room and cry over the loss of a relationship that had just barely gotten started. Or two, she could brush her hair and go after Seamus, hoping they could work their issues out.

It took her less than two seconds to decide. She loved Seamus.

"Let me grab my hairbrush. I'll use it in the car on the way over."

"Cool. Can I do your hair?" Kelsey asked.

"We could have walked faster," Alexis complained when they finally had snarled their way through traffic, parked the car, and went into the casino at the Venetian.

"But then how would we make a quick getaway if Ethan and Seamus are hurt?" Kelsey asked, giving a flirtatious smile to a man who gawked at her in naked interest.

"Good point. How reassuring to think they won't be able to walk home on their own."

Not to mention that with traffic as brutal as it had been, an anemic vampire with cataracts would be able to catch up with them. Cara crossed her arms over her chest and swallowed nervously. Maybe this hadn't been such a good plan. Like it was much of a plan. They were just going to hang around the Venetian and hope Donatelli sensed them?

This wasn't his hotel—he didn't have cameras and guards like Ethan did at the Ava.

"Let's go sit at one of the tables," Alexis said, hands in the back pockets of her jeans. Her eyes were scanning the room.

"Okay," Cara said because she wasn't sure what else they were going to do. They found an open seat at a craps table, and Alexis fronted her some cash.

It wasn't her game. Cara lost two hundred bucks in ten minutes and turned to Alexis. "This isn't working."

"The plan or the craps playing?"

"Both."

Alexis bit her fingernail. "Okay, I have an idea. If Donatelli is involved, and Ethan and Seamus are in trouble here at the Venetian like Seamus told Kelsey, it stands to reason they're in his suite, right?"

"I guess so." But Cara wasn't sure they could make that leap in logic, or how they could get into Donatelli's suite.

"It makes total sense." Alexis marched up to the front desk, told them she forgot her room number. "It's in my husband's name, Roberto Donatelli," she said.

Cara thought the clerk would tell her no go, but he just looked it up and gave her a new key card with a smile.

"Whoa," Alexis said as they walked away. "I used vampire mind control and it actually worked. I feel guilty." But it didn't stop Alexis from hitting the up button on the elevator and pocketing the key card.

While they were waiting, Cara tried to ignore the tugging at the back of her brain that something was off. The Venetian had a less fluorescent décor compared to some of the other casinos. It was full of wood, creamy textured walls, and elaborate frescos on the ceiling.

"Who is that?" she asked, gesturing with a slight tilt of her head. There was a man sitting in the lobby lounge with two women, his posture relaxed and arrogant. He wasn't even looking at them, but Cara felt . . . an awareness. There was a scent lingering over him, different from mortals. "He's a vampire, isn't he?"

"You're good," Alexis said, expression grim. "You just found Donatelli."

He didn't look powerful. He did look smarmy and self-absorbed.

"And now we know he's not up in his room," Cara said.

"Which is why it's the perfect time to head up there and check it out."

Damn. She had thought Alexis might say that. She'd bet her stripper heels—which were damn expensive—that she was going to regret this.

Once in Donatelli's room, she was convinced of it. The suite, lush in gold and burgundy fabrics with a king-size bed on a platform behind an elaborate balustrade, looked and felt empty.

"No one here. Let's go." Cara grabbed Kelsey's arm and retreated for the door, heart pounding.

"We should at least look around."

"For clues? Give me a break, Alexis. There's nothing Nancy Drew about any of us."

"My name used to be Nancy," Kelsey announced.

"What?" Cara looked at her in confusion.

"When I was mortal, in the fifties. My name was Nancy. I hated it."

Oh, my God. Cara was breaking into a vampire's hotel suite with a sword-wielding fledgling and a name-changing assassin-loving secretary. Where had the calm life of a mild-mannered stripper gone?

"Kelsey is a nice name," Cara said, for lack of anything better to say.

"I tried out Summer for a while, in the sixties and seventies, but it was too blond for me."

Alexis gasped, having wandered over by the bed. "Oh, that is sick. I'm going to be sick."

"What?" Hearing the horror in Alexis's voice, Cara imagined used condoms, sex toys, porn, a penis pump. "What is it?"

"Donatelli's underwear. They're briefs."

Cara glanced at Kelsey, who gave a snicker of amusement. "Geez. You scared me. I thought it was something really gross."

"This is gross!"

"There is nothing here," Cara repeated. "Let's go. I just remembered I said I'd start back at work tonight... they'll want me there by ten so we should go before Donatelli decides to come back to his room."

"Too late," Kelsey said. "He's coming in the door now."

"What?" Cara grabbed Kelsey and glanced around frantically, looking for a place to hide.

"Don't bother. He can sense us."

"Shit" was Alexis's opinion.

Cara looked around for a weapon. That lamp looked heavy, but it was bolted down, and Donatelli was already walking through the door with two women.

He stopped inside the doorway, expression unreadable. Glancing from one of them to the other, he finally settled on Alexis, who was still over by his bed. "Mrs. Carrick," he said. "What a pleasant surprise to see you this evening. You don't usually venture out of your husband's place."

"I felt the need to check out the Venetian," Alexis said, with way more aplomb than Cara could have mustered.

"Excellent." He smiled at Kelsey. "Hello, Kelsey. You're looking good, as usual. I always thought you should have been a supermodel, not a secretary."

"Thanks."

Cara couldn't gauge Kelsey's true feelings from her neutral, polite expression and she was impressed that Kelsey had pulled herself together. She had real reason to be afraid of this man. He had ordered her to be drained of blood, then had her tossed in Ethan's apartment like an empty blood bag.

"And I don't believe we've met." Donatelli held out his hand. "I am Roberto Donatelli."

Alexis and Kelsey were both playing it cool so she needed to do the same. She swallowed a gallon of spit and said carefully, "Cara Kim." She forced herself to shake his hand and concentrate on keeping her thoughts locked.

"Ah. Seamus Fox's new lover. It's a pleasure." With his Italian accent, *lover* didn't sound rude, but Cara sensed it was meant to be. That he was good at saying one thing and meaning another. "Allow me to introduce my friends, Kathy and Laura. They are in town from Oregon and I've been showing them the best spots in Vegas. Kathy, Laura, this is Alexis Baldizzi-Carrick, the wife of a business associate of mine. Kelsey, a close intimate friend of mine, and Cara Kim, a dancer down at the club Some Like It Hot."

Oh, he was good. Cara would give him that. He had managed to let her know he knew who she was, what she was. Intimidate Kelsey. And be the only one to call Alexis by her full given name, in an unfailingly polite gesture that clearly infuriated her. All while ignoring the fact that they were in his private hotel suite without his permission.

"Nice to meet you." Kathy stuck her hand out.

Cara shook automatically while Laura grinned. "We're here for our birthdays. We both turned forty this month, so we left the soccer games and the laundry at home and came for a wild weekend."

"Oh, well, happy birthday." Cara tried to pull her hand back. Kathy was gripping it too hard, and something about the glassy, drunken look in both their eyes was disturbing.

These were normal suburban housewives and Cara had a sudden, sick sinking feeling that Donatelli was toying with them. In what way, she didn't really want to know, but she couldn't imagine it was totally of their own free will. He was using his vampire influence on them and it repulsed her.

"We were just going to have a drink. Would you care to join us?" Donatelli asked, heading to the bar in the sitting room.

"Cut the shit, Donatelli," Alexis said, obviously tired of being polite. "Where's Ethan?"

"You've lost your husband?"

"Do you know where he is?"

"No." Donatelli poured scotch into three glasses. "Is that the reason for your charmingly unexpected visit? You think I know where your husband is?"

"Yes, I do."

"What about Seamus?" Cara asked.

Donatelli handed Kathy and Laura a glass each. They both tossed the whole thing back like seasoned alcoholics.

"I don't know where they are, though I imagine they're together, as usual. If I were both of you, I'd start to worry that maybe there is more than friendship between them."

"You're scum" was Alexis's opinion.

Kathy and Laura were starting to look confused. "Well, what happens in Vegas stays in Vegas," Kathy said inanely.

Donatelli smiled at her, clearly amused. "Come here, both of you."

They walked over to him. He put an arm around each of their backs and walked them over to the bed, murmuring lowly. They stretched out on the huge king-size bed and Donatelli bent over them. Cara was about to scream and yell and do something to stop him, when he stood back up.

Both women were asleep. Cara let out the breath she'd been holding.

Sighing, he walked back to the sitting room. "They were starting to grate on my nerves. I got them for a friend of mine, and he has the audacity to be late in returning tonight." He smiled at Kelsey. "You know my friend, Kelsey. Ringo would enjoy these women, don't you think?"

Kelsey didn't answer, tiny spots of red appearing in her cheeks.

"Leave her alone," Alexis said. "We're leaving anyway."

"Oh, you think so? But I'm not done enjoying your company yet. I was hoping we could play parlor games, have a few drinks, talk, and tell jokes." He opened the drawer of the buffet and rooted around in there. "I'd love for Cara to dance for us."

Cara started to back up, tapping Kelsey on the elbow to get her attention. Donatelli was starting to creep her out. He had something in mind. He was taunting them.

"Maybe another night." Cara shot a frantic look at Alexis, who was frowning and studying Donatelli's back. Alexis wasn't paying attention to her.

"No, you'll dance for me tonight." He pulled something out of the drawer, and Cara realized it was a thin, sharp wooden stake. "Ever seen one of these?" He pushed it into his palm, drawing blood.

Cara grabbed Kelsey by the arm and tried to run for the door. There was a rush of movement, air, a loud slamming sound. Cara blinked, fear freezing her to the carpet. Donatelli had Kelsey up against the wall, one hand on her neck, the other holding the stake right over her chest.

Kelsey looked terrified, her breath hard and urgent. Her eyes darted around wildly and landed on Cara, pleading with her.

"Let her go," Alexis demanded. "Kelsey doesn't have anything to do with this."

"But she does. She's here, isn't she?" Donatelli wasn't a big man. He was actually shorter than Kelsey, but he leaned forward and whispered to her, twisting the stake slowly. "Do you remember the last time we were together, Kelsey? This time it will be more than blood I'll take. It will be your life."

Kelsey whimpered as he pressed a little harder, breaking the flesh beneath her silk cami. The silver stained with fresh blood, a tiny quarter-size spot, but growing.

"Stop!" Cara cried out.

Alexis suddenly attacked Donatelli's back, but he knocked her to the floor with one sharp crack of his fist.

"Alexis!" Cara scrambled to her, finding her friend unconscious. Fear made her stomach flip. He'd barely touched Alexis. He could kill Kelsey before they could even blink.

"What do you want?" she asked him.

"I want you to dance for me. That's not so hard, is it? You do it every night."

"Will you let Kelsey go if I do?"

"Absolutely. Once you are stripped down to nothing and you've given me a full five-minute routine, I swear to you, on my honor as a vampire, that I will let Kelsey go. I'll let all of you go. And I'll even tell you where your boyfriend is." He caressed Kelsey's cheek, making her shudder. "What do you think? It's a pretty good deal on your part, don't you think? A bargain, given your experience."

It was meant to humiliate her, mock her. Cara felt nauseous at the thought of taking her clothes off for Donatelli, but one look at Kelsey and she knew she had to do it. Kelsey was crying now, blood tears streaking her pale cheeks, and her whole body quivered. Even her teeth were rattling. Alexis was still out cold on the floor. And Donatelli wouldn't think twice about killing all of them. She could sense that. He let her feel that. He allowed his thoughts of malice and cruel intent, amusement and lack of conscience, drift over to her, so she would understand he was serious.

"Do you have some music?"

He might be lying about letting them go, but it felt like he was telling the truth, and she wasn't sure they had any other options. In fact, she knew they didn't. Giving a desperate call in her head to Seamus, who very possibly needed help of his own, she watched Donatelli let go of Kelsey's neck and point.

"There is a satellite radio system over there on the desk. I'll let you choose the music."

How generous.

Cara found an R&B station with some thumping bass driving a soulful song. She started moving, her back to Donatelli, not ready to face him and his leering, triumphant face. It was harder than she'd thought. She felt cold and stiff, terrified and disgusted.

"Is that the best you can do?" he asked, scoffing. "It's a wonder you keep your job. Dancers are a dime a dozen in this town."

Coming to a complete stop, Cara clenched her fists. She couldn't do this.

A sharp cry of pain and a gurgling jerked from Kelsey. Cara spun around. Donatelli must have pushed the tip in, then pulled it back out, because Kelsey's shirt was crimson on every inch of the left side. Before she could even ask if she was alright, Donatelli reached out with his expensive leather shoe and stepped on Alexis's wrist.

Cara realized Alexis had been discreetly reaching for him, probably to pull his leg out from under him. But he came down on her wrist with enough pressure to rip a scream from her, the sick crunching of her bones reverberating in the room, jarring over the bass music.

"You're starting to irritate me," Donatelli told Alexis.

Alexis held her wrist limping against her chest and rocked back and forth in pain, her lips clamped shut.

"Leave her alone."

"This is getting redundant and tiresome," Donatelli said, voice hardening. "Strip for me, bitch, or I'll kill all three of you in the next thirty seconds."

Menace rolled from him in waves.

Cara pulled off her T-shirt and went into her Tuesday night routine.

Seamus grabbed his head in the elevator and cursed. "Damn, what was that?"

"What?" Ethan was using the wall to prop himself up.

"I felt . . . fear, or something. Pain." He glanced at the numbers lit up above the doors, suddenly anxious. "I could have sworn I heard Cara calling for me. She was scared."

They were flying downward past the fourteenth floor.

"What floor was Donatelli on when we went to his room before?"

"Before he tied us up?" Ethan shrugged. "Twentieth. Why?"

Seamus hit the button for the twelfth floor to get the elevator to stop. "Shit. I think Cara is in Donatelli's room." He didn't know why, but something was just telling him that he needed to get to her. That something was very wrong.

"Why would Cara be here at the Venetian?" Ethan asked, rubbing his jaw.

The elevator doors opened and Seamus hit the button for the twentieth floor. The doors slid shut again and they started back up. "You tell me. Can you call Alexis or are you still too drunk?"

"No, I'm sober now." Ethan shook his head. "But when I call Alexis there is a wall there. I thought it was because she was mad at me but . . . what if . . . what if something is wrong?"

Seamus watched his friend's face leech of all color. Ethan ran his hand through his blond hair. "Shit, Seamus. What if Donatelli went after Alexis and Cara while we were tied up on the roof?"

That's exactly what Seamus was afraid of. "I have the worst feeling about all of this. Ethan, you go in the front door. I'm going back up on the roof and fly down to Donatelli's balcony. That way we can watch each other's back."

"There are no balconies at the Venetian," Ethan said, his voice rising in frustration.

"Fine. We'll just have to rush him and hope we catch him off guard."

"If he's hurt my wife, I'm going to be very, very angry," Ethan said.

Seamus was thinking the same thing. "I know exactly what you mean. And when I have Cara safe again, I'm going to sit her down and propose."

The elevator opened on twenty. "Now, let's go."

Cara had her eyes closed so she could block out Donatelli as she moved, her jeans off now. But she couldn't ignore his voice, his insidious, hypnotic, amused voice. It was like a knife picking at her wounds, flicking at her over and over again.

"You remind me of Marie," he was saying. "Seamus's lover from the eighteenth century. She was more petite, that's true, but lush like you, with dark hair and fair skin. She was an actress, did you know that?"

Truthfully Cara hadn't even known the woman's name. Just that she had betrayed Seamus. She didn't want to hear it now, when she was already on display, vulnerable, being mocked and humiliated.

"I can tell from your expression you didn't know. That's a shame, because really you have a lot in common, and I imagine you would have liked her. Quite intelligent and cunning for a mortal, our little Marie, and while her career was based on her looks and her breasts, she was actually an astonishing actress. The whole time she had Seamus convinced she was in love with him, she was working for me. Fancied herself something of a vampire slayer, you know. Saw me as a means to an end. There aren't that many vampires who have the blood of an ancient one, and with Marie's zealous help, I was able to eliminate a number of them on the guillotine. Fox escaped, but many didn't."

Cara couldn't escape either. That was obvious. He wanted her trapped there, he wanted her to hear his vile braggings. He knew she wasn't going to take off her bra and panties, and he was going to let this go on and on until she lost it and crumpled in front of him and begged, cried. She had to work up the courage to finish this. She shook her hair back, rolled her shoulders and her thighs.

"Yes, I like that move."

He was heading toward her. Cara's eyes flew open when his hand touched her shoulder. God, he was going to kiss her. He was close enough to her that she could see the smoothness of his olive skin, smell his aftershave, register the lust in his eyes. She couldn't let him kiss her. There was no way. She would throw up, all over his expensive suit.

His hair brushed against her cheek as he glanced over her shoulder. His fingers played along the clasp of her bra. "Let me help you."

Skin crawling, heart racing, she tried not to show her fear, tried not to panic, tried to think. She was not going to let him do this to her. When he popped the clasp on her bra open, Cara stroked along his pant leg, searching for his testicles. She was going to give them a squeeze with every ounce of her vampire strength and drop the bastard to the floor the way he had Alexis.

His breath hitched a little. "Now you're being very agreeable. Isn't this much nicer? To the left," he murmured along her earlobe, sliding her bra strap down her right arm.

Good. He was giving directions so she could find his package, and she could end this now before it went a second further. If his fingers had time to brush against her breast, she was going to give him the satisfaction he was looking for and beg him to stop.

Without warning, there was a loud crashing noise and she jerked, startled. Donatelli wrapped an arm around her and pulled her against him, in what for a stupid second she thought what a protective gesture.

Then she heard Ethan's voice. "What the fuck is going on here?"

And she knew Donatelli had no such thing as protection on his mind—he was clever enough and fast enough to make this look worse than it already did.

Seamus came up behind Ethan, terrified by the horror and anger in Ethan's voice. But what he saw appalled him in ways he never could have imagined. His face went completely hot, then cold, and the room actually did a spin, like he was going to pass out.

Donatelli's arms were around Cara, and she was only in her panties. Red thong panties. Her bra was still hanging on, but only because her chest was smashed against Donatelli's. Otherwise it would have fallen to the floor, because it was unhooked and pulled down both her arms.

Her flesh was showing, everywhere, the flesh he had touched, made love to, and now Donatelli was touching it. Cara's arm was crushed between their bodies, her hand pinned against his groin, like she'd been groping him. Like they were lovers. Donatelli looked satisfied, triumphant, and he placed his lips on the top of her head, gave her a kiss. Whispered in her ear, like he was reassuring her.

It was like roadkill. Seamus should look away, needed to look away, but he couldn't. Not until he'd seen every gruesome detail, every inch of the damage.

"Are you okay?" Ethan was asking Alexis, who was on the floor clutching her wrist.

Alexis nodded and Seamus couldn't register what he was seeing. Why was Alexis there while Cara betrayed him with Donatelli? He spotted Kelsey on her knees as well, arms wrapped tightly around herself, tears staining her cheeks.

"Let her go," Ethan said. "And then I want to know what all this is about. Once and for all."

"Drunk wore off, Carrick? Damn. It was just too easy to overpower you before. I can't tell you the satisfaction I received from having you chained up, though I am disappointed you managed to escape."

"Let her go," Ethan said again, his voice like steel. He stood up and moved toward Donatelli.

"Alright, fine." Donatelli let go of Cara, who stumbled back away from him, her hand holding her bra in place.

Seamus realized she looked terrified, and everything in him thawed, shifted horror from her to himself. What the hell was he thinking? Cara wasn't half-naked willingly. Donatelli was at fault. When she came toward him, sobs started to wrack her shoulders, and Seamus reached for her, appalled at himself. Why had he just stood there and let Donatelli continue to paw her, scare her?

She curled up against him, hiding her face in his shirt.

"You're outnumbered, Donatelli. So tell me what it is you want," Ethan said.

"I want to win the election, of course. Are you so stupid you haven't figured that out yet? I want the power you have."

"And you'd kill me to get it?"

"I didn't think that was going to be necessary, but if I had to, yes." He shrugged, hands in his pockets.

"Why hurt the women?"

"They came here on their own." Donatelli looked offended. "I was just being hospitable."

"By breaking my wife's wrist?"

Alexis was on her feet now, some color restoring to her face.

"She attacked me. I was defending myself."

"And what did you do to Kelsey?"

Kelsey finally spoke. "He had a stake on me. He said if Cara didn't dance for him and take off her clothes, he'd kill me with it."

Cara clung to Seamus and she shuddered at Kelsey's words. Seamus felt all his shock, horror, guilt, collapse in on him and form a very hot, tight ball of anger. Heaven and hell, how could he ever make this right for Cara? She must have been sick, humiliated. And he was livid. He was six new words for pissed off. He was so fucking angry that if he moved one muscle, he was going to rip Donatelli's head right off his shoulders.

Ethan moved around Donatelli in a slow circle, expression feral. "Concede the election now or I'll kill you."

"I call your bluff," Donatelli said. "You've gotten tame in the last century. You won't kill me."

Seamus set Cara away from him and moved forward. "He doesn't need to. I will."

He wasn't bluffing. Not at all. It wouldn't be difficult for him to take off Donatelli's head, despite the law of the Nation.

The Italian must have seen his conviction. He took a long moment, where they studied each other, then he shrugged. "You are overreacting. I didn't hurt her."

Seamus flew at him, vampire speed, and pinned him against the wall, arm at his neck. "Keep your filthy fingers off my girlfriend, you bloody liar. You've shown no respect for Ethan or me, the law of the Nation, or these women. We're ending this here and now."

"It doesn't look to me like we're doing anything," Donatelli said, his voice tight but mocking.

Seamus jerked him back and snapped his neck, breaking it with a nice, sharp crack.

"Fuck, that hurt," Donatelli said, eyes glazed with pain, collapsing to the ground when Seamus let go of him.

"I'm calling our security," Ethan said. "We'll take Donatelli's statement of concession and broadcast it on the network immediately, and then security can escort him to New York, where he can await trial for treason."

"Treason for what?" Donatelli complained from the floor, looking in too much pain to move.

"Plot to kill the president," Seamus told him. "It's either that—which will mean banishment—or death. Your choice." A sick part of Seamus hoped Donatelli would taunt him by choosing death. It would be all too easy to justify killing him then.

"I don't see that I have much choice, do you?" He still managed to sound like a prick, even down on the ground curled up in agony. "I will concede. Does that make you both happy?"

"Immeasurably," Seamus said sarcastically. He hauled Donatelli to his feet for the sole purpose of punching him in the gut, when Cara called him.

"Seamus, the women . . . on the bed."

"What?" He glanced over at her. She was pointing to Donatelli's bed. There were two mortal women sleeping there under a glamour.

"What should we do with them?" Cara asked. Seamus noticed she had pulled her shirt and jeans back on. "I don't think they'd be here if they really knew what they were doing."

"I'll take care of them," Ethan said, immediately going over to the bed. He picked up both of them, one on each shoulder, and headed for the door.

"You are no fun whatsoever. Did anyone ever tell you that?" Donatelli asked.

Seamus felt his temperature rise. If he had to spend one more minute with this guy, he was not going to be able to contain his rage. "Cara, Kelsey, Alexis, why don't you go back to the Ava? We'll be back soon."

"Okay," Alexis said, with zero argument. Seamus knew then that she must still be hurting if she wasn't arguing.

Ethan returned. "All taken care of. They won't remember a thing."

"We're leaving," Alexis told him.

"Can you drive?" Ethan asked, touching her broken wrist.

"Cara can drive. We'll be fine."

Kelsey was out the door first. Alexis gave Ethan a smile. "Kick his ass," she whispered loudly.

Cara just went for the door and didn't even glance Seamus's way. He watched her go, worried. She was too quiet. That wasn't like her. And he would have liked to have given her a smile, to reassure her. But she just left, head down, shoulders rolled forward.

I love you, he told her mentally.

But like he had ignored her before, now she ignored him.

Ethan wanted to kill Donatelli. He knew one word of permission from him and Seamus would take his head off no questions asked. Ethan didn't blame him. He couldn't imagine how it must have felt for Seamus to see Donatelli touching Cara like that. But there were laws they had to follow, and while this method didn't satisfy bloodlust, it was the right thing to do.

Though oddly enough, Seamus had broken a number of their laws lately, which was completely unlike him.

"Should I kick your ass?" Ethan asked Donatelli.

The Italian shrugged, adjusting his jacket, moving up onto his knees. "How is my wife, by the way? I heard she was in Vegas for your wedding. I was devastated she didn't stop by to say hello."

The asshole. Ethan clenched his fists. "My sister is not your wife any longer. Gwenna was smart enough to divorce you over two hundred years ago." Thanks to Henry the Eighth and his lust for new wives, Gwenna had been able to legally sever her relationship with Donatelli. Emotionally, though, Ethan wasn't sure she had recovered yet.

"That doesn't change the fact that we were married for over three hundred years."

"Of which Gwenna regrets every one."

"That truly breaks my heart. And it's not true. We were happy before you turned her against me."

Ethan snorted. He hadn't turned Gwenna against Donatelli, but he'd been thrilled to help her escape him.

Seamus grabbed Donatelli and hauled him to his feet. "Quit your yapping. No one believes your sob stories."

"Let's just get this over, shall we?" Donatelli rolled his neck cautiously.

"Here, let me help you out the door." Ethan reached out and yanked Donatelli's wrist, breaking it more cleanly than Donatelli had done to Alexis, but snapping it in three pieces nonetheless. "Oops. Sorry."

Seamus grinned at him with sick satisfaction.

Ethan had to admit it felt better than it should.

By the time Seamus finally found Cara two hours later, he was sick with worry. He'd looked for her everywhere in the Venetian, the Ava, and all points in between. Alexis had assured him Cara had returned with her, and the dogs didn't look like they'd been left alone for long—no accidents on the carpet in her new hotel room.

He'd gone to the club and to her old apartment with no luck. No one had seen her. After wondering how rude it would be to call Dawn at midnight when she'd just gotten out of the hospital, Seamus had a thought.

Ten minutes later he was hovering outside the Resthaven nursing home, debating a walk around the perimeter of the building or a bold stroll straight into the lobby. He was on a gravel walkway that was separated from the long, low building by a row of indigenous drought-tolerant plants. The night was quiet, peaceful, and when he stood still and let his vampire hearing pick through the stucco building, he heard the low hum of ventilators, an occasional squeaking shoe on linoleum, and a TV droning softly. Then he heard Cara whispering, her voice gentle and full of love.

Seamus followed the sound, moving south down the building, until he reached the window of the room he was certain she was in. It was actually open, and not only could he hear her voice, he could feel her presence, smell her floral shampoo. Pushing the window open wider, he climbed in.

"Seamus?" Cara asked as she turned. She clearly knew it was him, because she didn't look the least bit startled.

"It's me." He put his feet on the floor and looked around the room. It was small and sparse, with a typical nursing home setup. Cara was curled up in an easy chair, and in the hospital bed a tiny Asian woman was lying, looking up at him quizzically.

The room was dim, just the lights under the cabinet lit, and the eerie green lights from a heart monitor.

"Are you okay?" he asked Cara.

"I'm fine."

She pulled her legs up in front of her, chin resting on her knees. Her hair was still done up in twists and knots, reminding him of how Donatelli had forced her to dance, perform. It made him sick all over again.

"Seamus, this is my grandmother, Kin Zan Kim. Grandmother, this is my boyfriend, Seamus Fox."

"It's a pleasure to meet you," Seamus said, reaching over and touching the older woman's thin, featherlight hand. She was tiny, the size of an American ten-year-old child, and her eyes were opaque, confused. But her skin was smooth, her hair still thick and black with gray shot through it.

She spoke in Korean, a quick torrent of words that sounded clear and cognizant to Seamus. He smiled at her and turned to Cara. "What did she say?"

"I don't know. My Korean sucks." Cara gave a small smile. "But I guess she approves of you. When I brought Marcus to visit her, she threw her tissue box at him."

So the prick had a name. "Smart lady."

"Yeah." Cara didn't move.

Seamus leaned against the windowsill. "I was worried about you." Terrified, actually, but he was trying to play it cool. She obviously had needed some space.

"I'm sorry. I just needed to see her."

"I understand." Seamus reached out, touching the twists in her hair, undoing them. He couldn't see them up like that anymore. It wasn't Cara. "Why did he put your hair up like this?" he asked in frustration, horror, guilt. It was a stupid, inane thing to say, but it was brutalizing him to think he hadn't been there for her.

Cara frowned at her knees. "Why did who put my hair up like this?"

"Donatelli." He fingered the strands, undoing all the twists.

After a second, she gave a small laugh. "Donatelli didn't do my hair. He's evil, not a hairdresser. It was Kelsey who did my hair. She was just playing around with it."

"Oh." Somehow that made him feel better. Though Kelsey shouldn't quit her day job. Cara's hair had looked rather ridiculous. "Cara... I'm sorry about Donatelli. It's my fault. If Ethan and I hadn't run off and gotten drunk because I was mad at you, none of this would have happened. Cara, babe, I'm so damn sorry he hurt you." He didn't know how to make that right.

She looked over her shoulder, up at him for the first time. "It's okay. And I don't want to put blame on anyone—we're both responsible for everything that has happened between us. We're *not* responsible for Donatelli or Ringo's actions."

Her fingers reached out, laced through his. "You told me that you don't know how to take care of anyone, don't know how to nurture because you haven't had a lot of relationships, but Seamus, I disagree. The way you care for others, assume responsibility you don't have to, that's one of your best qualities. You're a good guy, and you take good care of me."

He hadn't realized how much he needed to hear that. "But I wasn't there..."

She put her fingers to his lips, shushing him, and he felt pain, down inside him, swelling and burning. He couldn't live without Cara, without her love.

"That's okay. I can take care of myself. I don't care about what happened in there, you know. Donatelli meant to humiliate me, and he did, but I'd do it all over again to save Alexis and Kelsey."

"You're an amazing woman." He couldn't prevent himself from kissing the top of her head.

"I think my mom was an amazing woman." She glanced over at her grandmother. "She was a blackjack dealer, did I ever tell you that? And I don't think I ever gave her enough credit for her loyalty. My dad ran off, but my mom kept things going. She took care of me and my grandmother, who is really my great-grandmother, and totally unrelated to my mother. I don't think I've ever appreciated how amazing that was for her to do that."

Seamus looked at her great-grandmother, who appeared to be sleeping. "I think together they did a damn fine job raising you."

"You're a wonderful man, did you know that?" she asked, tears suddenly in her eyes.

"I resigned," he told her, because she needed to know. It hurt to say the words out loud, but it was important to him that he do the right thing.

"I'm sorry," she said, voice anguished, hand squeezing his. "That must have been hard for you."

"It was. But I've done two hundred years of public vampire service. Maybe I need a break, some time to focus on my personal life."

Her expression was unreadable. "Yeah? What will you do with all your free time if you're not Ethan's campaign manager?"

"Well, I was thinking of doing some political consulting and analyzing. Or taking Ethan up on his offer, and running the day-to-day operations of the Ava to give him time to focus exclusively on the presidency now that Donatelli has resigned and Ethan's a shoo-in for reelection."

"Sounds good."

"What about you?" He had no idea what she was thinking.

"I'm going to finish veterinarian school and see if I can work in an all-night emergency animal hospital. I'm going to give my two weeks' notice at the club and live off my gambling win."

That didn't tell him what he wanted to know. Did she want to be with him or not?

Then Seamus realized he couldn't wait for her to tell him what she wanted. He had to be man enough to lay it all out there, take the risk, let her know she was important enough to him to risk humiliation, rejection.

Seamus brushed her hair off her face and looked down at her, ready. "Do you have any idea how beautiful you are?"

"Seamus . . ." Her eyes dropped down to her knees. Even with the dim light, he could clearly see her long, delicate hands clasping her jeans tightly, desperately.

"I love you, Cara."

"I love you, too," she said to her knees.

He didn't think her kneecaps were going to answer, so he was going to just keep going.

"Never in my very long life have I felt this way about another person. Being a vampire can be lonely, and I've shunned personal relationships. But there is nothing I want more than to spend eternity with you." Seamus bent down in a crouch, got in front of Cara, lifted her chin up so she would look at him, stared into her eyes. "Will you marry me?"

"Oh!" She started crying, hiding her face back in her jeans. "I didn't know you were going to say that."

Okay. Seamus felt his stomach flip over, his heart stop. What the hell kind of a response was that?

"Well, I did. And I was kind of hoping for an answer." Sometime in this century would be nice. He turned to her grandmother, who was awake and watching them carefully. "What do you think? Is she going to put me out of my misery and say yes or should I just go home and drown myself in ale?"

Cara's grandmother said something, lifting her hand up off the bed. She repeated it, frowning, waving her fingers back and forth.

"I don't think she approves," Seamus said, feeling a little crushed. He hoped she wouldn't fling a water glass at him, further lumping him into a category with Marcus.

"No ring," she said clearly in English.

Seamus blinked. Cara gave a watery laugh.

"Damn, she's right. I should have bought a ring. First time I ever propose to a woman, and I screw it up." He sat back, letting defeat overtake him for a second. Then he thought better of it. "But we can pick out a ring together and go get married tonight."

"Tonight?" She looked at him in shock.

"Yes, tonight. Why should we wait?" Okay, so she hadn't even said yes yet, but he was tired of analyzing everything to death. Tired of worrying and waiting and wanting to be perfectly discreet and politically correct at all times. Seamus wanted to grab what he wanted and shout to the world. Within reason, of course.

"I love you. You love me. Marry me and fill my life with hot pink." He leaned forward and kissed her.

She dropped her feet to the floor and threw her arms around him. "Yes, you crazy vampire. I will marry you. Tonight."

Seamus let out a shout. "Yes!" He turned to her grandmother. "She said yes."

Cara's grandmother smiled.

Cara laughed and stood up. "We have to get out of here. I hear people coming down the hall."

Seamus heard it, too. "Did you hear that yelling? What was that?" someone was saying in the hallway.

He clasped her grandmother's hand and thanked her. Cara gave her a long, loving hug. Then even as the door was opening, Seamus was lifting Cara up and jumping out the window. They landed in a tumble on the gravel walk, just missing a cactus by an inch.

"Impressive move," Cara said, lying on his chest, hair falling forward.

"Thanks, I'm full of them."

"Let's go get married and then you can show me them one at a time."

"You have the best ideas." Seamus wrapped his arms around her and shot up into the night, his exhilaration sending them fifty feet straight up before he evened out.

He was in love and he didn't care who knew it.

"I can't believe he's doing this," Ethan said for the fourth time as they stood in a wedding chapel at two in the morning. "This is the tackiest wedding I've ever been to. I can't believe this cost seven hundred dollars."

Alexis elbowed Ethan in the chest. "Okay. I heard you,

you don't appreciate their choice. Now be quiet before *he* hears you. I think it's awesome that Seamus is marrying Cara. She's good for him, loosens him up."

"There is loose, then there is insane." Ethan shook his head. "They got engaged an hour ago. And this theme they've picked out is ridiculous."

Alexis fought the urge to roll her eyes. "Since when do you have such a stick up your ass? I think it's romantic that they didn't want to wait to get married. And okay, so choosing the vampire wedding package was a little odd, but I think it's meant to be symbolic. Like Cara has brought out Seamus's sense of humor or something."

Ethan made a snorting sound. "It's ridiculous. And I'm not wearing this cape." He shook the black velvet cape he was holding for emphasis.

"You're his best man." Alexis decided it was time to get tough. "Look, Seamus didn't like it when you married me. He thought I was all wrong for you. But he kept his mouth shut and supported you. You owe him the same respect. Put the freaking cape on and wipe the disgust off your face."

Ethan looked down at her, a sly smile turning up the corner of his mouth. "Damn, do you know how hot you are when you're bossy?"

"Put on the cape!"

"Yes, ma'am."

Cara walked up the short wedding aisle on the arm of her bodyguard Daniel, wearing a black velvet clinging dress with a red satin bodice underlay. She had a hood up covering her head, black fingernails, and blood-red lipstick on. Fog swirled around her feet as she walked through the chapel, done up Goth style and resembling a cemetery.

Kelsey and Alexis had preceded her up the aisle in short black cocktail dresses. Seamus and Ethan, wearing black velvet capes, were waiting next to the mock vampire priestess. It was crazy, wild, silly, over the top, and Cara was ludicrously happy.

She giggled when Seamus shot his eyebrows up and down and flashed her his fangs. Daniel deposited her in front of the priestess and Cara pulled her hood down.

Seamus took her hand, squeezed it hard, turned to the woman, and said, "I do."

"I haven't said anything yet."

"Doesn't matter. I do."

Apparently Seamus had caught the spontaneity bug. Cara squeezed him back and added, "I do, too."

"Alright then. I pronounce you husband and wife. You may bite the bride."

Seamus looked down at her, a very wicked gleam in his blue eyes.

"Seamus, don't even think about it," she said, trying to sound firm, but ending in a laugh.

He held his hand up to the priestess and her head lolled back as she fell under a glamour. "Any other mortals in the room?" he asked casually, glancing around.

"No," Ethan said. "Just her and the six of us."

"Good."

Cara wasn't sure what Seamus was planning to do, but his eyes were dark, dark blue. Like denim. And his grip on her was firm, solid. She closed her own eyes right before his lips made contact with hers.

He was so delicious, so firm, so good with that tongue. And when his teeth broke through her flesh, bursting blood from her bottom lip into both of their mouths, she swallowed a gasp. The pleasure exploded in her, around her, and she bit him back, blending their blood, their thoughts, their love, their everything, from two to one.

I love you, he said into her mind, before he broke away, licking his lips.

Cara panted hard, weak in the knees. “I love you, too.”

“Congratulations,” Ethan said with a grin. “Now get a room before you shock me.”

“Brilliant idea,” Seamus said, with a very hot look that told Cara she was about to learn firsthand about vampire endurance.

“Wow. If looks could tear off clothes,” Alexis said. “I think Ethan’s right. You two need to get out of here and go somewhere private.”

“That was a beautiful wedding,” Kelsey said, blowing her nose into a tissue and swiping at her eyes.

“Yes, it was.” Cara wrapped her arms around Seamus. “Now let’s start our honeymoon.”

“You don’t have to ask me twice, gorgeous.” He looked over at their friends. “Now, who wants to pet-sit for us?”

Turn the page for a look at

THE TAKING

the next paranormal romance
by Erin McCarthy.

Coming soon from Jove Books.

New Orleans, 1878

The latest yellow fever epidemic held the city in its iron grip for nine days and nights, the bodies piling up like corded wood in the cemeteries, in the hospitals, and in the streets themselves, as ordinary business and cheerful living bowed in deference to death. With nary a streak of sun in the sky, the shrouded city was quiet save for the constant clatter of carriages carrying corpses and the roar of cannons in the square to clear the putrid air. The tally of dead raised daily—dozens each hour—and the endless opening of doors to bring out a parade of victims to the carts and wheelbarrows waiting on the streets contributed to a weary denizen of despair, of darkness, of numb drudgery.

No stores, businesses, or banks were open, as those who could fled to the country, and all other conveyances were pressed into service as hearses, while the cloud of the smoke from burning bodies created a stinging mist that lingered for days. The agony of melancholy and the silence of profound grief crept into every corner, every house, as the disease swept mercilessly from block to block, taking the young, the old, the rich, and the poor with equal enthusiasm—the sick, the dying, and the dead all intermingling.

I performed innumerable Last Rites from morning to night each endless day as the plague raged on, both on those I knew and victims I had never before laid eyes on. Children I had only recently baptized, adults seeking absolution for their final sins on earth, those with no one to grieve them, and whole families who left this earth together, all received my prayer.

Specific tales of tragedy abound everywhere, from the death of a young bride on her wedding night, to the unfortunate end of the wealthy and proud Comeaux family, which dominated Louisiana business and politics for decades. Seven members of the Comeaux family sat down to dine, hearty and hale and confident in their place of power in our city, on the second day of the infestation, and twenty-four hours later all save one were dead. Camille, the Comeaux's youngest and unmarried daughter, is left at the tender age of twenty void of her entire family. One can only ask what such a loss would do to the state of one's mind and heart, and how many will be forced to confront such a future in the epidemic's aftermath.

—From the diary of Father John Henri,
Catholic priest

The Taking

Camille Comeaux lit the candles on either side of the French doors to the gallery, igniting taper after taper, and watching with pleasure as the flames cast dancing shadows on the wall behind, framing the doors with a moving, undulating arch of darkness.

"Don't light too many," Felix said from behind her, his hands coming to rest on her shoulders. "You'll risk a fire."

Enjoying the press of his strong fingers on her bare shoulders, Camille lit another candle and still one more, pleased with the effect, excited by the danger. If the draperies caught on fire, it would only be fitting. Conjuring the dead deserved drama.

"I want to be sure it works," she told him. She wanted that more than anything.

She knew that Felix didn't understand her drive, her need, but then she knew he was using her, the same as she was using him. He wanted her wealth, and perhaps her body, while she wanted—needed—his power. His magic.

"It will work," he said, leaning around her and snuffing the last two candles she had lit by squeezing the flames between the tips of his thumb and forefinger. "I don't perform any ritual that isn't successful."

It was easy to believe such confidence, and Camille studied his profile, pleased with her choice of hoodoo practitioner. Daring, bold, and successful, Felix was also singularly beautiful, with the thick dark hair and rich skin tone that revealed the African heritage of his mother's family, along with the narrow, aquiline nose of his French father.

At some point soon he would take her virginity, along with the vast amounts of her money he had already acquired. She knew that. Perhaps even tonight. Regardless of when it happened, it was inevitable, given the course she had set them upon, and she could not regret it. The future had been altered irrevocably when her entire family had perished in the fever four months earlier, and every day, every decision had led her here to this moment.

This was the night she would call forth her mother and father and sisters from the grave.

Felix stared at her, and she stared back, a smile playing about her lips. There was a question in his brilliant blue eyes, a doubt that she could see the ritual through to the end, and it made her laugh out loud. She had no doubts, none whatsoever, and she would do whatever was necessary to speak to them, to express her love, her loneliness, her grief and desperation.

"Are you sure?"

"Yes." Perhaps he thought she was mad. Perhaps she was. Certainly twelve months earlier she would never had imagined that she would be standing in her parent's bedroom *en chemise* with a man such as Felix, the expensive chest of drawers from France converted to an altar for his implements to aid in the ritual. A year ago, Camille had been a pleasant, content young woman of wealthy means, her days busy with embroidery, playing her instrument, receiving callers with her mother, and doing acts of charity in the hospitals of less salubrious neighborhoods.

But she was no longer that girl. She was a woman now, a manic, angry woman with no one to love her, and no one to live for. Camille grabbed the open wine bottle off the altar and drank straight from it, the sweetness sliding down her throat. "I am absolutely certain."

Felix didn't hesitate. He closed the distance between them and kissed her, a hot, skillful taking of her mouth that had Camille's head spinning and her body igniting as the candles had. He gripped the back of her head, his tongue tasting and teasing, his thumbs brushing over the front of her chemise, finding her nipples and stroking them.

Camille was always surprised at how good it felt when Felix touched her, how wonderfully free and alive it made her feel. She ran her fingers over his bare chest, excited by the hard muscles, by the power his body contained. Whether it was the wine, or the excitement, or the sexual desire stirring to life, she didn't know and didn't care, but she could see through half-closed eyes that the room was in motion, the shadows pressing in and back out again, the furniture crisp and sharp, the candles appearing pliant and alive.

Everything was dark and warm, the yellow glow of the tapers plunging the altar into light, yet leaving the corners of the room black and secretive. Felix slid his tongue across her bottom lip and she shivered, her body aching deep inside, between her thighs. He stepped away and turned his back to her, leaving her breathing hard and reaching up into her hair to pull the pins away, to let the brown tresses tumble over her shoulders. Her bare feet dug into the rug and she licked her moist lips, the heat from the sultry September night, from the candles, from her own pleasure and excitement, creating a deep flush on her face along with a dewy sheen between her breasts.

When Felix turned around to face her again, he had a snake in his hand, its long brown body wriggling in an attempt to escape. But his captor brandished him high in the air, chanting lowly. Camille hadn't known about the snake, had never guessed one of the baskets was holding a living reptile, and she gasped. Not from fear, but from excitement. This was right. This was magic.

Felix's hand moved the snake so skillfully that it looked as if it were dancing, its body moving to a rhythm his master created, a decadent primitive form of expression. A glance down the length of Felix's hard chest and past his trousers showed that his bare foot tapped out a beat, and with his free hand he pulled a stick from his pocket and hit the chest of drawers, the sharp rap of the rhythm loud in the closed room. The hand tapped out time, the snake did his dance, Felix's foot went up and down, but the rest of him held still—a hard, lean body of control.

"Dance for me, Camille," Felix commanded, his eyes trained upward.

She did, first swaying softly, hands in her loose hair, then she closed her eyes and let her body feel the rhythm. It started in her feet and worked its way up to her hips, to her shoulders, until she was careening to the staccato beat, feeling it from inside her, springing to life, wanting out, needing air to fan the flames.

"You have the power," he told her. "The magic comes from you. Reach for it."

It did. She could feel it boiling up in her body, and she would have it. Camille opened her eyes as she moved, dancing in a pounding circle, her arms reaching up and out, sweat trickling down her back, and she loosened her chemise in a sharp tug at the ribbons, wanting the air, wanting the brush against her bare skin, wanting Felix to see her, wanting to connect with her very essence, the heart of who she was.

Felix brought the snake to her, and where she would normally have recoiled, Camille didn't flinch or retreat, but instead danced for Felix while the reptile twisted and turned in front of her. They moved together, and she tore at her chemise with trembling, excited hands until she was completely naked, writhing like the snake, her fingers in her hair.

"You *are* ready," Felix said.

She was. She was ready for whatever this night would bring.

My life...

My love...

My Immortal

By *USA Today* Bestselling Author

ERIN McCARTHY

In the late eighteenth century, plantation owner Damien du Bourg struck an unholy bargain with a fallen angel: an eternity of inspiring lust in others in exchange for the gift of immortality. However, when Marley Turner stumbles upon Damien's plantation while searching for her missing sister, for the first time in two hundred years it's Damien who can't resist the lure of a woman. But his past sins aren't so easily forgotten—or forgiven...

"*My Immortal* is truly a passionately written piece of art." —*Night Owl Romance*

M174T1107

Discover
Romance